Economic Sex

Economic Sex

Ali-Janna Whyte

The Coach House Press Toronto

Published by Coach House Press
with the assistance of
the Canada Council and
the Ontario Arts Council.

ISBN 0-88910-279-1

PART I

Only One Week 9
sunday 9
monday 34
tuesday 48
wednesday 61
thursday 74
friday 92
saturday 104
sunday 120

The Hospital 127

PART II

Listen Nick 135

The Final Meeting 200

PART III

In the Beginning Before Noise 217

I

Each blade of grass has its spot on
earth whence it draws its life, its
strength: and so we are rooted to the
land from which we draw our faith
together with our life.

JOSEPH CONRAD

Only One Week

Either this kid needs a shake or I'm going to vomit the whole mess.

She sat opposite him wondering.

No. You are not alien; you are human. Physically anyway. You occupy space. An ordered heap of buzzing atoms. Blood, tissue, hair, chromosomes and bone. You talk. A muscle contracts and blood flushes through your interior. Your skin, paper thin, holds it all together. The skin is weathered. Healthy. And as your face moves I see the gleam through your tanned shaved cheeks. Smooth. Your lips move. Sensual, I think. Sensitive mucous membrane.

Her mind wanders.

I wonder about lips, wonder what it is that makes them so appealing. To touch lips. Or not to touch lips. Always looking at lips. Moist membranes. Word framers. Echoing that deep hollow chasm. Where speech comes from. That voice. That other being. Out There. Yes, there are so many considerations.

Cold sores. They ooze. Infection. Don't touch. Contagion. Like a hickey. Tell-tale. Rude. So déclassé. Dirty.

She looks down at her finished plate. Automatically checking her knife and fork. Finished. Together. Slightly resting to one side. Perfect. Good manners.

Or cuts. Like paper-cuts from envelopes. Perfect miniature scars. Or blistered. Or peeling like shale. Hollywood castaways. Dragging over soft sand dunes. *Waa*ter. One thing is certain, lips need moisture. A soft, moist, moving membrane. Needing wetness.

She looks up and into his mouth.

He has yellow teeth. They protrude. Buck teeth. Sort of. Where was his mother for that one? They've got the money. But he knows. He's grown a moustache to camouflage the imperfection. The moustache needs trimming. It's growing, evolving, forever changing. Right before my very eyes. Like Hitler. Zap. Fu Manchu. Zap. Father Time. Zap. With gray fleck.

She stares. Unabashed. Entertaining herself. Stealing his looks.

And then he moves. He puts his hand on the table, and moves the palm along the edge. His blazer buckles at the wrist squishing the brass button in a crease. What next? He reaches for his glass and continues talking, but changes his mind and rubs his eye. Still talking, he rubs his neck and goes for the glass again. The glass goes to his lips. He tips his head, the ice jingles, the liquid slips into his mouth. She watches fascinated.

You swallow again and I see moisture glisten on your lips. A quick lick. And you swallow again. Adam's apple bounces. (Why Adam's apple? But there is no time to think.)

He replaces the glass on the table. On the same spot. The wet ring on the tablecloth beckons like a saucer. He puts his hand beside the glass. Thumb tucked under. His gold family ring gleams. Brilliant. Bravo.

She touches the napkin to her lips. A gentle smudge of lipstick.

Meanwhile: they've covered the political situation in Iran, they've briefly spoken of his father's health, and they've even managed to comment on their next meeting plan. Actual time: twenty minutes. Real time: dense, thick, mythic, lifelong. And now. A silence. Looking up she sees that he is not focused on them. Wandering. She doesn't know where he is. It frightens her. She must entertain. Give something. Stoke the yang. Compliment. He wants a woman, his woman, to be an alert attendant. Time to stop playing the spying anthropologist. The talent scout. Some movement, she thinks, to snatch him back from his thoughts.

What can I slip in that will be definitive? Worthy? Of us? Us. Something new? No. Yet. It has to be fun or it will annoy you. New is weird. Out of pattern. It's entertaining, but it's also a strain. A delicate problem. She gently rubs her hands together. My palms are sweaty. Yes. That's it. I slowly twirl my family ring. The third generation bloodstone on my pinky. I know this information is going in, being filtered, a 'familiar' characteristic. Taking on a dimension through repetition. I gave you the story some time ago. Grandfather, on my mother's side, meets grandmother. On board an English ship bound for East Africa. Passing the Canary Islands in the moonlight, posed at a railing, they discover a common bond. Identical rings fashioned at the same jeweller's in London. Bloodstones with identical spots. Of the same blood. Love at first sight.

Fuck, I'm desperate. But I am drawing you to me. Helping you see my form. Giving presence. The pleasing traditional female. Even in the words I start to use. I say 'actually' and 'frankly' a lot. Tilt my head. Arch my neck. Pearls gleam. That helps you too. You start to smile. Ravishing my look. My contrived beauty. I want to tell you a story that will hold you. Give you pleasure. Entertain you. I read your signals and try to fit. Try very hard. I attempt to balance the familiar with an outrageous story. But yes, I know. The outrage has to flatter your experience, draw on your mythology, add to you. This is not the time to compete. Or show Otherness.

She talks about the bidding on the Kurelek at the Sotheby auction.

Yes, that got you. Fuel. But only for a little while longer.

We've lost it. And I have to admit defeat. The story is over. Finished. Kaput. The only problem is I want you. Seriously. Unprofessional for a lover. Unliberated for a twentieth-century female. But it's true. I want you. For life, Nick. But I am stumped. I've failed to reach you. The core. It's not from lack of trying. I've used every device I've ever been taught, even those I've learned from you. But it's obviously not enough. I've lost you. And now I have to ask myself if I ever even had you. Was I so far removed from you all that time? Or were you so far removed from me? Where are you Out There?

She looks at him hard. Their dance of movement still. She is staring.

He motions to the waiter. The check. His eyes shoot across the room, to the next table, to his hand, to the waiter, to the table, to the entrance, to the bill.

Well. Okay.

She brushes the tablecloth in the silence.

I'm exhausted and tired of trying. This is bullshit anyway. It's bullshit because I have had to try so hard. If you were really able to understand the Immediate, the Essence, the Known, I wouldn't need to be explaining all these things to myself.

He sat reviewing the bill.

Perhaps I made a mistake three years ago. That's one hell of a mistake though. Difficult, no, impossible to admit that I was so wrong. It's what's so difficult about letting you go. And you're too well bred to be overtly rude. To walk out. At least so I believe and so you want me to believe. Politesse. Image projection. And I'm stuck like a desperate heroine, bound and gagged, tied to the railway tracks, bobbing in a barrel, trapped under a fallen log, moving slowly towards the buzz-saw. Comic. I can't reach you. You're both the villain and the hero. Complete, unmoved, fixed. I yelp in terror and longing. Cursed. Tackled by fate. Fate.

I remember a moment we had shared sometime ago. I had pulled a silly gift from my luggage – Bullwinkle in bow tie. I gave it to you. The bow tie blinking. You laughed as you put it on the mantelpiece. Then you took the long-stemmed yellow freesia from the pink vase. One by one. Laying them gently in my open palm. One by one. And you held me. Close, so very close to you. The bow tie blinking.

It all seemed so easy then, so right. We had so much in common, we both seemed so confident. Grabbing life. Seizing the opportunity. Children of Good Fortune. Crazéd lovers. Mad cappers. Nicholas and Sarah.

But it went flat. We stopped believing, trusting. Or maybe the problem was that we started believing and that's how it got so confused. Suddenly the moment – Are You Really the One? The Chosen? – flashed before our eyes. Correction: my eyes. I don't know about you any more, Nick. Today I can say quite simply I feel I was bred for you. I feel Right with you. Damn it. Adam and Eve. Yes. The Chosen. But it's a revolting feeling because there is no sense of the mate. There is no sense of you. Like gulping polluted smoky air: I breathe and swallow, choking, coughing, but it's all I've got. Gasping for air. Choking.

She shifts, glances down at her costume. Her mother's ancient Madeira silk blouse suggestively open. Revealing the long line of inherited baby pearls. A yellow gleam. Age and tradition. Her lap is covered in an attractive woven wool skirt. She feels her legs crossed together. She pulls up her toe. Her black leather gold-clasp shoe reflects her impeccable classic taste. The shoes are tight. Squishing her toes. But she knows she looks good. The Image is Right. Suitable. She compliments him. His blue blazer look. And she likes the idea that they look good together.

A traditional couple. Groomed, nurtured, blinkered to believe this. Inheritors of the throne. Crowned. The Establishment.

Yes. I know this is what I've been bred for. A Romance with a Nice Wealthy Young Man from a Good Family. Romance meant to lead to Wedding Bells and a Lifelong of Bliss and Children. I, a professional, college-educated, Nice Young

Woman with good legs and a quick mind. The perfect match. And yet I sit opposite you and wonder why our relationship is so fucked.

He puts some money on the silver dish and stands up. She picks up her handbag and stands as he pulls out her chair. Walking towards the door. He places his hand on her back. A searing, red-hot iron. Scalding. But she doesn't jump. Calm. She maintains her dignity, her composure. Two young professionals out for lunch at Tavern on the Green. Spring. Central Park. New York. America. Image intact. Click.

Once outside she steps aside as he flags a cab. A pink oxford-cloth blue-blazer brass-button arm shoots up. A yellow taxi zeros in. Nicholas opens the door for her. She goes to step in, turns and smiles. 'Thanks for lunch, Nick.' He smiles back. 'Sure.' He leans forward and quickly kisses her on the cheek. He shuts the door, leans in the window to the cabby and while handing him a few bills says 'La Guardia.' He nods to her, a brief smile, turns his back and walks into the park. Click.

Sarah rolls down her window. The rush of warm spring air cools her burning face. She blinks. The blurry trees mesh with the mushy lawn. She blinks hard again.

There is no denying, Nicholas, that Origin is All. I understand that. It is the most important thing to learn in any system of thought or faith. It is the centre point. The birth of a union. Creating an idea. A person. Identifying who we are, at least who we think we are. It gives us a place in time, a concrete existence, history. Form. It is All. Beginning and End. Each of us is the First Born. Divine, sacred, all in one breath. We are all human, we are all divine. The trouble and the joy of it – we are not created equal.

Can you hear me? o nick, can you hear me?

A warm wet tear melts down her cheek, catches on the corner of her mouth and slips onto her lip. She blinks again.

On the plane.

Moving over the slowly turning earth. Going home.

14

Sarah sat by the window. Looking. At the cloud vapour on the wing as the plane ascended. At the bulbous cloud forms as the plane rose higher. At the sea of white as the plane rose even higher. At the distance. The miles of white. Curving into the horizon. That line where her eye could see no farther. The earth slowly turned. The speed and the direction of the plane taking into account that revolution. The understanding of the pilot amazed her. To pinpoint exactly the landing spot. Somewhere down there. Below that white sea. To know. Exactly. Where to go. The curvature of the earth, the direction. To move north, south, east or west. Could the pilot do it without a compass? That bouncing bubble of mercury pointing true to the Magic Magnet of the North. Yes, that is a given. A known. A scientific constant. Axis. A North Pole. A stationary point on the earth. Still. Frozen. Solid. Pinning together that bulging burning molten core. To the south. The plane buzzing about like a fly. Where to go to lay its eggs. Toronto. Lisbon. Tokyo. New York. Sydney. Moscow. Rio. Rome. All beacons. Of warm life. Bright pungent flowers in the world jungle. Beckoning.

oh god.

Sarah closed her eyes.

The world. The human world on earth. With all those little microscopic citizens in that vast cosmic nation of Humanity. Stuck on a twirling ball. Flying through space.

How does one begin to penetrate that white? How? Without a compass?

Perspective. How one sees things. How one sees outside of oneself. Finding oneself the centre of all things. All the time. With no compass. Taking direction. Taking flight. Moving with no maps. To go from A to B. B to C. And then back to A. Nothing could happen if there was no memory. Memory acts like a compass. It gives an orientation. A bearing. A place. From that very first moment. Those first explorations. Those first discoveries. That first family world.

Pushing her finger along a crack between two boards. Seeing the small specks of dirt clumped and collected in the space. The boards are dark. They are smelly. A moist odour. Wave-like lines flow through the boards. Grains. Knots. Grime. Crawling. Flat. Her finger following the straight crack to the end. Stop. A wall. Going up. A baseboard with moulding. White. Painted wood. Smelly too. Her finger follows the moulding. To eventually stop again. More moulding. Her finger hops to the new direction. Going up. Pushing her finger. Higher. Farther than she can reach on her knees. How far? Looking. Reaching. No farther. Reaching. How far? She could see farther, but she could not reach farther. Both hands touched the moulding. Finding indentations. Cracks. To hold on. Grabbing. Holding. Pulling with her hands. Up. Farther. Higher. Her face against the moulding. Smelly. Old wood. Pul-ling. Her knees touching. Her feet touching the ground. Hold-ing. For balance. One hand moving up. Higher. Along the moulding. How far? Looking up. Seeing farther. Her head moving back. Wobbling. Looking. And losing balance. Her tiny hands, her fat knees snapping away. Rocking off her pudgy feet. Falling down. With a thud. To roll back onto her back. To smell again the moist odour of the floorboards. Star-ing at where she had been. Seeing the wall and understanding it. The moulding went up, turned, went across, turned and came back down. To the ground. Leaving a great big hole.

Pushing with both hands. A big white wooden slab. It was not made of the same stuff as the floors or the walls. It was wood but it was different. It had a different smell. And it moved. And made noise. Push. Pushing it into the hole. A ga-clunk. Fixed. Like the wall. Now there was a new crack between the slab and the moulding. And it went along the floor too. The crack. Filling the big hole. Perfectly. Fingers went into the crack under the slab to pull it out. To open the hole. But no. It was fixed. No movement. It would not budge.

A boy opened the door. A little boy. 'What are you doing, Sarah?'

A brother. Not a sister. A sister is a girl. He is a boy.

He calls me Sarah. I call him David. He owns that. It is his. Name and label.

He carries me to his room. To see his fish. Tropical fish. Beautiful moving vibrant colours. All different. Black. Shapes. Orange. In tiny bunches. With whiskers. In a little ocean. Bubbling with life. Stringy plants and spotted shells. In gravel. Fish would die and float. And fish would give birth. All within a matter of days. And they would eat anything. All the time. Pecking. With their gaping mouths. I touched the glass. To touch a fish. It bolted away. Behind a plant. I hit the glass. All the fish zipped away. David said 'Don't.' He lifted the lid. Stink. Wet and rotten. He pulls out a dead one.

He takes some dry crumbled paper-like food and drops it in. All the fish come. Gobbling. All over each other. Stealing from each other. Big taking big. Little nibbling little. Little taking the crumbs from the big. Snapping. I put my finger onto the bubbling water of fishes. A splash. Then silence. They all went away. Down to the bottom. The food slowly sinks down like snowflakes. I want to put my whole hand in. Would they nibble at my hand like they do that mushy paper? Nibbling. Feeding. Or would they swim from my hand and hide? Why would they hide? How do they know that they cannot harm me, that their bites do not steal anything from me? How do they know they are powerless against me? How? Because I am bigger? But. How do they know that I am not good to eat? I have eaten fish. They are good. I have known them. Not tropical fish but other fish. They do not know me. They have never eaten me. They do not know if I am good to eat or not. But yes. It's true. I have only eaten them when they were dead. If I was dead would they eat me then? Did eating dead things give other living things Life?

Yes.

It must be so.

Would they like me if I was dead? They are frightened of me because of my life. I am not dead. And they know that. I do not know how to stop. Dead. Real dead. Like they do. Sometimes when Davey and I are playing I'll pretend to die. I'll even fall over. And close my eyes. But I'm only pretending. But when fish are dead they are really dead. They stop swimming around. And they float to the surface. Belly up. Rising to the surface.

Where would I rise to if I died? The surface? The tank. I can see the ceiling and no further, but I know that there is Sky. I cannot see it now. But I have seen it. Especially at night. I have seen stars. And space. I have stared at Sky. Up there. Fish cannot do that. Not here. In a tank. But maybe they could in the sea. Maybe fish stare at Sky too. If I died would I float up in Sky?

But the fish.

They are not interesting to look at when they are dead. I like them better alive. They are very pretty. To watch. To observe. Don't they like to watch me? Through the glass? I am behind the glass. To them I am in a tank of air. My brother and I must look as strange and foreign to them as they do to us. We have colourful clothes, and noses instead of gills, and arms and legs instead of fins and tails. And he and I have hair. But we all have eyes and we are all alive. Now. I want to put my hand in. To touch. To pet. Their Beauty. Their living Motion.
To know them so well as to almost become them. I am. A Fish. I am. Everything.

So much of what I am connects me to the world beyond my skin. How can I not be excited, fascinated, by what's outside of me? How could I possibly be neutral, blasé, and just not care? I can't. I get such a kick out of everything. Out There. There is so much to learn about. So much to know. I am just a spy upon the World. And I am very curious.

I go to put my hand in, and David says 'Don't touch.'

Davey piggy-backs me downstairs. To the back door. Looking out the screen. The man was feeding the ducks. He puts me down and opens the door. He says to the man 'I'll do it.' David takes some of the grain in his hands and all the ducks go quacking towards him. He holds up his hands. Above his head. The ducks quack. David says 'Don't – Stop – Go Away.' He starts to get frightened. He backs up towards the door. With his hands held high. Some of the grain spills out. All the ducks go shooting towards it. Heads bent down. Davey laughs. And then he calls me. 'Sarah. Look, Sarah.' And we watch the ducks. David throws some grain down on the step at the door. All the ducks come quacking at it. He opens the door and says 'See?' Triumph. And as he stands there smiling, some more grain spills out of his hand onto the carpet. All the ducks come quacking towards it. David says, 'Sarah, look, I'm the Pied Piper.' We decide to take the ducks upstairs to show mum. 'Come on, Sarah.' And we all go marching to mother. Single file.

We both get spanked. There was pandemonium as the ducks splintered off throughout the house. Quacking.

After we had cleaned up the smelly squiggly messes, we were sent to our rooms.

I had my own room. It had molding, colourful navy blue and white floral wallpaper, a glistening glass chandelier, a walk-in wardrobe, old brass-handled oak chests, delicately carved bed-side tables, taut mustard yellow linen lamps, a silver boudoir set, dancing porcelain figurines, Chinese vases in the win-dows, and a mammoth hand-carved four-poster mahogany white canopy bed. And a white carpet. These are the names and descriptions that others uniformly gave all those things. I had different names for them when I was alone. They had sacred names. Sacred meaning. Not just bed. No. The bed was many, many things. A chariot, a boat, a wagon, a house, a tree-fort, a throne, a dungeon, a mountain, a rocket, a barrel and a place to curl up and sleep – a cave. I also had a horse in my room. I would tie my school tie around the bedpost, move the pillow onto the corner for a saddle and then I would ride for miles. Over hill, over dale, all along the country trail. Some-times. Mad. Escaping. Hiding. Running from. Danger. Indians.

Cowboys. Magicians. Surly Lords of the Manor. The pack. Glancing over my shoulder. Sometimes I would run to. Danger. I have a secret. Top-secret. Information. Posse. Highway robbers. Messenger. From the castle. Or hunting. Galloping. Or strolling through a stream. Finding others. I was told that the mattress on the bed was made of real horse-hair. Antique. From England. So. A real horse. And at bedtime I would gallop to the rescue. Bareback. High-ho Silver. Geronimo.

The old Quebec wardrobe in my room was filled with linen. Blankets and towels. The doors were thin. And they kind of popped when you opened or closed them. I would stand and do that for a time. Opening and closing. Pop. Pop. I liked the sound. Discovering. That hidden music of any noise. I would stand opening and closing the door to the sound of the grandfather clock chiming in the hall. Pop. Tock. Pop. Tock. Pop. Tock. The heavy weights in the clock never let it tick. Only tock. Pop.

Across the Persian rug in the hall was my parents' bedroom door. Outside was a little wooden black doll painted in an Afrikaans military uniform. With a ratty khaki-coloured cap. It would always slip off if the door was bumped. Sometimes. If the door was pushed or pulled too quickly, he would topple right over. Lying on its face. Its chipped negro nose holding up the rest of that stiff body. At attention. Always. With the cap over there. And in my parents' bedroom there was a mirror. With a serpent bird taking flight off the top. It pulled away from the wood. Aching to be set free. That gold griffin. And there was also a little gold mark on the corner of the mirror. On the wood. I tried to peel it off. Once. Only. I was spanked. No. 'Don't touch.' Chippendale, valuable, 100-year seal, proof, antique.

Through my parents' bedroom was the bathroom. Hallelujah. Water. One place in the house where I could make a mess. All in the name of cleanliness. Steaming up. Fog. Seeing my naked body in the mirror. Jungle mist. Playing Tarzan on the pole over the tub. Climbing up beside the sink. A bird-bath. The shower. A waterfall in the cave. A wet toilet seat. And wet toilet paper. Yeech. Easier to pee in the shower. Clean. Isn't it? While the shower is running. Not in the tub. Unless you really have to. Pee and water. It's like water. Except yellow. My pee is okay. Comes from my clean body. Like my snot. From my body. I'll eat it. Not anyone else's. But mine. It's okay. Clean. But my hands would be slapped. No. 'Don't touch – Dirty.' But. She didn't know what she was talking about. What did she do with her snot? Didn't she have a clean body? Or. Is she telling me the air is dirty? If so. Then I say. Don't touch the air. Don't breathe.

Sliding down the banister. Plop at the bottom.

Crawling up the stairs. Up and down. Down and up. With Davey. On our bellies. Himalayas. Pyramids. Castles. Heaven and Hell. Poking our heads through the cage. Over the cliffs. To see. Before flight. In our towel capes off the seventh step. To the bottom. Superman. Batman and Robin.

The downstairs washroom was the hide-out.

I had my mouth washed out in there. With guest soap. Called my mother a bitch. I didn't know what it meant. But it really wasn't for the word that she washed out my mouth. My brother could call me that when he'd lost a game. We'd be playing. And I would win. He would get very angry. (Why? I had won. Fair and square. According to the rules. 50-50.) He would say that I had cheated. I would get angry, how dare he call me a liar. His greed pinching my pride. He would call me a bitch and punch me. Hard. With cruelty. In the stomach. I called him a bitch and punched him right back. Hard. Stupid. Power politicking only. Bitch meant no. No. Don't say, do or think that. Stop. Dead.

Well, mother and I were in the diningroom. I was drawing. I was very busy. She told me to go upstairs to get her purse. I said. Get it yourself. Startled, she said 'Sarah, don't you dare speak to your Mother that way. Now you go upstairs and get my bag.' I said no. She said, come here. I said no. I knew she would spank me. I started leaving the room. With the crayons. She came rushing up behind me. And whacked me on the bum. I said. With daring anger. You lazy bitch. Then she really got mad.

The diningroom was quiet. A still room. Formal. Venetian blinds and pewter. An oak table that was so shiny I could see my reflection in it. Chapel chairs from England poked under it. With maroon cushions. They were tied up at the back. So they wouldn't slip off every time someone sat down. Underneath was a coarse wicker seat.

Wicker, what is that?

Natural fibre.

Yes. Like the hay and straw in the barns. Like the bullrushes down at the pond. Like the corn stalks in the vegetable garden. And I would find other things like wicker Out There. In the Wild. That no-name unfamiliar land beyond the timber-fence boundary of our property. Stiff crisp plants would grow. On their own. With no one watering or cutting or watching them. Out There.

Inside our Fenced Property was the Familiar. The House, the Gardens, the Pond, the Orchard, the Fields, the Barns, the Sheep, the Ducks, the Chickens and the Dogs. And the Geese. No. Not our geese. Those geese would fly into the pond to feed and rest before flying south. Honking up there in perfect V formations. They belonged to Canada. Swooping down to gobble up the feed that had been put out for them. Not as a trap to kill. Only as a trap to see. They were beautiful. An arresting sight swooshing in and out. What a raucous. Beautiful. Full of rowdy Life. And then off. Away. Free.

Other animals would sneak onto the property. To see. To eat. To live. I would find them. Tracks of them. All the time. Wild deer would come to the pond. To drink. Leaving slippery two-toed mud tracks. And dogs. Coons too. And they would all go to the vegetable garden to eat. To snack. Fresh tracks at dawn. Leaving damaged lettuce. Broken corn. Squished tomatoes. Hollow cabbage. Dad said they were stealing our food.

Not just a little. But a whole lot. Too much. So. My brother and I made a scarecrow out of my snowsuit. Stuck it on a stick. I tied it up with string. For that real person effect. But. It didn't stop them. Not really. So. Dad put out traps. Huge iron jaws. In the middle of the corn stalks. Once pink pigs came from the neighbour's fields. A sow and her piglets. Going to market. To our booby-trapped vegetable garden. I tried to scare them away. Yelling and flailing my arms. She didn't like that. That sow. Her little piglets were frightened of me. But not her. She snorted and came straight at me. She was big. Bigger than me. I started to run. Down the path to the bottom of the garden. Running. Ducking behind the rusty garbage incinerator. Hands on. Peeking from behind. Then. A pained scream. The incinerator had been burning. Scorched hands and a stopped startled old sow. I. Running to the house in tears. She. Running away. Her little piglets clambering about her feet. Thank goodness.

I liked the animals. They were fun to watch. How they ate. Slept. And played. Except when they got angry like the crazy coon swaying in the lawn chair. Frothing. Dad killed it. Bang. With a gun. He said it was dangerous. Rabies. Sometimes he killed untamed rabbits too. Squirrels. And crows. With his shotgun. He would set traps for field mice in the kitchen and the basement. And in the sheep barns. He said they were a nuisance. They spoiled things. They were bad. So. He would stop them. Dead. I didn't think they were so bad. They didn't mean harm. How can a little furry rabbit mean harm? Once dad put out poisoned chickens for the foxes. One of his hunting dogs ate one and died.

That's justice for you.

There used to be a big brown toad that lived under the back step of the house. An ancient toad. My brother and I would sit and wait for that big fellow to come out. To sun himself. It lived in the crack between the two solid granite blocks. The crack would get bigger and bigger every year. I thought dad would kill it. Because it was spoiling the stairs. I would pray

23

for that antique toad. Now I lay me down to sleep, I pray the Lord my soul – and the toad's soul – to keep. I hoped it would get wise. One day I went to see if it was home. Nope. Either dad had killed it. Or it had moved. I didn't dare ask. Maybe dad would stop me. Dead. Too.

That House.

Pineridge.

All that limestone. All those windows and doors. Brushed by pine. Five fireplaces. Huge. On the highest point of land. For miles around. A gentleman's farm. On a clear day one could see across Lake Ontario to the shores of Grimsby and Beamsville. High up. Over the treetops. A bird's eye view. The towers of that fabled city Toronto scratched the distant horizon. Far away.

The house is very old. For the New World. Almost two hundred years. It is older than mother and father. It was bought from an ailing Scot and his four wacky sisters. Highland farmers. They had been poor, old, unable to manage. Drowning. In the wake of the Industrial Revolution. The house had been ramshackled. Run down. With no plumbing. An artesian well fed the wood outhouse out-back. There was another well. A drinking well with a cracked bucket. On the front lawn under the ancient apple tree.

So. My parents bought history. Rural Canadiana. They transformed someone else's hell into paradise. Creating the Homestead. On the Hill. The escarpment. The old rim of Lake Iroquois. Stuffing it with their assembled assorted ancestors' junk. Pioneers. Slowly putting the house together. Home. Using the best from their past and the best from the local area. Cast-iron porridge pots and wooden beams. Italian oils and sixteenth-century English wall cabinets. Brass fire dogs from the Continent and cold brick floors. Iron locks. With keys bigger than my hand.

I have seen proof of their beginnings there. Black and white photos. With a white border. Dated. From their first year there. Newlyweds with a first infant. Together they stand, grinning, in a newly cultivated garden. Click.

Pineridge. Rock by rock. Bound together by a pebbled crude mortar. With foot-thick walls. And sunken windows. A shelter. A fortress. To protect. To ward off that barren cold winter landscape. To ward off snow, rain, and sun. To protect us from all that Sky.

The plane was descending.
Sarah opened and closed her eyes.

Cards and ribbons interwoven throughout the banister poles. Changing the decor. Magical. Mystical. Red poinsettias. Crinkly silver wrapping paper. Ribbons. On everything. Mistletoe hanging from lights. Little lights. Twinkling. Bright. On a living tree in the livingroom. Cut from the forest by the pond. Covered with tinsel. Glitter. Glass. Throwing light everywhere. All of it held together by white hardware string. For effect. All in the name of Christ. That lucky bastard kid. God's son. Pineridge, the sacred. The cradle. Family and friends celebrate the living memory with raised glasses. A toast. A, B and C. Small presents are opened. The fire glows on the window pane. Embers ooze warmth. Milk and cookies are left for Santa. We go to bed with eager excitement. Holding our breath. Christmas.

Breakfast. Davey and I facing each other. Mother and father facing each other. In that sombre diningroom. Lime green bone china passed in front of our sleeping noses. Steamy porridge. With melting brown sugar. A huge silver spoon. A tablespoon. I couldn't even get it in my mouth. But Davey could. A foreign woman would swoosh in and out. Clearing places. Setting places. David and I touched toes under the table. Black oxford to brown oxford. Touching. Sometimes we'd kick. Trying to rest our feet on top of each other. We would make faces. Get off.

Sshh, children.

25

The black labs sat beside father's chair. Quiet. Obedient. Waiting. For a sign. The command. For the moment. From the Master. Ah. Tidbits. Tiny pieces of toast put onto their noses. Stay. Don't move. Stay still. Frozen. Stay. Until. 'Pay for it.' The dogs would salivate all over the carpet. Mother would complain. 'Dear....' So. Okay. 'Pay for it.' Tossed up in the air, and chomped into their drooling mouths. Gone in a flash. Wet saliva sticking to table legs and the backs of chairs. And dad's gray flannels.

And dad would pass mother the sugar. In an unorthodox manner. Throwing cubes through the ring at the bottom of the brass chandelier. Sometimes he'd miss. Plop. Straight into the orange juice. Mother would frown. We were not supposed to laugh. The children. Touching toes. And mother would go back upstairs to bed.

Off for the bus at the end of the lane. Snapping off icicles at the back door. Walking down from the house to the bottom of the hill. Stepping outside the car tracks. Undoing the coat that had been so carefully done up. You can't breathe when they do up that top button. Davey and I agreed. Waiting for the school bus. The big yellow bus with the name of the school stamped on the side. PRIVATE SCHOOL. Waiting. Racing the passing cars with our eyeballs. Who can go faster. Jumping into the puddles. Sneaking out on the ice. Testing. Who gets a soaker first. Who gets dirty first. You. Me. You. Me. Gotcha.

Sarah opened her eyes. Looking out. There were no clouds over Toronto. The plane descended over the lake, over the islands, and circled the CN Tower, waiting, waiting, and then down. Down to Terminal 2, the 427, the 401 to Union Station and the subway. Swirling down.

So much of what I am, who I am, is bound to that place. Pineridge. It is a sanctuary as well as a prison. Isolated and yet oddly connected to all outer worlds. Home. A living vibrant memory. My compass.

Opening the door to her apartment at Yonge and St. Clair. She noted that she would never get used to two-inch thick suburban walls. Imitation walls. Unreal and unfamiliar. She turned on the light. It would take more than just an evening to sort this one out. This mess.

Nicholas.

She wondered if she was just letting herself be overwhelmed by her emotions for the moment. If she was pretending to herself the effect this man and his life had had on her. She had clung to the romance of romance before. There had been others. And there would be more. That wasn't the point. She listened to her body. Quiet. Feeling the undertow. No. She wasn't pretending. The swirl was great. An internal tug pulled on her insides. Dragging her down. Down to a hollow aching pit. Aching.

She went into the kitchen. Flipped on the light. A drink. Scotch and lime cordial. No ice. One of his first comments. No ice? She had explained that the ice didn't affect the drink, it was the booze she wanted not the visuals. He had filled her ice tray that had been tucked away under the sink. He didn't take his drink until the ice was ready.

The telephone rang. She jumped, thinking of him. Guilty. Caught. But, she reassured herself, he never called now. Their arrangements were fixed up through his secretary. The one with the heavy New Joysey accent.

Hello?

The new man. Tony. The one she had met through her stockbroker. He had been nice. Inoffensive. Tame and pleasant. Understandable. She relaxed. Accepting a dinner invitation. They had been seeing a lot of each other. He had stayed with her several times. Taken the bait. Asked her about her trip to New York. The business. She casually answering fine, just fine. Friendly, casual with each other. Hanging up she was pleased he hadn't insisted on getting together tonight. She didn't want to be rude, but she had no desire to see him. None. Though it was odd in her mind, because he was one

27

person she could hug and mean it. A nice, clean, uncompli-
cated hug. Pals. The strength of their bodies together. Clothed
or unclothed. Neither needed the other so much that there
was that desperate sexual want. She caught herself smiling.
That's why we'll never get off the ground. She knew that she
would have to start pulling out soon. She cared enough about
him not to let the possibility of lust arise. If he started wanting
her then they would be in trouble. Because she didn't want
him. No desire, no need. Except for the hug.

And then there was Howith. The aspiring architect. The
only reason that they ever got together was the lust. Not love.
Just lust. They played romantics very well together. Each a
past master on setting stage, atmosphere. Seducing. She would
call him later.

She poured herself another drink. Selected an album. Rach-
maninoff. Sitting on the sofa. Slipping off her shoes. She closed
her eyes.

So much is dependent on what came before us. The genes and
the stories. Big boned, blue eyed, long fingers, thin wavy fine
hair, white and rich. Or. Petite, swarthy, stubby, olive toned,
black eyed, cloaked in a history of poverty and misery. Nurtured in a womb of love, lust, convenience, accident and / or
terror. Vice-versa. Topsy-turvy. In a cocktail shaker. Shook up.
And poured out. History.

The genealogy of our brains and our bodies. Our separate
mythologies. How are we bred? Who do you think you are?
The artificial as well as the real history. From the beginning.
What ancestors paved our paths with their eccentricities?
How does one remember Family? How are they spoken of by
others? How do parents retell their history, how do they trace
their growth?

How are we nurtured by our parents? What are we told to
value from Out There. The givens. To belong. And then, what
do we find. The acquired. To separate. What do we discover
with taste, smell, sight and touch? How do we play? Explore?

And know? Seeing something for the first time. Alone. How does one label it? How does one stamp it with the seal of human knowledge? How do we learn? All our unique experiences and perceptions culminate into an intimate ballet of thought. Gradually developing distinction. Form. Difference. Character. How do we become who we are? Do we resort to the givens? What we have been told. How to think. How to see. How to behave. Or do we explore? Finding words and feelings in ourselves to describe that Otherness. Out There. The inside and the outside of our minds. How do we become who we are?

I was nurtured in the embryonic stage by mother on stories of her somewhat blissful childhood spent in colonial East Africa. Tribal kings, hippos eating roses, nomadic Arabs, British diplomats, swirl as the backdrop to her ancestral home in Dar es Salaam. All sorts of treasures from this golden past linger around the house. Brass inlaid chests. Delicately carved swords in crinkled leather cases. Monkey furs. Etched silver ankle manacles. A dusty turkish coffee pot. Her father was a loyal British subject, and lawyer. He played the violin, read and wrote voluminously, adored his two precious daughters, and finally returned to England during the War to protect and defend his homeland. A great and good man. Her mother was there too, but few stories have been passed on. I have seen a photo in the family album. A group shot of mother's family. She and her sister perched like pigeons on either side of a great fan-shaped rattan chair by the Indian Ocean. Sitting square in the chair is my now dead grandmother, her little legs not quite touching the ground. Her hands are folded neatly in her lap. Around her neck – double stranded pearls. She has a weak smile, but her eyes stare boldly at you from the picture. My now dead grandfather stands at the back, one hand in his jacket pocket, the other holding an unlit pipe. He almost winks at you with his whimsical Noel Coward twinkle. Mother had been brought up in the tradition of perfect English school girls. Nurtured on British Supremacy, Imperialism and Days of the Empire. Both she and her sister were considered to be Ladies of Breeding. Much of her adolescence was spent in England, in London. It was during the air raids that she met my war-hero father.

Father's family, Empire Loyalists with pedigree genes, had moved Northward from Philadelphia during the Civil War. Plymouth Rockers. Quakers, doctors, respectable responsible homesteaders, pioneers, engineers, builders of nations, lawyers, Members of Parliament in Upper Canada, railway builders, financiers, entrepreneurs – all exist as characters in the Stauton family photo albums.

Mother and Father fell in love and were wed.

So. I was given a sense of family honour and destiny before I could barely walk. My blood and brains had Tradition stamped all over them before I could barely speak. I was taught about imperial majesty and pioneer power before I even knew the words. I did not judge these tales, these myths passed on to me. I believed them. My Elders. And listened. I trusted them. They were the Knowing, the Wise, the Truthsayers. The first gods.

I found I was able to verify most of these tales with physical fact. I applied the scientific method to my muddled myths. I would gaze for hours at the photos of the living and the dead who lie neatly in the family album collection. It was the best storybook I ever had. One day I discovered a dusty photo of my mother's mother and my father's mother. At the tender wide-eyed age of seven, dressed in embroidered lace party dresses that swoop floor length, they curtsey together to the poof of the photographer's witnessing eye. Somewhere back there the Society of Friends had pitched them together. Hamilton, Toronto, Philadelphia and England was at one time a small community of royal, loyal friends. So. As much as mother's verbal story came down that father had romantically married her, a foreigner, it seems that my great-grandparents from both sides of the family were close, or acquaintances at any rate.

Like-minded had met and married like-minded. Of the same drawer as my aunt would say.

I only knew one grandparent – my father's mother – a grande dame. She raised her restless children to be law-abiding WASP's. A matriarch, she didn't suffer fools, or nonsense. And she held the family reins in check. Watching all. She regarded the matrimonial choices of her five children as a necessary evil. Outlaws. Who were only included as family if they perpetrated the Stauton Family myths. Family First. The First Family.

All this ancestral intermingling funnels into the present-day appearance of myself and my two brothers: David Hilborn Stauton, the first born, named after my father, me, Sarah Elizabeth Stauton, named after mother, and George Stuart Stauton, named after mother's father and father's youngest brother.

Our heritage. Rich. Alive. Full of perky personalities and tantalizing tales. Past and present. Giving the Family a sense of Community, holding all the elements of Solid Social Fibre. Rooted in North America. Growing in Canada. We even have Red Indian blood mixed in for good measure. So.

Red, white and blue blood.

True Canadian Establishment.

At least, that is what I have been lead to believe. The given.

And then there is the acquired.

I grew up in the country. What I knew of city life was restricted to bimonthly visits to see my Grandmother in Forest Hill, a posh tree-lined residential district in Toronto, and to see my eye doctor who worked at the corner of King and James in downtown Hamilton. Community living was limited to interaction with my relatives and family. The clan gatherings.

And then there was Millwood. The local village about fifteen minutes by car from Pineridge.

Mother would have a mission. Shopping. With a list in her slanty large script. Sometimes I would go with her. To McQuire's. The grocer's. A small shop with a dark green awning. A big room with saggy squeaky wooden floors. The

McQuire family ran the store. I would stare at them. They were big friendly people who had different accents from the community I knew with my family. Clipped. And they dropped their *ings*. And they said *eh*. And they never wore gray flannels. Old Mr. McQuire had funny-looking glasses and an absent-minded air. His brother Jacob stood behind the meat corner. He would slash at meat and step into the cold freezer to get the cut mother wanted. He had a stubbled beard. A droopy cigarette always dangled from his mouth. Even while he spoke. There was a woman there with big brown eyes and bright red lipstick. Dressed in white, like the maid. Always smiling. Good teeth. June? No, maybe Joan. Often I would slip into the back room while they were loading up mother's parcels. The storeroom. Untouched privacy. Boxes. Dark and musty. Like the barn at the farm. And there were holes in the floorboards. You could see right down to the basement. Stuffed with cardboard. The McQuires' would call me by name. And they would ask me about my brothers.

To Addisons'. The glossy pharmacy, where I could find an unlimited supply of comics and candies. Mr. Addison was a friendly, gray-haired fellow with a fall-away chin. He was dressed in white. Like the milkman. He would give mother little white parcels.

To Doctor Rossway. The family physician. Rossway, mother would say, came from Scotland to seek Fame and Fortune in the New World. He wanted to become a member of Society. Mother used to find him repulsively friendly to her, especially with his salutations of 'Well Elizabeth, how are you today?' I have never heard anyone call mother Elizabeth. And we would sit in the waiting room of the doctor's office, mother would be reading a magazine and I would be watching the other people from Millwood come and go. Fascinated. I would stare. Spying on their differences. I had never seen any of these children before. We went to private school. Bus linked from the bottom of the driveway to the school grounds. And back.

But here, in Millwood, there were children who wore strange clothes. They were often dirty. Dressed in public in the clothes that we were only allowed to play in. None of the women in there looked like mother. She had a strength, an ordered proud beauty. Self-possessed, other-worldly. And she would not scramble after us like the other mothers used to do. She would order us back to our seats and that would be it. She used to speak to these people as she would the maid, the help, the cleaning lady and the gardeners. Friendly, but reserved. A child sees these things and adopts the manners. Recognizing early on that we were apart from. Separate. Different.

To the hairdresser's. There were many of them. Often little fidgety skeletal women who lived in tacky homes. Their front rooms would be converted into hair salons. There were always horrible photographs of women stuck on the walls. Fashion models. With buffoon hairdos. Teased. Glazed eyes and lipstick smiles. With necks that looked as if they strained around any farther they would snap. There were always magazines there that we would never have in the house. Film stars, glossy. Black-yellow-red. Screaming Scandal. Gossipy headlines. Elvis. Grimy, well thumbed. Mother said it was junk. She would give me a *Reader's Digest* to sift through. Under the dryer. But I was fascinated by this forbidden literature. Why didn't we have it? The school-bus driver, Grace, would always be reading that stuff. I liked her. So. It couldn't have been that bad. Those magazines.

To the post office. In our new look-alike button-curl perms. Mother and daughter pick up the deluge of mail. Bills, magazines – *Time, Reader's Digest, National Geographic, Life, Vogue, Maclean's, Harper's Bazaar, Country Life, Gourmet, Town and Country*, invitations and junk mail. A delight. Always different. And parcels. Reaching up on toes to unlock box 17. Finding the brown parcel ticket. Waiting in line. The first line I ever waited in. Recognizing decorum with strangers. These Millwood folk. Wait in line. To be handed a

33

parcel. Presents, books, records, clothes from relatives over-seas. From travelling parents. From travelling aunts. And responsible godmothers.

Sometimes I would go to Wilsons. The hardware store. But only with dad. A fantastic place. So many gadgets: pots and pans, paint, sporting stuff, western gear, tackle, guns, china, nuts and bolts. What a mission it was to go in and buy half a pound of nails. Or thread bolts. Or two yards of cable wire. Or fine-grain sandpaper. Dad would wait in the car. He always knew exactly what he wanted. He would give me a list in his hard, tight miniature writing. He would tell me to put it on the Stauton account. Mr. Wilson always talked to me about my father as if he were a buddy. He'd kind of joke. And then I would sign my name. Carefully. Sarah Elizabeth Stauton.

Then back home. Always to the house. Car-linked to Pineridge. The windswept farm on the hill. The fortress. The separate. The familiar. Home.

MONDAY

It was a quarter to eight when she woke. Damn. There was lit-tle time to put herself together. Her mouth tasted grotty. She needed to get ready not only for the office but for the evening with Tony. She rinsed out her liquor glass and filled it with orange juice.

She was late by the time she got to the office. Messages had already started circulating. The business world was clamour-ing about her. Demanding attention. Concentration. Her time. Yes sir. She gave her all. After all she was getting paid for this. Her career.

The magazine was in the final stage of production. Dead-lines had to be met. It meant pacing herself effectively, efficiently. The New York weekend had no place here. Little had any place here except for her judgement given in a

34

mechanical way. Yes. Nope. Maybe. Tomorrow. Now. Memos. Briefs. Letters. Action.

She didn't take lunch. There was too much to do. Besides, she rationalized, she would get a good meal later. And he would pay.

Tony would pick her up at the office. He always got away before the five o'clock traffic. The privilege of his position.

At 4:46 he walked in the door. Looking his businessman best. She shuffled together the papers, stuffing some into her briefcase. Checking quickly on the movement of the others. Yes. They would be ready by ten tomorrow morning. Good. On schedule.

They went to Luigi's Trattoria. One of his haunts. His smothered Italian blood. Passion for pasta. They drank wine, slowly. Gossiping. Talking business. Planning. Flirting in their friendly way. He took her hand. She resisted her natural impulse to squeeze back. Hesitantly she pulled her hand away. Talking, smiling, giving in a different way. He ordered dinner. Coffee and liqueurs. Taking her hand again. Gently. Persuasively. The booze had started pushing her towards him. Getting soft. Thoughtful. No. Not him Tony. Him Nicholas. She didn't want to think about it, so she let her hand sit in Tony's. She also decided that she wanted him at her apartment tonight. Knowing exactly what she was doing she slowly leaned towards him.

As they walked to the car he put his arm around her. He knew she would take him. There was no resistance. At the apartment, he gave her a gentle neck rub. Kissing the top of her head. Then he led her to the bedroom.

She didn't like sex with him. He jiggled. But he was a body. A warm companion. He slept peacefully beside her. She didn't move. She wanted sleep badly. But she couldn't get it. The luxury. Peace. Nicholas's naked form stood before her mind's eye. No. Too much. She had to think of other things. Push her mind to another place. Look at something else. Think. She thought of her mother. She thought of her parents' home. She thought of yet another story her mother had told her.

My conception. All I know is what I've been told. I also know that there is no doubt that one remembers the story the way one wants and needs it. So.

Once. While flying along in the open boat in Georgian Bay, Mother pointed to a long spindly island and quite matter of factly said, 'This is where you were conceived.' I peered at that island. Opposite the mainland. It was one of the last shelters for boaters and fishermen before the wild water of the Open. My parents had gone there some twenty-seven years ago. Wind-swept pines, arid gray-green-pink rock. For a picnic. Under the vast blue Sky. The sun brilliant. Warm. Inviting. Yes. I can understand the choice. I like to think that I was conceived in a love flowing from the Natural Way of Things. Not after some noisy, brawling, boozy, cocktail party in a stuffy house in the dead of winter in the electric-heated heart of downtown Toronto. No. Not I.

I was born April 4, 1955. No longer a desire, a wish, a longing. My conception is complete. Their desire to have a child is fulfilled. And I am. I belong to them. Their creation. Of their blood, but separate. All human, all divine. The chromosomic battle had produced a girl who they name after them. I am. To them, kin, One of the Tribe. A continuation of the Family. A continuation of the species, the flow of an idea and a belief in their matrimonial love.

I was pampered, cherished, scolded and spanked. My earliest memories are mostly those that jar me into a way of seeing myself. I was civilized according to my parents' perceptions. I was taught the habits of their civilization brutally. The gods told me how to be. A slapped curious hand, a spanked dirty bottom, a harsh word about when and when not to look. Told not to do something, when I knew I could do it. The contradictions. Not always given an explanation, just told. Taught about clean-dirty, tidy-messy, good and bad behaviour. Virtue and vice. Learning the Dos and the Don'ts. How to act to be acceptable. Civilized. Learning to conform. Discovering that some gestures had very little meaning except for some obscure historical precedent. Like how to hold one's knife and fork. This was important. A ritual akin to the Last Supper. Apparently it too shows breeding. How to shake hands, how to smile, not laugh. To stand, not sit. P's and Q's. Taught to be self-conscious in the presence of others. Other-conscious. Taught about uniformity. But learning too that the gestures and words had different meanings in public and in the privacy of the family. Learning that right and wrong were often a question of timing. How one ought never to scratch there. Or to pick one's nose. Never fart or burp. Taught to smother all natural impulses. I was jerked, pulled, pushed and prodded. Told to absorb the habits of my parents. Told to brush my teeth, comb my hair, shine my shoes and wash my undies. Control of oneself is all. Taught to be a a perfect little girl so that one day I could grow up to be perfect lady just like mummy. Taught to be good. Nice. Learning to kiss ass. Discovering that my getting was proportional to my giving what they wanted. Be good. Pat on the head.

But let's face it. I was being taught how to be proper and good not so much for me but for them. We were expected to be good children to fulfill their ideal of marriage. Heaven forbid that we actually didn't want to be any part of it. Just be their side-kick when they wanted to go into the Family Routine. Family unit comes first. Stauton always. Up front. On show.

And there I was. I am. And I had to figure out what this was all about. What is all this jazz anyway? I had to sort out the battle of perceptions. Mine and theirs. Who to believe. Faith. In whose perceptions. Me or you. Discovering that no situation is perceived the same way by any two people. Who to believe. You or me. Trust. Respect. Trust. Justice. I watched and saw that Father was a hard-working, tight-lipped, honest democrat and that Mother was a loud selfish gossip. An authoritarian. I learned about honesty, industry and hard work

37

from Father, and laziness, lies and entertaining from Mother. I also learned the subsequent rewards for each. Both have their advantages and disadvantages. And both had their reasons.

In the meantime I was jostled and jolted. Told not to be this way. It's not nice. Not becoming to a young lady. Be polite. Quiet. Don't shout. Quickly learning to internalize this dialogue. Do. Don't. Yes. No. Public. Private. Others. Family. Alone. Harnessing curiosity. Told it was desire. It was wrong to want. No. Figuring out that it is not wrong to want. What is wrong is to show something that they think resembles overt greed. Curiosity seeks explanation. Understanding. Desire seeks consumption. Control. Destruction. Learning that there are limits. To getting. Not necessarily to wanting. To know. Learning that it is more often than not a pedantic question of social appearances and economics. To parents. But a child doesn't want to be taught these complex adult games. I wanted everything. I wanted to touch, smell, see, taste everything. I wanted to belong to everything. To be. Everything. But they just wanted me to be good. A good girl. And they would hurt me if I didn't do what they wanted. So. Acting their way. Act good. Recognizing that of course you can do anything. Most things. Learning the tricks of the trade. Off. Doing alone. Stealing. Lying. Hiding. From them. To discover on my own. And I tasted that. The excitement of knowing you can. You are. Free. Realizing that when you deny the influence of others who want you to be something they want, you are free. In the meantime, quickly learning to be of two minds in one body. One for them. And one for me. Learning about the external NO and yes, and the internal YES and no. The squishing DON'TS and the liberating DOS. Developing the necessary Mind / Body split. Yes, you really have to spend so much energy convincing others that you are one of them. Yeah. Just like you. Actually you are much better than I. I have just a miserable little life and I want you to fill me with you. Please. Make me what you are. Yes. I promise. I will be your puppet. Hand springs and all. For you. I will belong. No. I promise, I am not separate from you. And yes. I will always, always, need you. But, you should really know what I will want. Some day. Only one thing. Yes, you should know I will always want freedom. Where I can be me. In fullness. I am. Complete. Without you. Without any one thing or person defining me. I am. Everyone wants that. Freedom. To be.

Dusk. After a four or five hour drive north with a stopoff at Freddy's Hideaway for a drink for the parents and a shot for the car, we kids would slip around to the back of the building and go down to the lake. To feed the trapped trout. Bread. A bubble, like an open sore on the water. Percolating. Starving little fishes. Going for crumbs. Then we'd all clamber back into the car. On the road again. Driving. Chauffeured. The roads getting narrower and narrower. Grass, cultivated trimmed grass would give way to burnt scraggly grass. Roadside mad grass. Untended. Untouched. Then the rocks. A streak here. A lump there. A lake on the left. Stretching away. The road would dip. More rocks. Boulders, cliffs, embankments, pink rock. The road no longer straight, a human invention, no, now it forms to the rocks. Twists, ducking in and out of the Forms. The Rocks. Big Rocks. Leading us to the River. A thrill in the car. Anticipation. Excitement. Knowing. Not just for the River, but for the way of life. The freedom.

Down the gravel drive. To the water's edge. The boats are waiting. They are covered. The tarps have water on them. The boats bounce gently against the bumpers. Waiting for Us. An invitation. Fill us. Use us. The boats. For the Escape. Loading them. Full. Dogs, groceries, booze, guests, family. Everyone finding their place. Their appointed spot. Dad at the wheel, sitting up on the back of the seat. In the big boat. Mother tucked down behind the shield. My brothers and I in the wood ski boat. There is no shield. It is open. You can feel the wind. The water. The sun. Watching Dad. He sits up on the back of his seat. So that he too can get the wind, water and sun. Mother protected, sheltered. Doesn't want to get fussed, her hair.

39

Especially when there are guests. The Image. On Show. They have to see it right. The North Country for the Weekend.

Anyway.

An hour by boat down the river. Indians, burial grounds, lost fishermen, drunk locals, long boats, the Sky – the vivid contrast of Sky to water, pink rocks, and the voluminous clouds. Dad in the big boat. Everything loaded to the hilt. Ploughing, not quite planing. Pushing water back, apart, separating the water before us. In our ploughing boats. Mother in the bow of the big boat ahead, dispensing drinks. Either she or Uncle George. Down the river. The route is always the same. Snug in here, close to this embankment, centre stream, know the depth. The water line. The rocks. Not like the highway where it's all spelled out for you. Here, just years of travelling. Indians. Voyageurs. Fishermen. Locals. Knowing the route. The way. Some spots are more magnificent than others. The hollowed-out rocks, like natural cathedrals. With altar pieces. Hunks of granite on their side. Leaning out. Balanced. Immensely quiet. Sacrificial blocks. A lost time. Before time. Our time. Glacial. Prehistoric. Tundra.

On one side of the river. The reservation. With one lonely Indian hut. A slapped-together log house, with a dirty mud path down to the water. The dock is hardly visible. A foot wide, with holes, sloping into the water. Reeds grow up through the holes. A little tin boat drawn up on the grass. The motor bent up. Rusty red. Filthy. Filled with water. We would go to buy our flagpoles from this place. Fifty bucks for a clean bald tree. The man was surly, dark. Rumour had it he spent the money on booze. Firewater. Looked half mad. Primitive. Yes. Savage. And poor. He had a woman, not a wife. We never saw her. No children. They had different rules. Laws. Wide-eyed and wondering, we were.

On the north side of the river were the white cottages. Figures that the white cottages would have white people. They had swing sets and yellow lawn chairs. Antennas. And their boathouses touched the water perfectly.

We would plough down the middle. You could always feel the Silence, the Permanence, from that dark side of the river. Even over the din of the boats. Even over the chatter of the guests. Over the tinkle of drinks. Over the friendly hand waving from the cottagers.

You couldn't talk in the ski boat. Not really. Too much noise. I don't like to talk anyway. I like to watch. To look, to smell. Rushing along the water like a god. Soaring. A high from the motion. Feel the cold roar. The dogs perched at the side with their noses out over the water. Ears flapping. Sniffing. Through the last little bay before the Open. A cluster of houses. The last point of contact with Civilization. Supplies. Gas and food. Two camps. Clarence and Maggie. Clarence Stout and Maggie Fish. On either side of the river. Arch enemies. We are neutral. Go-betweens. Touching both shores. Scuttling between their memory maps. Their ancient history. Before time. My time. Clarence on the gas pumps. Maggie in her store.

Approaching Clarence. He always knew. He'd be watching for the boats. Come strolling down from his yellow clapboard house. Slow. Over the rocks. Never wave. Strolling down the walkway to the pumps. Real slow. Hail Clarence. A railway cap on his sandy blonde head. Ageless. Never shaved. Stubborn stubble. Poking out all over his weathered face. Twinkling sky-blue eyes. He would say What's new Charlie Brown and tousle my hair. To me. Joking. Giving dad the gears. Kidding. The longest fingernails I've ever seen on a man. Real long. Yellow tobacco fingers. Export A. And he always smelled of gas. Talk about the weather, past present future. Talk about the winter. Talk about the fishing. Talk about the hopeless Stautons. Driving boats for twenty years and still don't know how to land the crates. Dad swinging in the tanks. In and out of the boats. Smiling. Mixing in the quart of oil to the gas. Fuel. Pumping the line till it was hard. Clarence never touched the lines. Your boat, you do it. Pushing off. A wave. And a twinkle. Then. Strolling up the path. Slow. To charge it. The

Stauton account. His back. Our back. Back to back. Moving towards Maggie.

The last spot before taking off through the harbour markings. She would be so friendly. Chatty. Aged. Years of living there. At the mouth to the Open. Wrinkled. Sun-eyed. Toothless. Perfect dentures. She'd sell pies. Blueberry pies. And fresh cranberries. She'd pick them in the outer islands. The Bustards. She married Harry. A guy from Point-au-Baril. I think. I might have that one wrong. Anyway. Mother would say he was a good-for-nothing who gave her sex. He was about twenty-five years her junior. A handlebar moustache, lamb-chop sideburns and a beer belly. He never did a damn thing except drink. That's still Mother's voice. He'd sit at the old ice house in front of the store. As we came in he'd wave. But he'd never come down to help us. There was a kind of honour system there. If you outsiders want to come and play hardy. Well, play hardy. Dad used to love it. In his broken-down felt hat. Brim down, sunglasses clipped onto his specs. Shorts, ankle socks and Wallabees. Dad up-north. He was so strong up there. So much himself. Skipper. Pioneer. Voyageur. He knew those waters so well. He knew those boats so well. He ought to. He made them. In the garage. His mistress, mother would say. He separated off part of the three-car garage. Making it into a workroom. During the winter. Fiberglas floating in the air. A pot-belly stove hooked up to keep it warm. A plastic tarp hammered up to the ceiling. Hours he would spend in there. Hours. After everyone had gone to bed. Only a single light on in the garage. In the night.

He knew his boats all right.

And Maggie would hail him. No one said hi David like she did. It was as if she were his sister. Familiar. But not too familiar. She knew her livelihood. She used to call Mother Mrs. Stauton.

Standing with Maggie in the store. Watching the boat traffic. Another consultation on the weather, gossip about the locals, the city folk. The who's-where-this-season ritual. Talk about food needs. The summer order. How much fresh milk, bread, eggs and meat we'd need. She had to order it up from the highway. So it would be ready when we next came in. And she would have boxes of freshly laundered linen to take. Towels with lots of starch. Snapping on the clothesline behind her store. Bundled up, then folded and put into cardboard boxes. Charged to the Stauton account.

Then the Open. Ready. Prepared. Full throttle. Away. Always rough. The boats must stick together. For safety. Against the roar. Dad would keep looking back at our boat. Stick to his wake. He'd point. Standing up. Colder. The boats banging the water. Spray over the bow. Over the stern. People snuggle. Adjusting the weight, trying to get the smoothest driest ride. The driver always gets soaked. Have to keep up the speed before losing daylight. An orange talon sky. Nothing but rocks bubbling out of the water. And bare islands. An occasional fishing hut with a crooked tin smokestack. Leaving the city, the people, the highways, the telephones, the cars, the human noise. Over the water. Away. The protected walls of the river giving way to the Open. Space. To the Roar. See for miles. To the horizon. White caps. Island dots. No one talks now. No one drinks. Like the dogs. Perched. Watching. Sniffing. Being. Soaring.

After a time.

Coming down. Who can spot the marker first. Looking, squinting. Looking for the buoy. Looking for the familiar landmarks. Burnt Island. Banging. Looking. The excitement. The reaching. Then. There. A bobbing Javex bottle. Full throttle. The spray. Holding. Holding. Then. There.

Aurora. Paradise. The Island. Our Island. My Island. The naked flagpole visible over the torn pine trees. The marker bobs. Across the Bay. Flat out. Aurora. Past the open gap. Past the isolated islands. The rocks. Aurora. We circle the island. Welcome. We're here. Aurora.

I could write a symphony.

Sing.

Dance.

Skip.

Jump.

We step out of the boats. Onto the dock. To the rocks. Up to the cabins. Unlocking the buildings. Unloading the boats. The dogs go crazy. Sniffing. Running. Swimming. Wagging. Jumping. The people are controlled but the feeling is the same. Boxes up to the house, suitcases off to various cabins. We're here.

For the summer. For months. For days. For hours on end. Multiple minutes. Here. Indefinitely. Pulling off shutters. Opening windows. The wind blowing through. Starting the water pump. Lighting the fridges. And the stove. Propane. Dad over at the wind tower. Unlocking the generator. Pulling down the blades. Swoosh, swoosh. Mother in the storeroom putting away the supplies. Everyone else is carrying. From here to there. There to here. Uncle George sets up the bar. Then. Slipping away.

To your own room. To unpack. I have the end cabin always. Down the walkway over the swamp. Opening the heavy pine door. Opening the windows. The screens breathe. My view across the water to the Open. High enough to see everything. As far as the Killarney mountains fifty miles away. Magnificent. The water is a stone throw away from the room. Kissing the shoreline. The marriage, the caress. Impertinent quiet pecks. And the hum. The distant faint roar of the Open. The hum. Dusk. Slipping away. I am here.

That feeling stays with you the whole time you're there. You can't get away from it. The presence of the Sky. The Open. The Water. The Sun. The Rocks. The Sky. Even when you fall into the rituals of the human. Cocktails, hors d'oeuvres, gossip, drinks. Tinkle, tinkle. Menus. The human adornment. The costumes. Decorum recognized. Dad changes into knee socks, and beige shorts that still have the crease mark down the front. And a polo shirt. Mother goes exotic. Flouncy. Pink and lime green with bright jingling jewellery.

Fighting the natural colours. The soft wispy grasses, the pastel rocks, the perfect pines. The dark stained cabins and the brick chimneys. Mother insists on the arrangement of chairs outside. A perfect semi-circle around the stone barbecue. With little tables for drinks and nibblies. The conquering ordering human. Mother the Imperialist. But. A ruby red blaze rips across the Sky. Marking another majesty. Sometimes it gets to be too much. Too powerful. Even the mini-imperialist realizes, or maybe senses, that she's only second in command. Dust to the impersonal Natural Order. The Atomic Buzz of Electricity. Something much bigger. Beyond our limited comprehension. But it's only touched. Ever so gently. A passing comment between guests. 'Such a beautiful sunset.' Trying to force it under control as if it were made to order. The earth turns slowly. The sun doesn't set at all. Ever. On top of the world. Everything human seems so far away. Below. Sitting. On top of the world. Aurora.

So rich. So much wealth. Money can't buy. The rules don't apply.

Here. Within the Sky.

How can you beat that feeling?

The Family was always more of a family up north. I'm sure it was mostly a result of the lack of telephone, TV, radio and Society. We had to turn to each other for entertainment. We always seemed to talk up north. The flow wasn't suddenly chopped in half by someone arriving. Or the telephone ringing. Or the intrusion of TV time. And no one had to go anywhere. To be somebody. And no one was going out. Away. We had to entertain each other in the luxury of Aurora's solitude. Bridge, puzzles, Scrabble, games, fishing, cooking, talking, dining. Oh yes. There were always Guests. Mother needed them. Otherwise I'm sure she wouldn't have been able to cope with the Hereness. Guests gave her a future problem. A planning problem. She would spend enormous time and energy organizing everyone to death so that all would have a Good Time. David

45

once said that he detested Forced Fun. It put mother into tears. On the edge she was. Almost always. She too. Struggling with the personal and the public. Caught between the Big Yes and the Big No. Squished.

The weather dictated everything there. It would determine our day's activities. Day cruises, exploring, picnics or fireside. Omnipresent weather. Coming in across the bay. The Open. Clear sunny weather. Knowing when you wake up in the morning before the seven o'clock skinny what the day would be. Not only the weather but also the human plan. The human ordeal. Mother orchestrating. Deciding what would be fun. She controlled the meals. The menus. And since everyone wanted to eat you'd have to bend to her. She holds the food strings. Catch her gist, her mood, and do what she wants. As children. Sometimes she would be outvoted. Only sometimes. The Men would want to fish. The Women would want to mostly sunbathe, read and gossip. Ergo portable sardines. And picnic. Then there would be the hunt for the good picnic spot. Filling the boats and taking off. Could literally take hours. I want a nice flat rock, Mother would say. Battling the natural flowing curving environment. That glacial toning. Wanting it to be like a floor. Finally she would get out of the boat, go over to the picnic hamper which was set up on a flat rock and sit down. On a cushion. Queen Bee. She would dispense the food. But it was all timed. You could only eat after you'd taken a swim. If of course you were going to swim. Always the same. And Mother would sip her sherry or wine and wait. With triscuits and cheddar cheese. Watching.

She always looked so uncomfortable. Sitting with her legs stuck out in front of her. With her crooked painted toenails. And she would wear a big flouncy hat to cover her face. She didn't like the sun. Gives her wrinkles. Bad for the skin. Cancer. Jesus. Why didn't she ever allow herself to be just a woman? Relax. Dad would bumble off. Do his thing. Fishing. Picking berries. Fixing something. Content. Mother would

46

always grumble and want to talk. Gossip. Orchestrate. Order. Puncture that Here Roar. With human entertainment.

Maybe she herself was confused by the roles. Man. Woman. Mother. Father. Male. Female. Not sure what to do. Power games and order are more easily understood. Yes. Order, repetition is understandable. Maybe it was the presence of her children, maybe she didn't know what kind of example to set. At Pineridge everything had its proper place. We children were kept out of her path by a variety of live-in help. But at the cottage, there was nowhere to hide us. We were living proof of her sex. Her animalness. Her loving lust for father. Well, shit, I'm trying. There we would stand. The children. Their progeny. Awkward, quiet, blond, inquisitive, delicately sturdy youth. Strangers. The contact consisted of giving us hamburgers and hot dogs. No physical contact. Ever. Never. That was lost long ago. And we would seldom see them touch. Display. Affection. Between them. Always masking the true sensuality of their bodies. The strength. The natural strength. Aware only of the appearance. The Image. The look. The Brady Bunch. The Stauton Show. In the Open Wilderness of the North Country.

Sarah woke early. She didn't want sex with him. She quietly got up. Taking her clothes into the livingroom. Going into the kitchen, putting on the kettle. Into the bathroom to shower. What had it been in the dream – somewhere up-north, in the boat, the Open, somewhere. She towelled quickly to dress quickly. She knew he would sense her wall. She would have to masquerade her early-morning denial of him or else he would be hurt. She set the breakfast table, playing Nice Girlfriend. Making it pleasing. She'd forgotten her perfume. He liked it. She went into the bathroom. Wiping it on her chin. There. Even if he sensed she wasn't willing he would appreciate her morning effort. It would be all right. For a while anyway. She could hear him in the next room. Getting up. She slipped out of the bathroom and went into the kitchen. When he came out, he walked to her, put his arms around her and hugged. Tight. Holding her. Murmuring. 'Good morning.' Hmm. Easy. Painless.

Now breakfast.

TUESDAY

Tuesday was uneventful.

Except that Howith had called. Would she be free later that night? He wanted to see her. But only after he'd finished the line drawings for the Edmonton project. He also had a squash game at the club. So he would be running late. So. In time for bed. Bedtime. She hung up. Cheap horny bastard. But they understood each other.

At seven she packed it in at the office. She'd have time to have a drink with a friend, and a shower before he would arrive. She called Barb. Yes. That would be great. They decided to meet at the Twenty-Two. While waiting for the subway to carry her down to Bloor she thought about Howith. Another satisfying dissatisfaction. A smooth devil. She was well aware that she wasn't the only woman in his life. But she would not demand more. She didn't give much. She did a mental comparison of Nicholas and Howith. No, Nick had some other element. A subtle softness. A human politeness. A soft spot. Somewhere. But Howith was cold. Dagger ice. No vulnerability anywhere. But it didn't really matter. Now. They both used each other anyway. For sex. Instruments. Object to object. Their bodies spoke well together. Purr and bounce. But sometimes it was a bit much for her to take. He had said once, somewhat matter of factly, that he wanted to jerk off in her mouth. She knew she would never do it. Not that she hadn't. It was his sucking whore fantasy that she was resisting. No. Not me, kid.

She pulled up her collar as the wind tunnel caught her on

the platform. She wished he would deal with the age-old problem of wanting his girls to be just like his mother. He never seemed to address that question. It made him truly impossible to be with for extended periods of time. He never let her be. He would judge. Her in relation to his mother. Act authoritarian. Pushy parent. Be this way. Big Daddy. No. No. He would never do. Just good sex. To a point.

She was meeting Barbara for a drink. Barb was the closest Sarah could find to a kindred spirit in the beautiful bowels of Toronto the Good. Barb could say fuck off and mean it. That's no mean accomplishment for someone who's been brought up to be a lady. She was also a generous, giving creature, sensitive to the balance of selfishness in all interactions. They understood each other very well. They could both fight and they both tried to love. It was Barb who had once said what a poetic touch it was to be involved with someone called How. Yes, they both watched very carefully. They both stared.

When Sarah entered the bar she didn't see her right away. Barb was at the counter smoking, sipping her favourite. Looking at her. Sarah smiled. God, we are such kids. Playing this assinine adult game to perfection. She sat down and ordered herself a dry martini.

Barb was excited, she was soon opening her new play at Adelaide Court. She only needed time now to get the publicity done. She was pleased. The actors and the actresses were good. The stage design was good. The theatre was good. Now she just had to work on the press. The critics. The ones who would pat her on the head and say well done kid, you're a star. Sucking the rest of the audience in through the holy words of print. As Barb spoke her body moved. She was sensual, aware of her sexuality, her womanliness, aware of her breathing. Her natural light. She could attract people without trying. She had that look.

Sarah always felt good too, passing time with her. She liked their presentation together. Their ambience. Uppity, witty, sexy women. When they were high they always attracted others. That evening was no exception. Before long two lone rangers from Winnipeg were buying them drinks.

Sarah asked them the time. They gave each other the eye. I got this one pegged. She waited. For the time. 8:46. Time to go. She was glad she'd had the third drink. She felt she needed it. Barb had noticed. Had ordered a double on the boys. In the midst of flight Barb leaned over and kissed her. 'You look wiped. Ease up.' Sarah smiled. Hugged her. The taller man who'd given Sarah the time zeroed in on Barb. She winked at Sarah and allowed herself the distraction.

Walking felt good. Cleansing. She wouldn't have much time now but it didn't matter. She wanted the air. Striding along Bloor Street and up Avenue Road. At Davenport she finally hailed a cab. As she climbed in the driver moaned. Why? He had found out recently that he had been rejected in his second application to community college. 'You know lady, I just want a trade. I want to get away from this shit.' He hit the meter. Well. She talked to him. What did he want to do? She noted he had a nice haircut but also a dirty neck. He didn't know, but not this shit. Slam. As she climbed out, she handed him a big tip. 'You know, if at first....' 'Yeah, I know. Lie, lie, lie again.' He should wash, she thought. That always cuts the first impression. Always. Is it clean? Is it ordered? Is it tidy? A civilized human being. Is it?

Her apartment too needed a cleaning she noted as she dropped her bills into the kitchen drawer. But How wouldn't mind. Besides, he was only interested in the bedroom. She preferred it. He didn't threaten her. She'd known others when she was younger who would behave as if the apartment was their own. Throwing their coats on the chair, they'd use her phone, long distance and local, they'd drink her liquor, they'd raid her fridge, smoke her dope, maul her record collection, maul her, presume they were going out together ergo it was okay, and not even ask. Without checking. Without respecting her life there. Her presence. But she had learned how to handle it.

How to stop being so polite. Hey, wait a minute. This is not a public phone, nor a pit stop. And you don't own me. Hands off. No. How wasn't an adept thief, nor an adept spy. He just wanted the lay. Fine. That she could handle.

The buzzer.

She slipped into the bathroom. Checking the look quickly. She'd do. She pinched her cheeks. Licked her lips. Tasted the liquor. No. He wouldn't like that. She grabbed a cough lozenge from the cabinet, popped it into her mouth. And opened the front door.

Handsome. Standing. Posed. Waiting. Ready.

A fucking commercial.

She thought of the thousands who stand at doors. Waiting. Admit me. Gimme shelter. She stepped towards him. Aware of his heavy wool sweater. He smelled of the outdoors. He had biked over. He manoeuvred her inside and closed the door. Kissing her gently.

He wanted a glass of water. He placed her aside and went into the kitchen. He turned and stood. Looking at her. Right. Kitchen. Water. She handed him a glass and pointed to the tap. All yours, baby.

He talked of his latest project. A design for the new community hall in Edmonton. It was a competition. He knew he would win. He talked quietly of the squash game, only to say he'd won. He talked of some of the people he'd seen at the club. Mutual friends. He made a nasty gossipy remark about one of her friends. She defended her. But it didn't matter. They never talked with each other. Only at. So. To shut him up she decided to put on an album. Change the subject. The tone. He didn't like rock and roll, he didn't like folk, and classical music didn't quite fit the mood. He liked the subtle approach. The cat motion. The romantic lay. She pulled out Thijs Van Leer's *Introspection*. Flute, soft jazz. A gift from another cold romantic years ago.

They sat on the sofa. He closed his eyes. Tired. With his large hand placed on her lap. On her thigh. Quiet. She too closed her eyes. Allowing the seduction. The music to enter. The quiet smouldering ballet of sound and motion touching them. He was kissing her ear. Her hair. Gently touching her face. Running his finger along her hip. Kissing. Soft. Pushing. Pulling.

The phone rang.

It was her mother. Prying, hearing the music. Are you alone? It was a rhetorical question. Would she be coming home for the weekend? Would she like to bring someone? Had she heard that Aunt Clare was in the hospital again? Sarah interrupted her and said she'd call back in the morning. She was busy. Her mother continued. Your father wants to know if you have his lightweight chisel and his black-handled hammer. Sarah laughed. But it was a real question. 'No mother, I do not. I must go.' But her mother would not let her go until she had finished with her. Had she seen her Madeira silk blouse? It had been up in the attic closet and she needed it for a dinner party at the York Club. Sarah lied. No. I haven't. 'Well dear, give us a call if you're coming home for the weekend. I have to know in order to get some food. Well, I have to go now dear. Do call.' Sarah noted that she never got the food, she just pretended the Need to Know. It was only an age-old power struggle so that Sarah would have to think of her before she moved in any direction. She hung up.

She looked at Howith. His eyes were closed. He also had what looked like an erection. She was not in the mood. Even the soft, mellow jazz turned her. But what to do? 'Would you like some wine, How?' He opened his eyes. Smiled lazily. 'Red or white?' 'I've only got red.' He nodded. And closed his eyes.

She walked into the kitchen. The bottle was open. It had been breathing for several days. She took a swig. Tilting the bottle up. The wine rushing in around her teeth, filling up her cheeks. She drank deep. Swallowing mouthfuls. A slight burn behind her eyes. Yup. That'll do it. She opened the whitewashed cupboard and pulled out two of her Waterford crystal wine glasses. He'd prefer that over the cheaper model she also had. He was an architect. Ergo an aesthetic snob. Besides, she wanted it right. Just for the record. She poured a mouthful into each glass. It was for sipping, for effect, not for drinking. She took another long drink from the bottle, then corked it. She took the bottle and the glasses into the livingroom. He was looking at a book. The biography of Georgia O'Keefe: *Portrait of an Artist.* She didn't like him touching it. It was one of her favourite books. His eyes raped the Stieglitz photos. Piecing the woman together. Hand to mouth. She gave him the glasses as well as the bottle. He had to put the book down.

Before long they were in the bedroom. She was looped. Not out of control. But definitely looped. She wanted to fuck. She dropped her clothes on the floor and slid into bed. He walked over to the cupboard and proceeded to strip. Off came the Irish knit sweater, slowly undoing the Oxford-cloth shirt, unbuckling the Ralph Lauren belt, untying his polished Brogues. He took the change out of his pant pocket and put it on the small table. He stepped out of his pants and hung them up in the cupboard. She watched. Watching him watch himself being watched. Stupid handsome jerk. He turned finally. Running his hand through his hair, he gave her a sly sexy smile. He stood naked. He came towards the bed. She pointed to the overhead. He stopped and walked back towards the door. She noted that he had a pudgy bum and a pimply back. She thought that funny. Them's the breaks kid.

Their seduction was slow. He always seemed to sneak onto her body. Purring. He never took her completely. He never acted honestly. Except when he lay on her. Then he would let her feel his full weight. He would push down on her. Hard. Until she had to push back to breathe. And they would push pull. Tight. Until she would release herself to him. Gulping. And he would push. Push.

Oh yes. She knew his type well. These cold romantics. With his thick-stick calisthenic sex.

They slept. He holding on to her. On his back. In the centre of the bed. His big hand on her chest. Holding her lung. She lay on her side. Beside him. Quiet. Obedient. For the night anyway.

The bubble burst. My first period. Strange things happening. Not sure what to do. How do you tell someone you are bleeding down there? A slow pain. This seemed to me a private thing. Hiding it. The bleeding. Smelling it, touching it, tasting it. Different from a scab or a cut. Keeping it to myself. Stuffing in a bundle of rolled-up toilet paper. A pad to hold back the bleeding. Didn't tell my friends. Peering with my silver monogrammed hand mirror. What's going on up there?

It was early July. The family had gone to my cousin's for a swim. And iced tea. I wouldn't. I sat stiffly, quietly, with the Elders. My cousin knew me. She couldn't believe I didn't want to swim. So. I told her. In secret. We went upstairs. Into her parents' bathroom. I showed her the blood-saturated wad. She gave me a tampon and told me how to use it. It hurt. But at least I could swim.

I bled for days. A whole week. I suddenly saw kids, girls, ladies in a different way. Bleeders. Monthly bleeders. Something given up. A release of the body. I no longer had a tummy, I had a womb. Now that's heavy duty. I didn't buy tampons. I mean, how do you ask a man for tampons? No. I couldn't. So wads. It was hard to play, to climb trees, to run with that huge pad between my legs. But I now had everything every lady has. To be a woman. Not just a kid. A girl. A teenager. A woman. Wow. I carried the Well of Life. Gaia. Mother Earth. Wow.

I discovered my breasts. No longer a little chest for Vick's Vapour Rub. No. Breasts. When I touched them I was amazed at the feeling. It was like touching the electric wire fencing in the fields. A jolt. An electric shock. But the feeling wasn't external. It was inside. It made me flinch. A total moment. A total response. A shock. A spark. A bolt of hot current. I liked it. Wow.

But. How the hell am I supposed to know what a woman is? I am fourteen. The only thing that tells me with any certainty is my body. Outside of that, I don't know. Mother is not a woman, she is a lady. So. How? I'm not shaped like Sophia Loren, nor am I Twiggy. And I still get a kick out of playing The Man from U.N.C.L.E. and watching Mr. Magoo on TV. Yet I bleed.

Yes, I am a woman.

Now what?

Late that summer I was sent to Calgary for several weeks to stay with distant relations. I don't remember why. They were distant relatives of my father. Aunt Bets. AB. Mother tells the story. First woman your father ever kissed. In London. During the War. Married a good-for-nothing professor of geography who was into Zen Buddhism and medieval flutes. Married below her. But she was in love. End quote. Aunt Bets is now dead. Last time I saw her was at the Tutenkhamen Exhibit in Toronto. She was alone. Bespectacled. Skinny. Looking like a tramp. She died in an institution. Alcohol. Mother used to say I looked like her. These things make an impression.

Anyway. I went to Calgary with excitement. But also apprehension. My first trip away from home. Away. On a plane. Solo.

Many things were different. Aunt Bets' husband, Paul, looked like Martin Buber. The first time I'd ever seen a beard on a man. Their two children were weird. Lucy, the hippie blonde, was never home, and Martin, the vicious fascist, wandered around the house threatening to kill his father. He carried a red switch blade. And wore black-leather boots up to his knees. So. Enter Miss Priss. The first opportunity to show my stuff. Amazed to discover how much I clung to the forced patterns. Judging them too according to the Learned Rules. Watching how they hold their knives and forks. Do they know the correct way, the proper way? Have they got breeding? No. They didn't. But they were relatives. Family. Kin. Sort of. So. I listened to them. They were relatives who didn't know the Right Way. Why? I listened to them. Being quiet. Observant. A good guest. Spying on their differences. Pathetically polite. At

55

the diningroom table. Not polite conversation designed to entertain. These were not people who paid for their supper with good stories masked by the flow of wine. On the contrary. Anyone who sat down to their table fought. Violently. Screaming at each other. One-upmanship. Diving for the Oxford English. Reciting tidbits from authors, politicians, philosophy. Impassioned arguments between father and son. I had never seen such vivid intent. Aunt Bets would bang the table with her glass. Quiet. Quiet. Then everyone would start banging the table. Quiet. Quiet. All shouting. Laughing. Screaming at each other. And then starting all over again. I was terrified to move or speak. Wide eyed and wondering. At their passion.

Their house was comfortable. Sloppy old sofas. A piano in the livingroom. A bin of flutes in the hall that Uncle Paul would play at odd hours of the day or night. Floating around the house in a baggy Moroccan toga. I had never seen a man in a dress before. I slept upstairs. In the tower. A circular room. With a cot in the middle. A battered fruit crate for a bedside table. Vines growing up all over the wrought-iron windows. Ivy Tower. Atmosphere. You bet.

I was in bed. Sleeping. AB and Paul were out. I heard them come in. Paul was singing a Gregorian chant. Well, it sounded to me what a Gregorian chant would sound like. Coming up the stairs. Knocking on my door. Feigning sleep. He came in. Paul. He came over to my bed. Weaving. Of course I was watching every move. He was wearing a shawl. (Later I learned this was a poncho.) What a weird guy. Bent over and kissed me on the forehead. I turned. Feigning the groggy wake-up ritual, smiling. He leaned over again, his hands placed on either side of me and kissed me hard on the mouth. Scotch. His bristly beard rubbing my chin. I fell out of bed. Scrambling to get away. He was startled. I darted down the stairs, rushed to the front door. Opening and running. I didn't know, I didn't care. Terrified. Ran and ran. Ran until my convulsive crying and breathing made me stop. I sat down on someone's front step. In my nightie. In the middle of the night. Alone.

Miles from the Familiar.

A cool full moon shone in Calgary.

What to do.

What had happened.

I was cold. Shivering.

I thought of that man. A father. A husband. Someone else's property. The sacred boundaries of First Family. The kiss. On the mouth. I thought of Father. I couldn't imagine him doing that. Not in a million years. A kiss. On the mouth. To a visiting cousin. A young impressionable guest. A young girl. No. He was decent. He respected the laws. The rules. This man was indecent. For all his pompous brilliance. His *gnothi seauton* injunctions. His proselytizing philosophy. The Right and Virtuous maxims. This man was no good. He did not respect his chosen duties. His title. His honours. Talk bigger than big. Smash meaning. Bigger than Big. But on the line forget it. Scramble. Musical chairs. Get your ass square somewhere. And lie. No. I never did. Honest. How rude of him. How very rude. My fear turned into anger. Rage. I was Father's daughter. And I was me. Nobody treats another that way. No one. Smothering me with his stinking personality and then expecting to suck my blood. One of Them. No. Never.

I went back to the house. Ready for a confrontation. An attack. The lights were out. Except the light going upstairs. I went up. The house was quiet. Everyone in bed. Revolting. Coward. Sick little man.

Breakfast the next morning. As usual. I was helping with the dishes. He came over to me. Commenting on how long my lashes were when I wore my new contact lenses. Internally screaming: *Have you no shame?* Externally polite, quiet. Not prepared to make a scene. Would look odd. Out of time and place. He didn't even notice. He went over to Aunt Bets and kissed her. She unaware of the previous night's incident. I was disgusted. This blowhard. No. He would never do. No values. No respect. No beliefs. A liar. So. There it is.

My first encounter of the unfamiliar male kind.

One clicks into mind. I have no name for her. I remember only that she was attired in black leotards, imitation pearls and a skimpy pale pink blouse. She wouldn't wear shoes in the kitchen on those cold bare bricks. No, she wasn't protecting her kidneys. I remember her bending over the dishwasher. I could see her underwear under the leotards. Red with black lace. She was two-faced. Black and red. Kissing ass with my parents but as soon as their backs were turned making faces, retorting, swearing about them, in front of us. The Children. She behaved towards us as if we didn't have a life of our own, thoughts of our own. As if we had no being, no existence. She would dump patronizing bullshit on us. And she wasn't afraid of us. The Children. Unlike the others she didn't bend to our wishes, nor would she scold us. She'd just ignore us. On top of which she was a terrible cook. The food all tasted the same. Slop.

Once I refused. I would not eat the watery spinach. I was grabbed from my high chair and with great rapidity shoved into the broom closet. The door was slammed shut and locked. The light was switched off. I was startled and frightened. After a seemingly suitable period of histrionics I quietened down and considered my fate. How to overcome her. She after a while said 'Will you eat the spinach?' No, I whimpered. Nothing happened. Hard to work sympathy on someone when they don't give a damn. Suddenly I had it. 'I want my Mother.' Poke her purse. Threaten to steal it. Yes, that was it. Silence. I screamed. 'I want my Mother.' The employer. I knew this. Mother's power. My power. I went into histrionics again. Screaming. I was let out. Dragged back to my seat and plunked down. She said through gritted teeth, 'You will eat this spinach.' I said through gritted teeth, 'I will not.' She took my nose between her forefinger and thumb, clenched tightly and jammed the spoon of spinach against my clenched teeth. I breathed hard, through my teeth. Determined that she should lose. Fie upon you. Fie. She slapped me across the face. Startled and shocked that someone would dare do such a thing, my mouth fell open. She shoved in the spinach, smirking. I spat it at her. She slapped me again and I knocked the spinach and the rest of the meal onto the floor and went wild. Kicking, screaming, biting, crying, fighting. The body was in full revolt. A full explosion of the mind. Revolt. Blind. NO, NO, NO. I don't remember what happened. Except that the next day she was fired.

Mother said she was a horrible woman. I agreed. Horrible. Woman. Mother asked me what I wanted for my birthday. I said a guitar. She nodded. And gave me a string of imitation pearls.

These things make an impression.

Sarah woke up. It was night. Howith was on his side. Heavy breathing. She turned away from him. Falling again into sleep.

Ballroom dancing. Round and round and round. For two long years. Old Mrs. Hawks thumping the piano on stage. With elbow-length kid gloves. Yes. It was cold in there. The separate schools unite. Boy meets girl. Girl meets boy. The dance instructors act as chaperones. This was business. Big business. So. Fox-trot, rhumba, waltz, jive, two-step and Viennese. At twelve years of age. Girl meets boy, boy meets girl. Be nice children. Be good. The boys were supposed to lead. All in the pressure of the hand on the back, boys. Be gentle. Swirl, turn, dip, stop, pause, glide – effortless. Natural. But the girls were always much better at it than the boys. And you would have to yank one around after you with your hand. And then make it look as if they were doing all the work. Pushing. Shoving across the floor.

Sitting on wooden chairs in crisp party dresses. Waiting. For a tall one. At least. To be twelve and asked by a thirteen year old. To dance. Well. Jesus. Waiting. In black patent leather shoes and white cotton gloves.

Little ladies, little gents. High steppin' to Mrs. Hawks' mushy glove thumping. For two whole long years.

Waiting to make your feet work. Left then right. Right then left. Left. Right. Right. Left. Left. Right.

Like the gymnasium at school. Private school. Morning chapel. The Scriptures. The organ blowing away while everyone filed in. Left. Right. Praise to the Lord the Almighty the King of Creation. And on. Rise. Sit. Rise. Sit. Rise. Sit. All the uniforms clean for the school day. Rise. Sit. Rise. Sit. I had shined my shoes. Brown. Rise. Sit. Rise. Sit. Every time I stood up I would shine them again on the back of my knee socks. Every time I sat down I would deliberately put one shoe on top of the other. To make it dusty. Rise. Shine. Sit. Dust. Rise. Shine. Sit. Dust. One of the older girls had been standing. And then instead of sitting, fell forward on her face. Into the chapel chairs. With a clatter. A small group of girls went ooohh. And another group of seniors helped pick her up. She had fainted. Meanwhile the rest of the school was following the ritual. Rise. Sit. Rise. Sit. (Shine. Dust.)

The classes were small. Everyone knew everyone else. Everyone knew everyone else's parents. Let's face it, everyone knew. There were good girls and there were bad girls. The good girls always looked pretty. Their mothers had combed their hair. And they always got good marks. Top of the class. The bad girls usually had freckles and didn't do well in class at all. But they had spirit. I knew them all. I liked them all. At different times. Good girls and bad girls all knew how to climb trees and run.

Recess was spent playing in the woodland on the edge of the mountain beside the school. Recess was always followed by games. Field hockey. Good girls, bad girls alike. A team. Slashing. Running. Passing. Playing. Hard. To win. Everyone else knew everyone else. Passing. We all knew what to do to win. We all knew. Yes. We all knew how to be kind and cruel. We all knew.

After games came drama. Putting on the school plays. The productions. My first role. The alligator in *Peter Pan*. A big part. Dragging myself across stage in deep green. Bellowing.

Tick-tock. Tick-tock. Then. Later. The Queen of Hearts in *Alice in Wonderland*. High C. H'off with 'Is 'Ead. The King of Hearts had been one of the good girls. Finally to have a dramatic role. *Long Day's Journey into Night*. Playing the mother.

And back to chapel. O Canada. Our home and native land. Watching the clock. Passing notes. Inside the hymn books. Under the prefect's nose. Hee-hee. Our Father Who Art in Heaven Hallowed Be Thy Name. Thy Kingdom Come. Thy Will Be DoneOn Earth as It Is in Heaven. Heads bent. Tunics creased. Ties crooked. Looking down at those shoes. Looking down the row. Good girls have shiny shoes at the end of the day. Bad girls don't. Lead Us Not into Temptation. Good girls always sang. I thought that was pretty easy. I liked singing. So did the bad girls. So we all sang. Together. In chorus. Always. The Power and the Glory. Together. Every day. For Ever and Ever. Amen.

WEDNESDAY

When she woke in the morning she realized how hungry she was. She had no intention of cooking his breakfast. If she woke him now they would have time to go to Fran's. Did she have enough money? He never paid. For her. Big on dutch treat. The simple economics of their relationship. She also knew he would want his mornings morning. After all, that's why he was here. She could feel slumber in her body. Still. Lingering. She touched her breast. She could smell their sex. And his bitter sweet sweat. Yes. She wouldn't mind giving. Touching. But it would have to be quick. She was hungry. She leaned over to him. Kissing his arm. His shoulder. He, with closed eyes, turned towards her, his hand going immediately between her legs. Good.

He wanted to have a shower. And he didn't have time for

breakfast at Fran's. How 'bout a cup of tea here? She lied. She didn't have any more tea. She persuaded. Come on. A steamy cup of coffee at Fran's. Eggs and bacon. Bran muffin. He was towelling dry. No. He didn't have the time. Coy, she offered to make it her treat. He was putting the change back into his pocket. Tying up his shoes. He had a presentation at 9:30, he needed time to prepare. Fine. So. She wanted him out. Out of her place. Out. She lied. She was also in a hurry. Had to go to the bank. Well, I guess I'd better go, he said. Yes, it's a pity. She sent him one of her warm smiles. The one that brings them back for more. He sent her one of his.

When the door closed. She went to the kitchen and put on the kettle. Checking the fridge. Fried egg and raisin bread. She heard the paper boy plop the paper at her door. She flipped on CJRT and listened to the BBC news report. Sadat had been shot. Suspected terrorists. She flipped the egg. Muslims and Arabs want the U.S. out. Want Israel out. Salt. S.A.L.T. She thought it wrong to give Israel to the Jews. The Allied forces after the war giving away something that wasn't theirs. So easy to give something away when it's not yours. When you don't want it.

The newspaper hadn't caught up with the headlines on the radio. Trudeau was gleaming beside a gloomy Thatcher. The Constitution Is Released. She read that the U.S. was spending 200 billion dollars on military defence per annum. Reagan warding off Russia. Protecting his own. Property. Capital. Flexing for the public. Press. Gulp. The tea was hot. Increased taxes. The government's reason for living. We will protect. Our good nation. From all that unfamiliar Evil. Out There.

After a shower she gave a quick look to her little black book with gold trim. She would be playing squash after work, and she was going to lunch with a man who worked for a radio station. A business lunch. But she would have to be careful. Radio people were inverted snobs. Always knocking the Establishment. Lusting after their idea of the Powers that Be. They damned everyone who wasn't directly involved with media.

Press are like that. They want everything they think the Establishment has. Money and power. Impact. She would have to dress down. No suit. No classic gold jewellery. No pearls. She could get away with a wool skirt and a turtleneck and a sweater. Quasi-collegiate. Hey guys, relax. I'm really one of you. Neo-nothing. Insignificant. Honest.

She got to the office to the customary deluge of messages. A note from Tony. Call before three. She wondered what he was doing this afternoon. She glanced at the calendar on her desk and saw it was only a week and two days away from her next rendezvous with Nicholas. Nick. He had said it would be something of an occasion. The Vienna Spring Ball in New York. White tie. Ladies were allowed to wear pastel colours only. It sounded fun. Nick. She wanted to call him. To say hello. Just hello. But no. He didn't like her calling at the office. Only if it were for business. What flight? What time? How long? She looked at the calendar again. Her period was late. She had missed it last month. She didn't panic. What's the use of panicking? She would wait. Her phone rang.

Business as usual.

Lunch was uneventful. A bearded heavy-set fellow in a badly cut leather jacket with the lining hanging out slugged beer. And gossiped about the so-called personalities he worked with. Press are big on press. Storytellers. Going Bigger than Big. These Rulers of Reputation and Inflationary Thinking. She knew that among these people she too had a 'personality.' They judged quickly. On Image. Presentation. That's why she was so careful. Never too much. And never enough. Always important to have good press. Reputation. She hated having to convince these bastards she was okay. Unless they were producers. Real producers. They were a different breed. They would see her, not the poisonality, the Image. She insisted on paying for her own lunch. He could pay for his own beer. She went away from the meal satisfied. He had talked a lot. Had given her a lot of information. He had been so intent on impressing her magazine image that all she had to do was listen. He was a useless pawn in a battle he would never understand.

Back at the office Tony was on the phone. 'Would you be interested in Scrabble and some unbelievably good dope some evening soon? Tomorrow?' She hesitated. She didn't want to sleep with him. She lied. 'Sure, but Tony, I have a big presentation on Friday morning. I'll have to make it an early night.' She thought of the advantages of going out with someone who knew nothing about one's business. 'Okay, we'll make it early.' Good. She had full intention of only playing Scrabble. He always had good dope.

After work she managed to get herself a lift down to Hart House. The phys-ed complex at the university. Sliding in under the pretext of being a student. 741331745. No one ever checked. She went down to the locker room. Cath was there.

They had been university chums since first year. They had sat through an eclectic music course together. Music of Non-Western People. Learning to enter cultures by the sound they make. Peruvian, Ethiopian, Balinese. Chinese. Now Catherine worked as a researcher for the Hospital for Sick Children. At a shit wage. But she had desires to be a doctor. And every little bit helped. You can't battle for money if you have other priorities. She was from Montreal. Westmount. She was struggling. Even though she had had the luxury of private-school education and travel abroad. She would not take money from her parents. She wanted to stand separate. To think for herself. To be. Self-sufficient. Look ma, no hands.

They had played squash regularly for several years. They played a good game. Together. Well-matched.

They placed a bet. Winner gets the choice of a movie.

Sweating, they slugged it out with each other. Playing strategy, playing let, playing hard. Cath had better control of the backboard, but Sarah had a better serve. They interspersed their game with tidbits of news. Cath's boyfriend had an interesting job offer from Ottawa. He was a doctor. How was

Nicholas? Sarah gave a factual account of her weekend in New York. What she had done. What she had seen. The Museum of Holography. The Broadcast Museum. Keeping it neutral. She didn't want to lose the game. They played several sets. Pushing their bodies. It was a good game. Better than most. They came off the court. Exhausted but excited. The high lingered. They decided to run the track upstairs. To run out the excess energy. Sarah had won. She wanted to see a German film up at Eglinton. Cath winced. She lived downtown. It was a long way to go. They compromised and decided on a French film playing at Bloor and Yonge. As she went up the stairs, Sarah briefly thought of her disappointment in Cath for not fulfilling the bet. She would have gone anywhere if Cath had won. But then, she reasoned, you're being unreasonable.

Once on the track. They split up. Running their own pace. Noting the others. The hard-core athletes. Broad-backed men. Toned-down women. Running. Round and round and round. Concentrating. Sweating.

Sarah could smell herself. She could feel the sweat on her back. On her brow. Her arms glistened. She felt good. Alive. She started slowly. Getting the rhythm. The stride. Watching her breathing. Running. Watching her feet. Her mind wandered. She thought of her older brother, Davey, the marathon runner. She seldom saw him now. He worked hard too at his engineering business. He had a wife. A child. But then, he never called either. The thought bothered her. She pushed harder. Focusing again on her body functions. She could feel her body twisting, resisting the push. She pushed harder. She knew she could stop, but she knew she didn't have to. Her abdomen ached. She wondered about her period. The thought bothered her. She pushed harder. She passed Catherine on the track. She didn't even see her. She ran. She thought of Nicholas. No. She ran harder. Digging at the air around her. Pushing it back. Pushing it under. She was running. Challenging. Her life force. Running. Blind. She ran. To break. The body. She ran. From function. She ran. From her soft, female form. She ran. Gasping. Pounding, pounding the pain. Pounding. She tripped. She was only aware of something hitting her shoulder as she fell. She felt her ankle twist. She lay on the floor. Tingling. Quiet. Staring. Catherine's face. 'Are you all right?' Sarah slowly sat up. She smiled, wincing as she felt her ankle. Yeah. She stood. Tried her ankle. It would be all right. Cath was watching her. 'I guess I tripped.'

They went down to the locker room and showered. Exchanging tidbits. Talking about work, mutual acquaintances, family. Swapping shampoo and towel. Sarah felt shaky. Rocked. But this was not the time to think about the run. Later, much later. After the movie.

She picked up the mail as she went into the apartment building. A letter from a Dutch friend. She would save it for later. She sat down. Wishing no music, no calls, nothing. She was exhausted. But not enough. The run haunted her. She was frightened. Frightened to discover how intent she had been. She had been running too hard. She knew it. Running to destroy. What? She must be careful. Very careful. She didn't have as much of a grip as she thought she did. She had to answer herself. Why? She couldn't push it away any longer. Deal with it. The aching. She would have to dig. Very deep. She would have to help herself. She would have to get an understanding there would be no reason. For anything. Yes. She needed an answer. She couldn't live like this. It demanded too much from her. It sucked on her. Sucked life. She needed a reason. For Nicholas.

Growing up. Higher. One watches some people more than others. Watching the private show. Watching a human. Looking at Mother. The first female model. Watching her movement. In the air. Naked. Lumpy naked. Clutching a towel. On the cold bathroom floor. Shutting a door.

Watching mother. Watching mother watch mother in front of the mirror. Become something, someone else. Another Image. Another person. Multiple. The preparations could go on for hours. The bath would be the penultimate moment. The smell would waft through the entire house. She always smelled of bath. Always. Clean. Sweet. Unsullied. Then she would start the layers. Foundation. Colour. Swabbing it down her neck. Rubbing cream into her body. After, of course, removing all hair. Plucking, pulling, shaving. To get a bald body. Sweeping back those lines. The life-earned creases. Mother used jars, creams, lotions, sticks, pencils, lipsticks, polish, glue, creamy white, orange, chalk. Then she sprayed herself. First with perfume, then with a sticky, stinking gold can. Hairspray. She would stand atrophied in her bra and nylons with girdle. Then the smile. Always. She walks to the bed. Everything is perfectly laid out. Evening gown, suit or dress. Clean. And accessories. Belts, pins, scarves, gloves, purse. And separately in a little heap. Jewels. They always go on last. The final coronation. Shifting, tugging, pushing, piling it all on. Over that lumpy nakedness. Hiding her body. Before the flow of sweat smudges all that effort. Again. To make her dirty.

There she stands. Ready. Untouchable. Unapproachable. Clean. Ready. For presentation. For the public. On show. Ready for take-off. She turns off the TV which has been droning in the background. Tidies the room. Pulls the bedspread taut. Presto. Nothing ever happened. You'd never guess. The labour. Now, effortless and fantastic. She is completely transformed. Costumed. Contrived beauty. She smiles and looks Nice. Matching everything. Lips, shoes, purse. A ribbon of colour. Co-ordinated. Into a package. A beautiful portable parcel. And proud too. Elegant. Self-assured. Now. And tough. Almost militant. In her waddle. (The girdle produces a waddle.) Not sexy. That has nothing to do with it. She radiates power. Presence. Her mind spreads over everything. It is in all the rooms. It is through the entire house. The tidiness. The contrived order. Revolving around the Queen Bee. Queen Mother.

Mother. The Creator, the Giver of Life. Who wants nothing

from you. Except obedience. My first female model. A battle always. The Yes No Push Pull Dialogue. Give and Take, Take, Take. Using devices. Seduction with money, candies and clothes, but only to get what she wants. Obedience. Tidy children. Order. For that perfect Image. The symbol of the perfect mother. An entertaining bitch. And a spying beauty. Consuming all. Stealing material even from her children for her performance. To have the gossip. The power of information. Soft, but underneath very hard. A curse on me to say 'You're just like your mother.' Trembling in belief and disbelief. Trusting, accepting, but denying, battling. Do everything to separate. But see too her fantastic power. Her control. Watching her, listening to her. Greater than manipulation. Much is intuitive. Forced habit. Learned from her mother. Who she hated. I can see why. She learned seductive power from her. Manipulation. It was the only way to beat her. I too. Learning the tricks. Playing the game. Of poisonality. Pushing back the sacred. As she must have done. Burying. Deep down. The private voice. The Right voice. Hiding the good. Masquerading the First Form. Learning too to entertain and to lie. Hand springs and all.

In the bedroom the bestseller books are piled four rows deep. The latest magazines are in a neat stack beside the bed. The TV control sits on her dressing table. And she would sit there in the morning. In bed. Watching the *Today Show. America A.M.* Watching from the middle of her room. And she would sit. There. In a huge king-size bed for the Queen. And she would give brief audience to her children there. We would kiss her cheek quickly before we left for school.

And she would be up there at the end of the school day. Near the window. With the bird's eye view. She would listen for the bus. She always knew. She would hear you come up the stairs. Even if you went quietly. Even if the television was blaring. *The Merv Griffin Show.* Who's there? I'd wander into her room. A dumb magnet. She would notice my appearance first. Uniform untidy. Pens and pencils jammed into my pockets.

My hair a mess from being outdoors. In the wind. My green tunic needs ironing at the end of the day. The school crest is falling off the navy blazer. I was told to clean up. Give the blazer to the maid to sew. Mother would never sew. What? A lady of leisure? No. Only much later. Needlepoint. For the grandmother Image. And then she would pry. Spy. What happened at school today, dear? But I could only speak during the commercials. I would tell her some. Not all. So she would leave me alone. So that I too could watch some TV before doing my homework.

I gossip. Tell her a story about one of her friend's children. The society kids. So that she would make the comparison. Judge the race. Seldom would I tell her of my friends. My real friends. Sacred. Too precious for mother's organizing greed. Besides she didn't think they were important if they weren't a recognizable name from society. She would brush my hair. Come here. I would pull my head away from her. And she would yank on the knots.

Children on display. After a dinner party. We would have to file into the livingroom to say good night while the guests were sipping their coffee and liqueurs. Before bridge. Smile. Fuck. Smile as if your entire life depended on it. It doesn't matter in the slightest what the guests think. You are performing for the Queen Bee. Say good night to all the guests and the parents last. Dad and then Mother. You know you've done it correctly if she kisses you. Quickly on the forehead. If she notices you. If she has stopped talking. A public show. Look this is my daughter and my sons. Gossip won't you about Liz's beautiful perfect well-mannered children.

Fucking ridiculous. Before the guests would arrive. No Sarah, not that skirt. Wear the dress with the little blue flowers. Don't argue. Don't sulk. Do as I say. And your white ankle socks. Not your green knee socks. (Doesn't she know that ankle socks always slide down into the bottom of these patent-leather shoes?) Don't argue. It is the right thing to wear. The Right Thing. Father too would ask Mother what is

69

the attire? Sports jacket – suit – black tie? How to fit in, to conform. To fit perfectly. To go to someone's house and have it look as if you are giving the party. A natural. Belonging. Everywhere. The family photo. Click. For the record. Perfect. Click. The Stautons.

And if they were going out. Dad would dress in two minutes. Shower and shave. Slicked-back black hair. The moustache trimmed. Fingering through the tie rack. This one. Cufflinks. And a quick run downstairs to shine his shoes. But before he goes, a clothes brush across his shoulders to wipe off dandruff.

Dad would stand in the hall. His coat on with the car keys in his hand, he would tell Mother he was ready. Just a minute, dear. Another squirt of perfume, change the gloves. Fur coat. Waddle. Clop. Clop. Clop down the sixteen stairs. To present. Elizabeth. Phenomenal. Bustling into the kitchen to tell the help what to give the brats, oops, the children for dinner. Swirling. Tidy. Order. A touch of theatrics for all who are watching. Everyone watches. Come on, David, we're going to be late.

Then later. When I was nearly asleep. The dogs would bark. Clop. Clop. Clop. Up sixteen stairs. Mother would be talking, yakking, gossiping. Drunk. Dad was miles away in the kitchen. Letting out the dogs, having a glass of milk. She would groan. Shutting the bedroom door. Slam. The little wooden soldier would topple over with a clatter. At attention. Father would come up. The dogs behind him. He'd turn off the hall light. And the dogs would settle down on the hall rug. Mother would be in the bathroom yakking about something. Turning on the hall light. The dogs would scatter. Clop. Clop. I snuggle down. Turning away. Into the depths of that canopy bed. Feigning sleep. She pushes open my door and switches on the bright light. Are you awake, darling? Fuck. She comes over to the bed. Talking at me. Leans over. Perfume and booze. A drunk sloppy kiss. Embossed on me. Wet. Good night, dear. She would touch my face. With her face. And all that dirty greasy make-up. Repulsive.

On the weekend I would have to stay inside to help her. I was the girl. Not the boy. So. Preparing for the guests. Helping the maid. Recleaning what had been cleaned the day before. Not like the boys who got to go outside to help dad. You had to work hard for him. But at least you were outside. You got to play with dirt. Gardening, pulling weeds, in the flower garden, in the vegetable garden, trimming the hedges, riding in the wagon behind the tractor, picking fruit in the orchard, cutting grass. Moving things, trees, boxes, stones, raking and hoeing. In the sun. In that warm sun. Getting smelly. Dirty. Bending, stretching to the orchestra of wind sounds. Or. Downstairs with dad in the basement. Smelt of wood, paint, varnish and mildew. Dusty. Dank and dark. Water seeping in through the limestone floor. Helping dad. Holding lumber, boards, getting hammers, screwdrivers, and sitting as a dead weight. Dad would seldom talk, he would do. Mother would never do, she would always talk. And you would do.

She would talk about not being selfish. Always better to give than to receive. So give to me sweetheart. Help the maid. I'm your Mother. Do as I say, not as I do. And she would watch to make sure you did it right. I was in training to be a lady. Just like her.

By virtue of her role she felt entitled to some sort of special treatment. Lady. Mother. Wife. Volunteer. Socialite. Never woman. I never heard Mother describe herself as a woman. Female sex. An animal creature called human.

And from her I learned not to trust. Anything. All the gestures, all the fancy movements were only contrivances, devices to get what one wanted. I watched and witnessed her. The Imperialist. Imposing her law, her vision on us. Her clothes, her colours, her idea of what we were supposed to be, not what we were. Squishing down. With don'ts. How horrid her mother must have been. And her mother before that. Or the person responsible. For those laws. To kill love. To kill genuine trust. To kill caring. Maybe it's just ladies. Ladies. Ladies taught not to like themselves. As women. From day one. Taught at an early age not to believe, to see, in themselves. As women. As girls. As kids. As people. Heaven forbid that one should become critical. Heaven forbid that one should learn to say no. Or ask why. Drummed. Beaten with that fear of isolation. Aloneness. Singular. Spinster. Don't fit. Don't belong. To a family. To a man. To society. Ladies are not meant to be alone. They always belong. They are the connecting glue. Wives. Absorbing sponges. Till death do us part.

Push. And pull. Yes. And no. Give. And take. Sell. And buy. Lady. And gent. The dynamics demand each other. Need each other. Give a worthy performance. A worthy product. Something that men want, and are willing to buy. An Image. A concept. Ladies of breeding. Sold. At the highest price. Like cattle. For cash. But. There are a lot of lemons. Women fake it. Their market value. Don't they?

I was learning.

Mother knew I understood her. She was frightened of me. Of exposure. So. She sent me away. To relatives. To camp. Pushing me out of her territory. Her ordered kingdom. No. No questioning Rightness here. No rebels to the rule. Pushing me away. Exile. And I would pull away from her. I would leave her court and go to my own room. For hours. With books. Strengthening myself behind my closed bedroom door. I would spend hours in there. Hidden. Out of her sight. Reading. Day-dreaming.

One day I had returned from school and was on my way upstairs. Something was different. No TV blaring. My room had been entirely rearranged. My books were in boxes. My clothes were on the bed. All the furniture, except for the bed, had been pulled out and replaced by granny's older beat-up pieces. It was a violation. A slap in the face. How dare she? I got angry with her. What's going on here? But my anger was never as efficient or as spectacular as hers. She glared at me. And then laid into me. This is *my* house. And I will do as I damn well please. What could I do? I got the picture. Loud and clear. I stood at the top of the stairs. She at the other end of the hall. The gulf of stairs between us. She stood at the banister. Like an orator. Burying me in her anger. Standing between me and my room. Control. Blocking me from what used to be my space. My sanctuary. Banished. Telling me it wasn't mine but hers. All of it. Hers. Property. Ownership. It exploded in my head. Hers, his, mine, yours, theirs, ours. Have and have nots.

Everything is owned by someone. At least, everyone believes they own things. Somewhere. Stamped with their seal. Ordered. Made human. Clung to. Possessed. Coveted. You own what you alone have the strength and determination to claim. Oh sure, you can pay for it. You can inherit it. You can kiss ass for it. You can even steal it. Just guard it with your life. Those things. And call them yours. Your kingdom of things.

People groom children as things so that they too can be owned. Coveted. Possessed. Clung to. My son. My daughter. All mine. Stamped with the family label. Family. Stauton things.

So, there I was. A fourteen-year-old child. A woman. Alone. Stripped of what had once been mine. I could never call that house my home again. It was only property. Props. Her property. All the items in the house lost their connection to me. They were her things. Now. Owned by her. I had no home. No place, no security. No props. No supports. I owned nothing.

Except for one thing. She didn't own me. My body may have been in her house, I may have been eating her food, but I had my own soul. Sort of.

I found her repulsive. A liar and a cheat. Some mother. The very idea of her touching me appalled me. Tainted, soiled, contaminated. She chased me around the back room once, poking at me, mocking me. Don't touch me. Don't touch me. I squeezed down behind the piano. Crying. Hating her. Her brutish bigness. She couldn't believe it. Laughing at me. Her moody child. I could only see her odious lumpiness. Always pushing in, crowding, altering, stamping, ordering. Going for complete and absolute submissive control. Mine. Triumph.

Conquest. Owned. Chained. Mine. No. Never. Never. I am not a thing. You do not own me. And I will never ever belong to you. I own me. You bitch.

The only item I ever touched of hers again was a crushed white beaver coat. It hung in the back hall. I would hold it. Smell it. Cling to it. It smelled of her. It was soft and warm. Fuzzy. Like a great big gentle bear.

Everything else I would steal.

THURSDAY

She woke slowly. Feeling the body strain from the day before. She had slept badly. Dreaming of her mother. She got up and looked at her calendar. She had made a mistake with Tony. It would be impossible to meet him this evening. She had her volunteer English class. Something she had started several summers ago while at college. Students from around the globe relied on her to give them insight into and understanding of the English language. The powerful English-speaking culture. And the Canadian point of view.

She would have little free time. She must call him. Perhaps she could set up something for tomorrow night. She looked at her calendar again. Dinner at her cousin's. The Sinclair brothers in Hamilton. A theme party. The Great Gatsby. No. Tony would not fit there. An Italian businessman who smoked dope and listened to New Wave wouldn't fit in that neatly with the Hamilton WASP scene. Her parents' children's friends. He could handle it, but she would feel uncomfortable. Off-balance. Responsible for his pleasure. She'd invite another type. Ian, the social-climbing Osgoode lawyer.

She decided to spend the weekend at her parents' home. Yes. She would phone. And she would invite Tony for a Sunday walk and an early dinner. Yes, that was more suitable altogether. Her parents wouldn't mind. They liked meeting her dates.

Her abdomen ached. Reminding her again that her period was overdue. She took a urine sample figuring she could drop it off at the pharmacy on the way to work. She would find out tomorrow morning. Odd the sensation of not knowing. She felt a bit foolish. But she didn't have the confidence to dismiss her fears. She wasn't really anxious, she just wanted to know.

As soon as she arrived at the office she phoned Tony. His secretary said he wasn't expected in until 11:30. Sarah laughed. How does he do it? She said she'd call back later.

The magazine was print-ready and there was little else she had to do. Except start on the next month's issue. Folders were already piled on her desk demanding attention. She settled in, sorting, editing, clipping, adding, rewriting, deciding. It was 12:45 when she looked up. She called Tony. He was agreeable to the plans. He apologized. Said he too had forgotten she had had the class. Oh Tony, dear sweet Tony. They laughed. Sharing a joke. Later, she felt a pang of guilt. He was too nice to be fucked around. It was silly to lead him on. He was already thinking of her in terms of marriage. The perfect mate. There were too many presents. Too many considerations. Too much thought directed her way. Too much giving. She liked him. A lot. But she wasn't there for him. The balance was off. She wondered how it could be that she was in love with a man who of late had turned his back on her when they had had sex. She recognized she seldom relaxed with Nick. They seldom laughed. Now. But enough, later. Back to work.

Her class was at eight. It would run for two hours. She had some time after work to pull the class notes together over a sandwich and a glass of milk. There would be a short review of last week's material, some new handouts, some practice. And then she'd encourage some conversation. Today's subject. What would you do if your daughter arrived home and said she was going to marry a man from another ethnic origin? Yes. That would keep them busy.

The class was an odd assortment of people. Two Japanese men, both married, both on visiting fellowships. Specializing in cancer research. Their temperaments were quite different. One was an avid redneck nationalist. The other was religious, into Zen and the universe. Calmer. Mellower. There was also a Brazilian doing graduate work in forestry; a young jocular fellow. A bearded Argentinian studying Marx and geography. And two Mexicans. The older was male, fortyish, working under a Mexican government grant to increase North-South relations. And the woman, younger, unmarried, taught at a secondary school in Mexico City. She was in Canada to study English. The conversation classes covered what her structured university classes did not. They were a good bunch. Interested in learning, interested in the dynamics of the class. There was the added advantage that they were adults. They had chosen the course. It was free. Sarah enjoyed it. It was a look for her at the world unfiltered by the bias of media or the ambiguity of history textbooks. The direct voices gave their own views of their history, their religions, their people, their customs. And they were all tolerant and accepting of the other members of the group. The Mexican government man amicably exchanged hellos with the Argentinian Marxist. The Japanese men were always polite, attentive, nodding. They were all diligent workers. Always prepared. Tomorrow thinkers. Ready.

After the structured half of the class Sarah directed their attention to the topic for the evening. She preferred to let them speak. Seldom interrupting the flow. The language errors didn't matter as long as they spoke. The correction would come later. As they fine-tuned their views. Then they might glance at her to help. To aid explanation.

The smaller more fervent Japanese man readily spoke up. With humour, he explained that the situation would never occur in patriarchal Japanese society. 'A daughter would never have the freedom nor the leisure to discover men from the rest of the world. Besides, it would never be allowed.'

The Argentinian spoke up. 'But what about love?'

'What about it?' said the Jap, smiling. 'Why couldn't she love one of her own people?'

The second Japanese man spoke up. She would of course be encouraged to pursue a relationship with a man suitable to her upbringing. She would be taught that financial considerations would have to enter into it. She would have to be made aware of her background, her privileges, her needs. And she has her own family to think of. She is responsible to them.

'Surely the girl would be allowed to make up her own mind,' said the unmarried Mexican girl. 'Love is a difficult thing to find. To know.'

The Mexican man laughed. 'But it was the family we are talking about. What would happen if she brought a truck driver home? What would her parents think.' He would never allow one of his daughters to marry out of the Mexican family, nor out of her class.

She snorted. 'Isn't the question of religion and money their affair? Not the family? Besides, it sounded as though his financial situation really is the determining factor, not his race.'

He answered brusquely. Like a parent. 'Don't be silly. Of course, it's the family's business. It is business.'

Sarah interjected. 'And you?'

She asked the young man from Brazil. He smiled. 'When I was working one summer in Cyprus, I fell in love with a Greek girl. I wanted her to come back to Brazil with me. But she would not leave her family. Her father, her mother. And I would not live with her family. She was to be my wife. But her people had a terrible attitude towards South Americans in general. They were ignorant of our history, our people. Even she. She thought I was born under a palm tree. She didn't realize that we too have American colour television, German cars, Russian tractors and Japanese technology.' He smiled again. 'As you can see, we did not resolve our differences.'

Sarah asked the Argentinian. What would you do if your daughter wanted to marry an American?

'If it was for love, I would not stop them. But if it was for the American passport, the supposed American dream, we would talk.'

The others laughed. The first Japanese man spoke again. 'If my daughter wanted to marry an American for his passport, I would not stop them.'

Men and daughters. Men and wives. Never men and women. Economics and love. Racism and opportunism. Belonging and separate. The marriage of two opposites. The conversation swirled on. The class lasted longer than usual. They continued speaking as they left the room. The Argentinian asked Sarah what she would do. 'If I were the daughter or the parent?' she said. Either. She considered it a moment. 'I would like to believe that I would be supportive of any choice my daughter made. And I would like too to believe that my parents would respect my decision. Even if, in later life, it might prove to be a mistake.' He asked her if she had ever taken such a man home. She replied yes. But she added she had never married one. The Mexican nodded his head. So there. The Argentinian nodded. Wondering.

Enough. She was the teacher. Something to hide behind. Besides, they certainly had no idea of her private life.

As she walked home she felt again the freshness of the cleansing cool night air. Congratulating herself on the success of the class. A lot of meat there. Food. Fuel.

She thought of her own father. That quiet hard-working shadow. And some of the men she had taken home over the years. Only some had ever got there. The threshold. Entering into what had once been her life. Her home. Watching them carefully. How would they see her anew after being there. Seeing the castle, the fortress. And tradition, establishment, security, money and mother. None of them saw what she saw. None of them knew what she knew. And she would be silent. When they wanted her.

Digging deep to find them. The first. Buried under layers of memories, layers of ritual. Trying to find type, continuum, juggling in one's mind the presence, the behaviour, the movement through space, the look, the Image, the touch. Deliberately seeking those who didn't fit. Knowing that I wanted and needed the experience. Deciding on a method. A reason for perusal. The male creature. Man. The unfamiliar, the unknown. Those with the get-away power. Money and cars.

The virile jock was a terror to me. His body signified one thing only – sex. Steamy sex. Impossible. Society. Reputation. Whore. Father was not like these men. He was quiet. Sure, these other men were attractive as hell. I liked their sense of Self. Their immediate understanding of who they were. So here. Not even an invitation, or a demand. Only a completeness. I have excess. Overflowing with Self. Take me. Some stupidly call this chemistry. No. A living breathing Being. Yes, of course, there are possibilities of spoilage. Of vanity. Ruin. But it depends on their balance, their conditioning, their exposure. Young playful boys grow into virile sexy men. No? They have beginnings like everyone else. How they are taught to value their manliness. One thing is certain, they grow touching themselves. They know their bodies. That comfort of skin, of muscle, of sex. Warm life. Taught that it is clean, natural. That's the chemistry. But a good girl is taught that she can't touch. She can only look. And only briefly. Glance. Never stare. And by all means don't touch. A good girl saves her hereness for tomorrow. Planning. Waiting. Preparing, ordering, grooming for the Big Date. The Chosen One. The one who has also been planning, waiting, preparing, ordering and grooming for the Big Date. The good girl. Both from Nice Families. Ready. Steady. Go. Groomed for Families.

But everyone knows that good boys and good girls don't make it in a capitalist society unless they inherit a bundle. It's so easy to be good when you've got dough. Good boys become bank managers, CAs, lawyers, company men. Sexless intelligent responsible status-quo nimnods. A good girl knows this. A good girl must be protected. Her goodness, her station, her sex. She must marry well. Marry good. Above all, marry. To a boy. Not a man. Never women. No. Always girls. And boys.

It's knowing the double standard. Bottom line. A good girl sells her goodness. Carefully. Discreetly. With titles and time. Boyfriend. Never boyfriends. Drinks, dinner and theatre. Never just out. His family's for the weekend. Never just weekends. He's picking me up. Never pick-ups. Romance, not sex. Bottom line. Reputation is all. Wooing everyone. See. No hands. They're clean. Honest. Wine, bourbon, sherry. Silver, flowers, porcelain. Silk, suede, wool. Family, art, language. Never ever beer, brawls and beautiful bodies. Convincing whoever the hell it is that she's oh so fine. Refined. Taught by a mother who's done the same thing. For centuries. Tilt your head, dear. Suggests submission. Attention. Caring. But only if he's worth it. Stoke that ego. Stoke those flames so he'll do for you. Prove himself, his manhood, to his lady love. His princess. Lying treasures at your feet. Demonstrate your humble worthiness. Your goddess-like virtue. Clean. Unsullied. Good. Holy. Above it all. A precious commodity. Worth owning. And for the rest, fuck 'em. For fun of course.

Reputation is all. Maxim: Be good, honest, decent law-abiding citizens and no harm will come to you. But let's face it, this kind of information is for those who already have. Most things. Creature comforts and more. Sure, don't rock the boat. You don't want to lose all those things. I was brought up to be a decent, law-abiding human being, a lady, that was what was intended. But I'm not. Not really. How can I be? I own nothing. I have not inherited anything. I am poor. I have not married money. And I make a pittance in a man's world. I survive. I struggle. I only have what others would call class. Those fools. Sucked in by the Heritage Image. I have suave, style, mannerisms, stories. And my sex. And I also know that I will have to fight every inch of the way to get from have not to have. It is, I know, all a question of performance. How one does it. With halo or horns. We Ladies of Breeding.

I was fourteen. And I was now a single solo woman. On my own. After I returned from Calgary, I was taken out of private school. And told that I was going to the local high school.

David's expenses at his private school were used as an excuse. I was told I would get my fair share. Later. Grade 13 in Switzerland. I didn't mind. I wanted to be separate. I wanted to roam. Out There. Learn. To know more about what was beyond the parameters of my cloistered trapped existence. I was sent to high school in Burlington. Grade 9. It was *huge.* Immense. Three thousand students to the 247 I had previously known. And I was at the bottom of the pile. No prefect system, no chapel, no choir, no houses, no girl guides, no ballroom dancing. No patterns.

Alone in the New World.

The differences. Clothes, not uniforms. And boys, good boys and bad boys. Everywhere. Costumes and fashion identified what kind of girl you were. Mini, midi, maxi, pants, jeans, hot pants, shorts. Which group. Clique. Labelled. As one of *those.* Amazing how quick, how efficient the process was. Girls would dye their hair, smoke in public, wear boots and Levi jackets. Swearing. Fuck you. Streetwise and loose. And other girls would wear hand-crafted smocks, leather moccasins, jingling copper jewellery, burn incense in the lockers and have very kinky curly hair. Unkempt. Spacey. Children of nature. Effortless Eves. And other girls would be decked out in Simpsons-Sears January Sale attire. Red, white and blue, with perfectly tied-back hair. Suburban sophisticates. With red nail polish. 'Just like mummy.' Crispy critters. I experimented with each group. Weaving. Trying them all on. The wardrobes, the values, the voices, the accent, their language. Getting to know one in each group. Well. So I could learn. Understand their differences. There was no one in school like myself. No one knew about antiques, private school, clubs, Society, or the Beauty of the North. That part of my life had no meaning there. I had a clean slate. And likewise I discovered that my life at high school had no meaning for my parents. To them it was a place where I went to school. But they didn't realize that I saw different things. Learned different things. Spying. How poor, middle-class people lived. How they behaved, thought.

What they believed. What they wanted. What they were. Without knowing the Right Way. Just different. Like the tropical fish. Different. Separate from me.

I seldom told these people where I lived. The big house on the hill. The fortress. It was an isolated island. Removed. If I did, the idea was either met with resentment or ignorance. So. I seldom took people there. The house would become a freaky museum. A fantasy house. And I hated that. Girls would jump on my bed luxuriating in it. Wowing everything. Being amazed at the silver. Stupid. Teaching me to look at it all in a new way. A status way. A money way. Not just a bed. Not just a fork. Building a new wall. A new understanding between public and private. It was much easier just not to take people to Mother's house. No one seemed to understand why I hated it there. And Mother would tell the maid to give the kids milk and cookies. She would so completely wow them. jesus. no. As soon as I saw that whoever I had brought home was being sucked in by the performance I would back out. They couldn't really see. They were blinded by her Niceness.

I sought out boys. Debating with myself about the situation in the back room with pen and paper. I am now fourteen and three-quarters. I have my period. My breasts tingle and I like touching my crotch. Feeling me. Gently. Rubbing my hands over me. I like touch. I like my body. And when I look at other bodies, I want to touch. I would like other bodies to touch me. But I know that the unwritten law is that I am not meant to be touched until I marry. The idea. Find someone suitable and then wait until I am at least twenty before I hop in the sack. Yeah. Sure. No. That I would not do. Six years of waiting to be touched. No. Sounds pretty stupid. But how? The reputation of a Good Girl from a Good Family in Society was at stake. Can't blow my Family's sense of security. Nor their idea of my future marketability. Family disgrace. Family shame. Family honour. Playing with fire. That Zena Cherry Reputation. I too have to protect my virtue. Their virtue. Not loose, free, easy: a whore. No. Maintain the tight, controlled, lady-like posture.

Above all. Be careful. And don't get caught.

I would need a nobody boy. Nobody of importance. Not at school, that's gossip, scandal, a label. No. No discretion among friends. Nobody among the children of my parents' friends, that was worse, that meant marriage material. Lock and Key. Egads. No. Besides, I would have to be on good behaviour. Always. No. He has to be an outsider, someone who doesn't count. An outlaw. One who'll never threaten my position of goodness. My virtue. My reputation. Well. How? I might as well make it entertaining. So. An International List. A hit list. A class list. One from every country around the world. Out There. A wonderful idea. And educational too. A bit of glamour, exotic, possibly erotic and, most importantly, removed. Hidden from the spies. Those who'd tell. Blow my cover. That I want to touch. To be rubbed. Caressed. Loved. Used. That, yes, I want sex. Steamy sex.

Pete Pearson. The first. Numero uno. My first date. We met outside at a high-school football game over a bottle of Southern Comfort. He. A high-school jock hero. High profile. Ergo: I would have to be careful. Lady-like. At first. I was fourteen and seven-eighths, he was seventeen. He responded to my awkward flirtation. Liked me. Asked me out for supper and a movie. God. I was so naive. But eager.

We arranged that he should come by at 7:30, he arrived at a quarter to ten. I sitting in the big Windsor arm chair in the livingroom looking out the window. Quiet. Dressed to go out. Like one of my parents' cocktail parties. Anxious. Where is he? Wondering if something dreadful had happened to him. My parents waiting for him too, to meet him. Quietly. He arrives. At the back door. I smell alcohol. He says, 'Let's go.' I say politely, 'Wouldn't you like to meet my parents, Pete?' He grunts. A swift handshake. My parents exchange a glance and I am gone. We are too late for the film. We go to the school parking lot. He asks me if I want to learn to drive. Yes. I do. Really. He pulls me over to him. Says 'Hold the wheel.' I do. He puts his arms around me, his hands resting on my breasts. He pokes

83

through the blouse to my little nipples. I panic. No. No. The car's moving. I hold the wheel. He kisses me. No. No. I find the brake. Open the door and get out. He's chasing me. Come on, Sarah. Just kidding. Come on, I'll teach you. To drive. I believe his talk. I like him. His sex. I let him touch my face. He is gentle. At first. Then he gets rough. Coming on. Rubbing himself against me. Breathing heavy. Holding me. Tight. I hate this. Jerk. I get away. Running across the football field in the dark. He running after me. Tackles me. I start crying. He stops. Okay, okay. I'll take you home. My first date, home by 10:30. Humiliated and horny. Excited by it all but damned if I'll ever be treated like that again. Having to face my parents. 'Nice date, dear?' Jesus. 'Yes, we just had some Cokes in a restaurant. He's pretty boring.' Meanwhile. Figuring it out. So. This is it. The game. Say anything. Do anything. To get it. To touch. That forbidden fruit. This is it. There is no more to it than that. Sex. It's either yes or no. Simple.

I jumped around. Further exploring boys who talked of football, hockey, TV and beer. No threat there. Not at Pineridge anyway. My 'visible' friends were the kids from the nice suburban area of Tyandaga. These were the people I took home. Show and tell. Strictly platonic. Pals. Never went out with any of the boys from this group. Curbing the impulse. The desire. Holding back the curiosity for their bodies. No. Not these Nice Boys. Only those I never have to associate with again. Maintaining the Mind / Body split. One for me, and one for them. Spying and stealing kisses from those generous care-free unfamiliar boys. Out There.

Then came the big break. I was off to Florida. With a group of girls. I was sixteen. Got a summer job through one of the nice girls in Tyandaga to work in her father's hotel. Brilliant. Legit. And I saw him the first day I was there. Ed. The sexy beach-bum lifeguard. Blonde. Lithe. Perfect for me.

He asked me to a Pink Floyd concert. I didn't know what that was. But sure. It was fantastic. An All-American extravaganza. Smoked pot for the first time. Sitting in the rafters of a huge auditorium. The lights swirling around. Ed sexy, Ed cool, Ed casual. Necking in the car on the way back to the hotel. He asked me to his room. I was nervous. This is it. 'Yes.' He closes the door and turns to me. He attentive. Not pushing. Not rough. Touching me. Gently. Rubbing me. Gently. Nervous. His fingers touching me. Inside. Frightened. Nervous. Wet. But. He. Ed. He didn't push. He helped me. Touch him. I saw him enjoy. My touching. With the lights on. Like children. Wide-eyed. Exploring. Around ears. Along backs. Down legs. Tickling, sucking toes. Nibbling, licking. Fingers, feeling, firm. Pressing me. With rhythm. With slow motion. Careful. Gentle. He asked me. Could he. Enter. Could he. Come. In. I. He. I. He. Touched me. I aching for pleasure. For him. I. I. Said no. Not this time. Did he understand? Anxious. He smiled. Yes. But touch me. Here. Hold me. Here. Finally coming over my legs. This. Here. What? Touching, tasting. Sticky. Lying beside me. Happy. o ed.

I moved in. The perfect arrangement. Sleeping with a man. Sharing his house. His life. His habits. No spies. No threats. And I was watching everything. Playing Woman. Cooking, cleaning. Giving to Ed. Wearing his overalls. Swimming in the pool at night. Skinny. Learning about his music. That Rock 'n Roll Blues. Meeting his friends. And I had the title. Ed's Girlfriend.

I don't know if he loved me. Really. I never allowed myself to trust him that much to find out. Besides, I knew I was leaving. I was going to Switzerland. Ed. The first on my International Hit List. Ed. The American from Chicago who sold cocaine on the side to keep up payments on his motorcycle. Sexy, kind Ed. There were tears, there were phone calls. By both. And I left.

I went to Europe. And there were many. Countries, Cultures and Men. To discover. To explore. To touch. To know. I justified my good girl status by not taking birth control. Never tell a man you are on the pill. It is instant whore status. You'll get treated like one. Keep the balance. And I tittered between affairs and fucking. Mistress and slut. It's all a question of reputation. Who knows what. All for a simple hug. A little caress. Warmth. Skin on skin. o touch me.

And then I came home to Canada for college.

Some were more important than others.

Marcus. I had met him at a meeting of the Study Elsewhere Committee in my fourth year at the University of Toronto. Liquid Brown Eyes. A beard. A light physique and outspoken. I noticed him. He had a foreign accent. An outlaw. Ergo safe. He also had presence. He wasn't afraid to speak out. A casual arrogance. Solo.

We met by accident. I was going to another friend's place for drinks. Hurrying up the subway stairs. There he was descending. Carrying books. Wrapped in a Burberry coat. We had to speak. We knew each other. Arranged to have coffee sometime soon. He later told me he noticed me too at that meeting. Tits under a T-shirt. So. The perfect start.

Meeting again on the street. Two in the afternoon. We both had separate classes to go to. But something in the air. We went for coffee at the Backyard Café on Avenue Road. Downstairs, cosy, artsy, music, students, comfortable. Café au lait. We talked philosophy until seven. We talked about ourselves. Seeing, watching each other. Here. Two voices weaving in and out of the fluid of our being. Together. Argumentative. Discussing. Debating. Jesting. Teasing. Gentle. Reaching. Haggling Hegel. Discounting Kant. Hopping over Hobbes. Flashing our literary wares at each other. Flashing our active selves at each other. Comparing experience. Matching time spent in Europe. The U. S. of A.

Dusk. Getting late. Intensive. Eyeballs floating from the coffee. Time to go. No. Yes. Time to go. Walking me to the door of the house in the Annex. An awkward moment. Another coffee sometime? Sure. A closed door. He phoned me later. Huffing. He'd just finished a history essay. Inspired from the afternoon talk. I was startled. Flattered. He asked, What are you doing tomorrow night?

A film. Back to the house. Upstairs. Into the livingroom. In our coats. Couldn't find the light switch. I felt a hand on my face. Being drawn towards his shape. A kiss perfumed with passion. Want. In our coats holding onto each other. Pulling me to him. Moving up. His hands on my ass. Moving up my back. To my face. o marcus.

He stayed till breakfast.

The next day at five I was waiting for Philip. A Family friend's daughter's ex-beau. Ergo: a Good Boy. Someone I had to be Nice with. Self-consciously Other conscious. Dressed in the style of Family. The Stauton Look. On Show. The door bell. I went downstairs. Marcus. He was as startled as I was. Here. Gave me a box of something. Obviously I'd been thinking about someone else, waiting for someone else. Confusion. Awkward. He said, 'I'll call you.' Closing the door. Gold wrapping paper and a brown linen ribbon. Godiva chocolates and a thank-you note. Meditating on the gesture. Believing it. Taken in. Swirling in the kindness. The thought. The door bell. Shit. Philip.

It was at the door, Marcus later said, when he decided that he wanted me. In his life. A full person. Not a fleeting image. Within two weeks we were solid. In bed. Loving all the time. Touching all the time. Devoted. Impassioned. Like animals, licking and sniffing, romping and playing. Giving warmth.

Soon too I met the fabric of his mythology. His Belgian mother, his older philosophy-student sister, his step-brother. They lived in an apartment in Rosedale. A downtown fashionable area. For the Established. I met many of his radical friends. Impassioned communists who'd actually read Marx. Italians. Jews. Disenchanted spoilt WASPs. All alienated outcasts. Thinkers. Self-imposed exiles. The life I wanted. Solo. Individuals. Coffee cups. Canvases. Courvoisier. Late-night discussions of politics, economy, power and people. Involved, heated, intense, violent. Living with the world view. Developing a framework. A perspective. A working philosophy. Reasons.

Marcus never knew his father. Neither did his sister. Bastard kids. With no sense of familial history. They stood clean upon the world. And they called their mother by name. Maria. She was in good shape. A promiscuous broad in blue jeans. Honest. Straight from the pelvis. No ties. Ropes or chains.

Marcus and I became a couple. In Toronto. Only. Proof to his friends and his family of our romance. But something was wrong. Something prevented me from giving fully. Holding back. I felt like I was being used, experienced, experimented with, the Canadian WASP. But then too I could see and say to myself that I was spying on this Belgian communist. We were attracted yet oddly repelled by each other. Physically yes. But let our heads get into the act. We wanted to be kind, but we were leery. Wanting to believe, but never trusting. We had separate lives. Separate mythologies. I was one type of person with Marcus and another with Family. Like always. The Mind / Body split. Never complete.

Marcus denounced Society. As I did. Its pretensions. Its falseness. He mocked all Family stood for. As I did. He hit Formality with his Informality. He met my polite conservatism with a sexual casualness. Spread eagle. He met my strong feelings of nationalism with Marxism and corrupt capitalist property rights. The price. And he played seriously. We both did. Attempting to destroy established convention and replace it with the New Order. Marsar Inc. He'd pat my belly and say 'petite Marky.' I his sow. I the producer. Generating him again.

But wait a minute.

Wait a minute.

He was knocking *my* family. My beginnings. Where I had come from. And he'd never even been there. He didn't know anything about them. Only through me. How dare he. Presume.

Daring me to pull down my pants on the street one day. 'You're so tight assed.' I looked at him. Unzipped my pants and pulled them down. And looked at him. Well, he said, you're still wearing underwear. Marcus never wore underwear. Constricted his balls. Oh Jesus. I never had balls.

I began to challenge too. Why did he live in Rosedale? Or the equally fashionable Cabbagetown? Talk's cheap. Talk big, denouncing convention, but why did he wear a Royal Canadian Yacht Club polo shirt, when he wasn't even a member? Why wear a Burberry? Why smoke Davidoffs? Talking about the last girlfriend. Quote. Magin, a rich broad. But dumb. Unquote. You mean you didn't cut it. She wouldn't buy you. Living on the fringe. Seeing, touching, smelling, but not being. Not having. Security. For tomorrow.

He saw everything, every product, every person, every eating and living establishment as a reflection of money and class. He knew that the value or level of class or Image was entirely dependent on money. Hard to pretend to be a gentleman or anything when you ain't got dough. Dough lifts and separates. Buying time and leisure. Freedom.

Marcus wanted to make clear that all the actions in his life were choices, and not some response to mindless inherited convention. And, I would ask, is it choice to smoke a cigar? Isn't it more a symbol of power, macho manliness, recognizing that hundreds of slaving minions burn in the tropic sun to produce a white man's fancy? Isn't it more revolting to emphasize the choice, the conscious choice, of knowing the injustice, the economic slavery, than to do so as a result of blind, innocent, inherited convention? Yes. Monkey see and monkey do. But. Men were not born with cigars in their mouths. They get put there.

But I admit. Half the problem. I liked Marcus with a cigar. There it is. I liked the Image. The Hemingway figure. The Man's Man. Smoking sweat. And we were going out together. Labelled the Wasp and the Communist. Cross-breeding, hybrids. Others judged, we judged, and we would cling to

89

those labels whenever we fought. Losing Us. Our New Combined History. Whipping each other. With Old History. With our fabricated mythical singular solo selves.

I finally dared to take him to Pineridge. A black-tie Christmas dinner. The underground rebel drawn out of hiding. So. Everyone wants to see. He wants to see, spy, and judge them. And they want to see, spy, and judge him. Okay. Hoping to shock them all as well as he. Shake it up. Shake it out. That sense of the dice. Wondering about the odds. Wondering about the outcome. The idea of squatting down and saying, 'Okay baby, come on!' Rattling one's fist, throwing. Releasing. History.

Talking Marcus into it first of all. Said he would do it for me. Went so far as to buy a tux. (Buy? Not rent? I got suspicious. Buy for me? Why? What kind of choice was that?)

But. He looked good. Dashing. In his cummerbund and all. Davidoff clipped and trimmed. Puff puff. But he blew it. When the family was gathered around the oak diningroom table preparing to settle in for the traditional poker game, he was asked if he could play. With cigar in mouth and scotch in hand he broadly beamed and answered yes, of course. And he sat down. They had not asked if he would play but if he could play. Seduced. Playing bigger than big. The game. He was taken to the cleaner's. Cute. The Family thought him cute. A cute communist. Patronizing and smug in their knowledge of having made an ass of him. Never took him seriously. How could I after that? He fell for it. Any fool would have played that one differently.

We finished with a bang. I went hysterical one night. Collected my belongings and left. Taking the cab to my apartment. Well. That was clean. Severed. Another blow-up on the phone for his ego and we were over.

A closed book. Slam.

Back to 'visible' dates with gentle, tame creatures like Philip. The lavender Gatsby figure. He and I talked about books, biographies, plays, theatre and people. Polite people. Civilized and passionless. Occasionally holding hands. With this Nice Young Man. For the Public.

But I started wondering. Wanting. Other men again. The style. Watching men walk. Their rhythm. Noticing it in women too. The sensual. Pulling away. Back to the unfamiliar. Out There. Seeing others. For coffee. Tea. Drinks. Lunch. Dinner. Movies. Bed. Looking always. Some better than others. Knew what I liked. The hug. The sex. The caress. Deep. Full. No words. Big strong silent men. Not squirters. Liked lusting. The feel of a man. Liked sex raw. Honest. Touching. Feeling. Exploring. Loving. Here. But to a point. I mean. I knew the tricks. What I had to do to get that hug. Selling myself. A surface self. Telling them whatever they wanted to hear. Business, art, politics. Crooning, kissing ass, bending double. Submissive female. I let them smother me. Give to me. Touch me. And always splitting before it got too heavy. Finding a good sexual partner is tricky business. You have to put up with a lot, them as people I mean, with feelings, emotions, needs, families, history. After all, they're not just objects.

I didn't take any of them seriously. Why? What for? None of them could offer me more than what I already knew. Understood. I never took any of them to Pineridge. There was no point. They wouldn't fit. The drawer. The Image. And I couldn't be bothered having to explain one to the other. Again. Some got it into their heads that they wanted me for keeps. To own me. Marry me. Quickly easing out. Lady-like. Replacing with a less emotionally demanding stud. Getting someone who didn't understand control. Power. Toying with them if they thought they did. The politics outside of the bed. Humour them. Make them think they really are necessary for your survival, happiness and health. Stoke baby, stoke. And as soon as it would happen I would leave. I could not abide anyone telling me how to be. To be. No. You do not own me.

I learned never to mix friends and lovers. Messy. Take Eric. I genuinely liked him. Funnier than most. Dry ironic wit. But he wanted me. Too. Wife-material. No. No. He wanted me too cuz he thought he was getting class. Buying history. Getting Initiated. Poor Eric. No. No. Just another one chasing the pack. I am not your meal ticket. Your entré. I am a woman. Female. And I only want a man. Male.

My cycloptic eye would constantly rove, always looking. For Him. The Male. Out There. Who wants to give. A hug, a kiss, a caress. Without the Demands. The Rights. The Possessiveness. You're mine. I own you. Now do as I say.

Aware always of the difference. Between lusting and loving. Lusting took from others. It wanted. Contact. Raw. Body to body. But loving. That was something different. I never said it. Not once. To any of them. Knowing that those words were sacred. To be used with certainty, finality, commitment, truth. With life and limb. From one complete being to another. Fullness to fullness. I love you. Looking always for that one. The one I could say it to. In the meantime, waiting, watching. Filling the waiting with lust, affairs, tête-à-têtes, and strangers. Yet in the waiting quietly seeking. The sacred. Where someone could stand opposite me and say they couldn't own me, and that they loved me. And not want to possess me. Just love me. I don't want to love someone who needs me. I want someone who can stand on their own. Solo. Complete. Free from me. Free to love me.

FRIDAY

The following morning Sarah went into the pharmacy on her way to work. Walking up to the back counter she felt she was walking into the barrel of a pistol. Russian roulette. She gave her name and waited. Bang. Yes. The result was positive. She thanked the white coat and handed him five bucks. She walked out. Down the sidewalk. Crossed the street. Waiting for the streetcar. Standing. Waiting. Blank. She stepped into the car and sat down. A Filipino couple stood in the hollow space of the car. The little woman was very pregnant. They were standing together, they were not talking. She had her hand on her coat touching her belly, absent-mindedly looking out the window. Her scarf flapping in the breeze. He was staring at his feet. After two stops they got out. She stepped down first and started swaying up the street. He followed her staring at his feet. Sarah watched until they were out of sight.

She thought of her own body. Her poor body. It was only doing what it was told. And she had fucked it up. She wondered about the new life in her. The child creature, the fetal form, sucking on her. The growth on her insides. She felt her lower spine pressing against the seat. Her belly nestled in her pelvic bone. She wondered if the child was comfortable. She was. She thought of the recent men. Nicholas, Howith, or Tony. She didn't know. She had no idea who the father might be. She thought of her own father. She thought of her brother who was also now a father. How could a man really know? Marriage was no security. It was the woman who decided on loyalty. Fidelity. The woman chooses the father. When a woman says yes to a man she opens up her womb. She gives herself up to the life flow. But fucking around. Playing. That was her risk. Her joy. Her responsibility. Playing. With fire. Life's light.

There was no question in her mind of what she had to do. Abort it. Kill it. Scrape out the child. The baby. Smother the fire. Clean herself out. She considered the three men. She thought of each, in turn, as the Other. The donor. Father. A child of sex with Howith. A child of friendship with Tony. A child of. Of. A child with Nicholas. The first two didn't count. The child was a mistake. Happy sperm finally finding a playmate. But Nick's child, that was another thing. Another thing all together. It was better, easier, that she couldn't identify the father. It made the feeling less acute. Even so, the notion that it might be his, theirs, burned in her. A red-hot poker slowly scorching her. Blazing through her mind and her body. She sweated. No. Not our child. Our child. She clung to the fact that she didn't know. She could only guess.

When she reached the office she closed the outer door and phoned the hospital. Thank god for Canada. Thank god for OHIP. She had to make several calls before she knew exactly what she had to do. First, she had to go before a board and get a rubber stamp of approval that she was mentally unfit and financially incapable of being a mother. Then there was an appointment with a gynecologist. He or she had to determine how old the fetus was. The age of the infant would determine the nature of the abortion. Whether it would be only a scraping or involve induced labour with her uterus injected with a saline solution. The idea of a kid roped down within her drowning in poisoned salt water horrified her. If she was going to be an accomplice, a murderer, she wanted to do it cleanly. Quickly. Humanely. The whole process would take a couple of days. Time was of the essence. Again, depending on the age of the fetus, she would have to take a day and a night in the hospital.

She looked at the calendar. They said that she would be over it physically in a day. Amazing. They also suggested she take an appointment with a social worker to help her through the time. For adjustment. Fuck that. She didn't want someone, some stranger, patting her hand. There. There. No. She would deal with it on her own. She had gotten herself into this.

She made two appointments for Monday morning. They felt sure she could have the operation by or on Thursday of the same week. She looked at the calendar again. That gave her a day to recover before seeing Nick. Was that wise? She would have to speak to the doctor. The guy in the know. She hung up. Staring at a Bic pen with a gnarled top. Well, Gaia.

Back to business. At four the lawyer called. Was tonight still on? Tonight? The Gatsby bash. The Sinclair brothers. Oh yes, Ian. She masqueraded her forgetfulness with times, costumes and directions. 'So, your place at six?' Great. She had met the guy during college. She played good girl with him. Mary Tyler Moore. He never touched her, not really, and besides he was too wowed by her family connections to know how or where to begin. But he was good for this sort of thing. He would be presentable. He would hold his own in conversation. He would fit. And he would not cling to her. He would be working on his contacts, spying and stealing, which would leave her free to catch up with family friends she hadn't seen for a while.

She decided to stay at the office until five-thirty. That would give her fifteen minutes to change. That would do.

She hurried into her flat at 5:47. Swinging open the hall closet, she pulled out a black velvet dress with sequins. She had stolen it from Mother. It had been in the attic. A 1930s Paris original. Sexy and very flattering. More or less of the right period. And attractive. Sarah could never have afforded a dress like it. Shoving around the shoes and boots in the bottom of the closet, she finally found the pair she was after. Dangerous pointed black spikes trimmed with bits of sparkly glass. Great for boogie. She dumped the clothes on the chair and sprang into the shower, blow drying her hair in four minutes. She decided to wear it up. A quick makeup job. And for effect, a false mole. Perfume. Doorbell. Shit. 'Just a minute.' Wrapped in a towel. She opened the door half an inch. 'I just have to throw on my dress. Make yourself at home, the bar is in the kitchen.' She sped down to her room, grabbing dress and shoes as she went. Presto. He thought she was glamorous.

The ride to Hamilton was uneventful. Polite. Charming flattery. He may have been a lawyer but he was thick.

They pulled in the driveway, Sarah silently congratulating her aunt for pulling off yet another extravaganza. The house was floodlit. Hot pink and lime-green balloons were billowing out of the twenty-foot windows. Two Bentleys were parked on either side of the flagstone front steps. A red carpet came down to the gravel. There was a butler standing outside handing people glasses of champagne with a strawberry as they walked into the house. Sarah's date said wow.

Inside, the cocktailing was in high gear. The costumes were lavish and fantastic. Boaters, flappers, peach silk, black tie, all swirling under the hall candelabra. An orchestra jazzed away. She danced. She chatted, she drank, she flirted, she ate, she waltzed, she touched, she whirled. Strange to think of these people she'd grown up with. It was only yesterday that they had played tennis, football, tag, ping-pong, soccer. She had swum here often as a child. Jumping off the white tower. Thirty feet down. The skirt on her pale blue cotton bathing suit flashing up as she flew away. She loved these people. They were as brothers and sisters. Even today. But it was different. The discovered reality of the economic strength of their families in the local and even in the national community pulled at them. Pushed them. Contorted them. Prodded them. These young traditional adults were now competitive, ambitious men and women. It had been bred in early. They hadn't had much choice. One of her cousins came over to her. They shared a joke. He had just returned from a tough year of working with the family company in London. Her date lumbered over. Wanting to cash in. Sarah could see the gleam in his eye. She excused herself. Leaving him to it. Slipping over to the bar. She didn't have to wait for a man to get her a drink. Besides, the bartender had known her for years. He gave her the usual. Bourbon and lime cordial, no ice.

She walked out onto the flagstone terrace. The view extended down all the way across the valley and the lake to the lights of Toronto. There were several couples sitting outside. The storm lanterns flickered on the glass table tops. She walked to the top of the stairs that led down to the pool. It would be warm enough to swim now, she thought. Naked, in the moonlight. No. She would scandalize not only her date but the family. She returned to the cha-cha of the party. Her cousin came over to her and silently, and quite solemnly, slipped the empty claw of a crab under her dress strap. 'Your date forgot to give you a corsage.' They looked at each other and laughed.

The band closed up the floor at two but the party blasted on till well after four. Sarah discovered her date talking to one of the prettier girls. She hoped they had exchanged numbers. He guiltily stood and quipped, 'You've been neglecting me. Didi here' – he turned and nodded at the trophy – 'has been kind enough to look after me.'

Sarah looked at the couple. She looked at him. Pretentious asshole. 'That's great. I'm sorry, but I just had to catch up with some old friends. Thanks Didi. You know, we should really get together some time, the three of us, in the city. For drinks or something.'

'What a great idea,' he said. Sarah snoozed through the rest of the exchange. Nodding, dipping, smiling. Finally ending the dance with an injunction that she now wanted to go home. He had the wheels. 'Sure, Sarah.' Smiling. Contact. Take-off.

As they drove through the night back to Pineridge. Ian asked her whom she had spoken to. Who was that? How are they connected to the group? What does he do? She suggested he read Wallace Clements' *The Canadian Corporate Elite*. He looked at her in the light of a passing motorist. 'There's no need to be so bitchy. I'm just trying to be friendly. I haven't spoken to you much all night.'

'I'm sorry, Ian. Guess I'm tired. Would you mind if I turned on the radio.' Sarah let the alcohol and music carry her through the night. In the chauffeur-driven automobile. To the house. Pineridge.

He looked at the carriage lamps twinkling around the house and said 'I've always liked your home.' He walked her to the front door. Taking her arm. Playing the I've-got-a-date-at-the-door scene.

She ducked out. She leaned forward and kissed him on the cheek. 'Thanks Ian. It was fun, wasn't it?' He held on to her arms. He leaned forward and kissed her. Hard. On the mouth. With cold narrow lips. Then released her and skipped down the steps to his getaway car.

'I'll call you soon.' I hope not, she thought, as she went into the house. Wiping her mouth. Turning off the twinkling carriage lights.

97

The dogs came running down to meet her. Tails wagging. She let them out. Walking across the gravel to the field. They scampered off into the night. She whistled softly. To remind them not to roam, just to pee. In the dark she could see their luminous eyes looking at her. Staring. 'Come on, let's go.' The jingle of their chains. Betraying an inquisitive sniff here. A sniff there. 'Come.' She turned and walked back across the gravel. It was a clear night. Bright. Darkness. A full moon. Stars. Space. Looking up. Through the night. Released from the pull. The gravitational pull. Into Sky. Floating around the earth. Observing. Watching. Now there were political satellites up there. So. Propaganda spies. Are we getting closer? Seeing ourselves. From the outside. From the inside. Staring out, staring in. Tightening that human knot. Are we getting closer?

Climbing the stairs to her room. She heard the furnace. The rumble of stale hot air breathing through that old stone house. The house was cold. She was sure her father had turned down the thermostat again. Fuel costs. Energy conservation. Not like her mother who wanted a temperature that wouldn't remind her there was temperature. With no thought given to the expense. That little switch would be pushed up, and pulled down. Mysteriously from 70 to 57. From 57 to 70. The breathing house. Sarah liked the cold. It was an excuse to get cosy. Warm. Comfortable. Light the fires. Put on a sweater. Snuggle. Cuddle. The cold made her aware of her body. Its suggestions. Its cold points. Its hot points. Its needs.

Her room was dark. She remembered the days of running from the hall and jumping for her bed. Frightened of the bogeymen underneath who would snatch at her ankles. (Odd she never thought of bogeywomen.) She slid off her dress in the moonlight. The claw fell to the floor. A worthy token. A keepsake. She picked it up and wondered how it was that they couldn't play tag or hide-and-seek any longer. Only adult games. With booze, sex and money. Adult touch tag. Adult tackle tag. Adult hide-and-seek.

She lay in her bed and could see the night out her window. The bright darkness. Earth's blanket. Night. Snuggling. Seeing the stars and the distant shore lights on the opposite side of the lake. Iroquois. Ontario. Quiet Earth. Calm.

His presence slowly came to her. Naked. Standing. She had slept with him in this bed. On her raft. On her island.

When she had been younger she had promised herself that she would sleep on her wedding night on this bed. He, the Chosen, would sire. And she, the mate, would conceive sons and daughters in this bed. She would give birth and die here. She would be Queen. No longer a lovely little princess. He would be King. Master. Adam and Eve. Sacred. Divine. Human. Loving under a full moon. Life's light. Touching. Naked. Together.

But now the King did not want her. Nor her kingdom. And the lovely Queen carried a child. A half child. A sacred infant. Her first born. Murdered before it even saw Earth.

o nick.

Our first born.

She touched her belly. Her child. Softly. Alone. In the bright night light.

She dreamed of Alicia.

Alicia and Alberto.

Alberto was a Yugoslav freedom fighter, a heavy-set lumberjack from Alberta, with seven bullet holes in his left leg from the Great Civil War. A big man, he never lifted a finger to work on the property. Unless to tend to his paprika at the bottom of the garden or to grind his coffee beans in his brass cylinder. He tolerated us only, but he seemed to have a particular fondness for George. Bambino Georgio. Calling Mother 'missus' and Father 'Mr. Stauton.' He was a proud quiet man. Somewhat isolated in that big rambling house. Tucked away in the servant quarters. Reading foreign papers and listening to short-wave radio while sipping slivovich. He used to hand-carve his walking canes and then stroll for hours up and down

99

the gravel driveway. One hand behind his back. The other on his stick. Head bent. In all weather. Every day. We never walked or played on Alberto's path. It was his. Sacred.

And then there was Alicia.

Alicia. Alberto's bride. She had married him in her fortieth year. She was a virgin. A Catholic. An Italian from a family of seven brothers and a seafaring father. From Trieste. Alberto had gone to her father, explained that he had had a wife who was unfaithful, and by her had had one bad daughter whom he now never saw. He was seeking a good woman. A clean woman. He showed his war medals. His bullet holes. He showed his gold. His teeth. Bargaining for Alicia. Her father consented. Sold. They returned to the New World, Alberto on workman's compensation and Alicia began a job with us. As a servant. A maid. A cook. For nine years.

She was uncommon. Different. She had olive skin and dark eyes. Thinking eyes. Not demanding, or questioning, or blank eyes. Thinking eyes. She was not oblivious to you. As a person. She did not see the Image or the Object. She saw you. And she had beautiful gray-fleck black hair. Long. Coarse. Twisted up onto her head in a bun. Soft gold earrings hung from her floppy ear lobes. Draped in crucifixes and a white maid's costume. Portly, five-foot-nothing, she would mama mia her sore feet after climbing stairs. But Alicia, dear Alicia, was most different in her love. Her giving. She was kind. Generous. And, to us knock-kneed, knee-socked children, uncommonly emotional and physical. In a flurry of passion she would clasp us to her breast, hug us, scold us, kiss us, smother us, pamper us. And she never spanked. But she would in her fractured English make it clear when we had displeased her. Hurt her.

In the morning she would come to the bedroom door. Arch her finger around the side and wiggle it. Softly cooing. Coo-coo-ree-coo. Italian for cock-a-doodle-do. She would do it for some time. Softly, standing outside the door. Wiggling her finger. Coo-coo-ree-coo. Until we answered her. Coo-coo-ree-coo. Then she would disappear. The finger would slip away.

And it was time to get up.

She was a good cook. Greasy, rich soups. Pita. Stretched paper-thin across the width of the kitchen table. Fresh homemade bread. Palachinka. Filled with jam and honey. Filling the house with her baking. Spicy, garlicy Italian food. Sips of black potent coffee. Espresso. And she was always there. With an attentive ear, a sympathetic heart. Soft Italian murmurings. Cooings. Always. Warm.

She worked hard. Scurrying around under Alberto's monosyllabic direction. Adored. Placing his meal on the table. Placing the children's meal on the table. Clearing his place. Serving his coffee and our dessert before she'd even taken care of herself. And she would make our beds. Pick up our discarded clothes. Do up our boots. And comb our hair. Gently. And she would stand at the sink washing dishes, singing hymns and arias. Ironing. She sang well. With deep mournful wailing amens. The only time she ever went out was on Sunday. To church. Dark foreigners would come to pick them up. Alicia would be dressed in a simple buttoned-up navy-blue dress and she would wear a hat with black fur trim. Alberto wore a dark brown suit, a yellow shirt, an orange necktie. Held together by a big gold tie clip. And when they smiled their gold teeth would gleam. Together. And then they'd all talk funny.

Alicia. Dark, foreign, Latin, giving, loving, dominated by a young cool white Anglo woman who gave her orders. Gave her menus. Gave her work. I never saw Alicia get paid. I knew only that they had come from Italy to be with us. I saw another world through her. A world totally removed from everything I knew. The sacred. And the Family. She would tell stories of her youth. A young niece of her father's in Firenze had left a two-month-old baby in a carriage while she had gone into a store to buy meat. Rats had come. Eaten the child. o really? Wide-eyed wondering youth. Gobbling up the tale. The horror. The mystery. o alicia.

I learnt about loving from her. If I hadn't known her, I doubt I'd believe it was possible. It was her sense of faith, her trust.

Be it education or religion or her family. One thing for certain. It was there. Without demanding anything in return. We didn't have to perform little services – no curtsies, nor bargaining. We did not have to win her.

One day. Alicia was sitting in the kitchen. Crying. Holding her rosary. Rocking. I had come back from school. Her face was blotchy, her eyes red, her bun of gray-black hair untidy. I was horrified to see her in such a state. 'Alicia, Alicia, what's the matter?' I placed my cool school-girl hand gently on her heaving shoulder. She looked up at me. With those thinking eyes. o alicia. She smiled at me bravely. Through her tears. 'Ah Sainte-Maria. Sometimes I just don't know. I just don't know. I don't believe in God, and it frightens me so to believe this.' She sobbed. I asked, 'Alicia, why don't you believe in God?' She started to cry again. 'I've been a good woman all my life. All my life. And I have never asked Him for anything. I have been good. And now I know I will never have a child of my own. No bambina mia. No bambino.' She saw me listening to her, watching, feeling her. She pulled me to her. Holding me. Smiling. 'But God is merciful. He has given me beautiful adopted children. Familia Stauton. And bambina Sarah.' She wiped her eyes. 'Silly Alicia, silly Alicia, no?'

O Giver of Life, Taker of Life. I must always remember. You are not God. God is useless. You are man and you are woman. Only. Men and Women.

It had been a picnic up north. On an island of rock and pine. A sunny, pleasant day. The picnic was over and we were filling the boats. My uncle's boat and Father's boat. I wanted to go with my uncle. To sit in the bow. To feel the rush and warmth of summer air going back to the island. There was room. I was told by Mother to get in Father's boat. I said no. I would not. I would have to sit in the back with the hamper and the coolers. Tucked away with the dogs. The boats were full. The ropes were untied from the rocks, and I was standing on the shore.

Mother said, 'Sarah, you're holding up everyone else. Get in.' I looked at her. And then said no. The others laughed at this defiance. But she knew. 'Well then, we'll just have to leave you behind. Let's go, David.' They left. The boats gurgled away. Finally picking up speed, disappearing around the edge of the island. And I was left alone.

But I knew they would be back. They wouldn't leave me. I waited. For five minutes. For half an hour. Sitting on a rock. Waiting. Listening to everything around me. The water. The gulls. The wind. The whistle of the trees. Waiting. I was impatient. Waiting. I walked down to the water's edge to get a better look. No. Nowhere in sight. I ran up to the top of the hill. Looking. No. Nowhere. It had been easily two hours. I started getting frightened. They wouldn't. They couldn't. Waiting. A bit nervous. I started thinking of rattlers, wolves, bears. I thought a rattler would come to eat me. I went down to the water's edge. Crouched down. Frightened. My back to the water. Rattlers like to sunbathe on the rocks. They like to sleep under trees. They look for prey on land. The island was not safe. My back to the water. Watching the rocks. Rattlers can swim too. That's how they travel. I looked over my shoulder. Into the water. Scanning the shoreline. I looked back to the land. I was terrified. Where were they? Where are they? I was tired. But I couldn't sleep. A rattler could tell. Would come then. Where are they? I started crying. I can't cry. Then I can't see. Wiping my eyes. Where are they? Still and quiet, crouched in the midst of all this noisy nature. Tense. I have no place here. I am not a rock. I am not water. Where are they? Scanning the islands, the rocks, the Sky. Crouched at the edge. Still. Tense.

Then I saw him. Dad. He was on top of the hill and walking towards me. I stood up. o dad. Crying. I didn't believe you would. I was crying. He beckoned to me. I went running towards him. He was gruff. Had turned his back and was going back down the other side of the hill to the waiting boats. I followed him. Crying. They were all watching me, except one. I

103

looked at Mother through my tears. She had a drink in her hand and was talking to someone. I got into Father's boat, and sat down in the back. Beside the dogs. Looking out over the water. Looking at the island. I was silent.

I must always remember. You are not God. You are human. Man and Woman. Only. o giver and taker of life.

SATURDAY

She woke. It was late. The sun was streaming in across her room. Edging up her bed. She put her hand in it. Could feel the heat. The warmth. Against the windowpane several flies were buzzing, attempting to get out. One of the black labs lay beside her bed. On its side snoozing in the sun. There was wind. She could hear it. See it in the trees. Her father was going to a shoot today. He always shot better when there was a breeze. He would concentrate more. The clay pigeons bobbing, bouncing like real birds in flight. He was one of the best shots at the club. He had been voted president last year. By his comrades in arms. He had at first quietly accepted this honour but had since declined. He did not feel that a man with diagnosed throat cancer should be the spokesman for the club. He had probably gone out there already. Her younger brother George would probably have gone as well. George was being slowly initiated into the ritual. The men's shoot. Ladies were only allowed to shoot on Wednesday afternoon. And every second Sunday. For two hours.

Sarah liked shooting. But only up north. She enjoyed the ritual. The atmosphere. The early rising. The expectation. Of the hunt. The heavy weather duck clothing. Cartridges slipped into a gun belt. Heavy waterproof boots. The thermos of hot coffee. Stalking or sitting in a blind. Listening, waiting, watching for those dark spots in the sky. The decoys bobbing. The dogs would always know when they were going to a shoot.

They could smell the remains of the ancient dead birds in her father's coat. They could smell the guns. But the dogs didn't go to the club shoots. They only went to the marsh. Up north. At the club, quiet businessmen, gray-haired businessmen would stand and shoot with the agility, speed and excitement of a young boy shooting his first squirrel. They were good shots. Most of them. Steady. Constant. Cool. Persistent. Competitive. The women were reluctantly allowed to stand with them. Some women never even tried. They hid in the clubhouse out of the cold, away from the thunderous bang, sipping gin and tonic. But other women would. Like Sarah's aunts. Her father's sisters. They too were excellent shots. Such beautiful women with their gray-streaked hair. Raybans and khaki green. Swinging to the motion of a flying bird. Pull. Swing. Bang. Hit. Some men didn't know quite what to do with these dames. Didn't know how to handle it. How good they were. Especially when they would drink too like the men. Scotch. The only real difference was the lipstick on their sunburnt faces and the weight of their guns. Ladies had made-to-measure Purdey's.

Sarah remembered the last time she had shot. Up north. Thanksgiving weekend of last year. The fall colours had been magnificent. The marsh clear and cold. Stalking the ground for pheasant. The dogs running ahead to flush out the whir-whir of the birds. She had been walking with her younger brother. Their guns were ready. Loaded. Unlocked. Resting on their crocked arms. The autumn sun warming their backs. Ten feet away from them a female popped up and tried to dart through the underbrush. Sarah pulled the gun to her shoulder. Tight. Sighting. Squeezing the trigger. Bang. The bird dipped and fell. A lab came running from another bush passing in front of them and went in for the bird. That afternoon she and her brother had cleaned it along with two that her father had shot. Pulling out the feathers, the down, slashing off its head, the tips of its wings, its feet. Pulling out the innards. Saving the livers, kidneys and heart for breakfast. The cook had prepared the meal with wild rice and fresh garden beets. Her first wild bird for the season. Her father had been proud of her. His favourite daughter.

The dog sat up at the end of the bed. Turning, looking at her. Breakfast? She heard Mother on the phone in the other bedroom. Yes. Now was the time to slip downstairs before she got cornered and told to reiterate the evening's events. No, she didn't want to get into it just yet. The gossip. The costumes. The date. Not on an empty stomach.

The kitchen fire was smouldering. Her father must have started it before he had left. She grabbed a small log from the wood pile at the back door and threw it in on the coals. It was cold outside. And cold inside. Except in the kitchen. She could imagine that Mother was going to complain.

A pot of fresh coffee was on the stove. And some of her father's hand-baked biscuits were already cut and ready for toasting. A bowl of fruit had been cut and prepared. She heard her mother coming down the hall. She entered. Fully dressed, carrying her breakfast tray and her purse. 'This house is cold. Your father seems to think we still live in England. You've got the fire going. What a good idea.' She walked over to the window and turned on the portable radio. MOR. Middle-of-the-Road gook. She carried on. She was going to play tennis today at the Thorn Club. She would be back for a late lunch. Would Sarah set the table for six and make sandwiches? Some of the ladies were coming back as well. She would have to buy some sherry on the way home. She turned and walked out looking for her coat. She came back. 'Oh yes, how was it last night? The Gatsby bash. Did they have a good band? Were Uncle Tom and Aunt Elena there? Barb and Stew? Who of your crowd?' She pried. Sucking for gossip. News about the Hamilton crowd. Community. Society. Sarah was curt and brusque. Her mother noticed. 'What's the matter with you? Crummy date?' She tried unsuccessfully to extract more details from her daughter then turned and walked out. 'Make twelve sandwiches.'

Sarah looked at her coffee. Now cold. Her mother still mesmerized her. Stopped her. Dead. Confused her. Controlled her. She realized she must not come home so often. There was no point. The pleasure she derived from the house, her father and brother did not compensate for the presence of mother. Sarah's emotions would get jumpy. Agitated. She would continuously be violated, ordered, whipped with questions. Never allowed just to be. Calm. No. It was not good for her. She had enough on her plate just now.

Sarah decided to get the sandwiches ready and out of the way. She did it quickly with the fire hissing in the background. Deciding too that she would make a point of not being in the vicinity when the ladies came back from their tennis game. She would have to find a costume to wear to the Vienna Spring Ball. Once that was done she would go outside. Down to the barn. The pond. Maybe over to the Bartley's. Away. Out There.

She went up to the attic. Her mother's old clothes hung like carcasses in the gloom of the musty room. She found an old chest with her name on it. In child's print. SaRaH ElIsAbEtH StAuToN. Her camp trunk. When she had been ten and eleven she had been sent to a private girls' camp. Tanamakoon in Algonquin Park. She had hated it. Forced fun. Classes from nine till four, in the middle of a forest. Making crafts. Clay canoes, dolls and painting dumb pictures. Told to sing camp songs. Get into it. The group effort. Make friends. Play tetherball. Tent duty. Cleaning up other's messes. The Rules. Cleaning, when there was no need to clean. Again. She would have preferred another month at Aurora. But she had been sent away. Her mother had said it would be good for her. Good for what?

Her best friend there had been a girl from Detroit. Ann Spitz. They used to go out late at night, down past the boats, away from the buildings. Into the night. Along the water's edge, over the rocks. Sometimes slipping. Getting soakers. Sneaking like Indians. Until they came to a clearing. There they would build a fire, a small fire. Enough to warm their hands and dry their shoes. And they would talk. Sometimes they would fall asleep. Curled up beside the fire. On the cool damp earth. Under the sky. Waking. Stirring the ashes. Scooping up the lake water in their hands to douse the fire. Stirring again. And sneaking back. Over the rocks. To their tents. That was the best part of camp. Sneaking out into the quiet sombre wilderness alone. Together. She never told. She never exposed. The sacred.

She finally found it. A pale blue satin evening dress. Old-fashioned and a bit snug. But it would fit in well with the New Yorkers. Nicholas would like it. She would fulfill his fantasy. Beautiful girl descends from The Tundra. Glistening in sequins and white evening gloves. To Be with Me.

She heard a car. Her father's. The Mercedes. She went down to greet him.

As always he had done well. 25-24. He had won a bottle of Glenfiddich. George's score had been good for a beginner. 14-17. He showed signs of being a true Stauton. They went in to change. Asking her about lunch. Where was mother? Sarah explained that lunch was in the fridge and Mother would be returning later. With the other ladies. She added that she would not be in for lunch. She did not give a reason. They did not ask why. They understood. Like an echo. Her mother would have wanted to know. Would have insisted that she speak even when she knew. Would force her into a lie. She would have insisted too that she stay. To help. Handmaiden on the table. Even today. And Sarah was a Working Woman, not a volunteer servant.

She pulled on her boots. Found some old gardening gloves and went outdoors into the cool spring air. The crispness banged into her lungs. Sharp. Clean air.

Walking over to the Bartley's. Over the fences and fields. Annie Bartley. Fuzz-top. Curly. Sarah had loved Annie dearly. They had been the best of friends, inseparable until grade 8. Then Annie had left private school. Gone away. Gone public.

Their house was a zoo. Literally. Horses, dogs, cats, strays, guinea pigs, hamsters, gerbils – all scurrying around. The kitchen was a disaster area. But I loved it. It was the antithesis of my own home. No 'live-in' help. No heavy-handed Mother power-tripping in party dresses. There was only Sue. A smiling friendly woman who played with her kids. Building things, cooking things, making things. Old Sue. Never had to put on airs with old Sue. She never scolded us. She encouraged us to explore, to discover. To play. With mud even.

Annie and I smoked our first cigarette together. In her bedroom. The parents were out. They never had babysitters. There were always enough children about to look after the others. One cigarette for both of us. The thrill was lighting it, taking a puff, then putting it out. And starting all over again. Playing. Acting. Grown-up. Adult. Imitating the great smokers. Marlene Dietrich. Humphrey Bogart. We had a garbage bin beside the bed. We tossed the used matches in there. Silly girls. There had been a lot of paper in the garbage bin. And with astonishment we watched flames leap out of the canister. Jesus. Smoke filled the room. Flames licked the bedside table. We ran into the bathroom. Taking small glasses of water back to the room. Throwing it on. That billowing smoke. Charcoal black filling the little room. Finally, bravely, grabbing the bin and rushing into the bathroom. Where? Under the shower. Blasting it with more water. More smoke. Jesus. All for one lousy cigarette.

We had cleaned up as best we could. But the house stank. We went to bed. Trying to sleep. Other little heads popped out from bedroom doors. 'Go back to bed,' we hissed. Waiting for the gods to descend.

Mr. Bartley came rushing into our room. He dragged Annie out of bed, demanding an explanation. She cried. Telling him everything. He spanked her. Yes. And he spanked me. Then he called my parents. It was the middle of the night. Come get your daughter. Jesus. Father came. I was scolded again. Sent to bed immediately. Well. It was the middle of the night. I was told that I couldn't see Annie again for a whole day. I bowed my head. Taking punishment. Knowing damn well that I would see her at school the next day.

They had a lot of property all along the edge of the escarpment. Limitless fields. Tumbling over rocks. Folding. Paths everywhere. Some for the horses and ponies. Some for the cows. Fields. Trampled by tamed animals.

The horse. Big Red. Monstrously big. Huge. With a head bigger than me. And huge brown eyes. We had to bury him. Dug a pit. Tractor had to drag him over. I always thought horses died standing up. Don't they sleep that way? Strange, the pit sagged. Always thought of Big Red whenever we played in the fields. Asleep in that pit. That huge horse covered with a little dirt. Red. Belly up. Under Sky.

And Annie had a great barn. Bigger than ours. The smell was different. Ours smelled of sheep. Theirs smelled of cows and horses. Straw and urine and pellets and dung. With a hayloft second to none. Bales of hay stacked high. We'd make forts. To hide in. From barn rats. And barn cats. Above the quiet cool machinery.

Then we would walk across the field back to her house. Annie was so brave. Never afraid of the horses or the cows. With their big brick heads. Sometimes she would run up behind the gray pony and catapult herself aboard. Bareback. Galloping. Round and round. I never got used to it. To them. I was scared. Those wild horses with knotted burrs in their sweeping tails. That walk on the path as it clung to the dips and slips across the field. Well worn. From years of walking. By animals. By us. We used to run along it. Pretending to be horses. Jump the stream. Jump the logs. Snort. Canter along the final stretch to the house. Annie's fuzzy head bobbing along in front of me. She was so small. Smaller than I. But fierce and with much energy. I liked her body. Compact. She had little feet and squatty little hands. Stubby like an animal. Strong nails, yellow they were so strong. More like claws. And her feet. Pudgy toes but padded, from being outside on the gravel and in the fields. Barefoot. Unlike our house. Sue didn't insist that the kids wear shoes. Filthy was good. Natural. We'd play hard. Only had to wash when we wanted to. Even eating with dirty hands. Grabbing an apple with a filthy little paw. Feet tucked under a cushion in the sofa. Indian corn and squash hung from their fireplace. The mantelpiece was not crowned like ours with priceless inherited Zing Dynasty jade trees. We were allowed to make noise. We would often play the piano together. Heart and Soul. Or Chopsticks. Again and again. Changing places on the bench. Alternating parts. Alternating hands. Our little feet swinging. Sometimes we would pretend we were in a rock band. Like the Beatles. Or Herman's Hermits. Singing lead vocals. Grinding pillow guitars. Snapping out Led Zeppelin drum solos on the table top. Dancing together.

And we would sing hymns too. 'Bring me my bow of burning gold, bring me my chariot of fire. O clouds unfold ...'

And we would sing about holding hands in the fields with country boys. James Taylor. Glen Campbell. Gordie Lightfoot. Softly awakening a need.

Then Annie went away. She went public. So. I found a new friend at private school. Sue Grant. Her father was square. Really a square man, in the way he used to dress and cut his hair. I don't remember the mother well. They had a small yapping Pekinese dog. And lived in an old limestone house in the country as we did. They also had a swimming pool and a skiddoo. We had neither. Learning early that you can get what you don't have at someone else's place. Friends are a valuable commodity. There is a lot to see and do Out There. Susan was freckled. Athletic. Strong. I liked staying over at her house. It was more of an adventure. I would stay there for a full weekend. Going to school on her bus. Mother wouldn't call me there. She couldn't chase me there. It was long distance. And Sue and I would smoke cigarettes by the pool when her parents were out.

Then when I had been taken out of private school and put

into public school I met Doreen. She lived in one of the little clapboard houses on the edge of the Bartley's property. They paid rent. Which meant that she was poor. Like Millwood folk. She too had the strange accent. She was loud, quick-tempered and amusing. I liked her. Like playing with a servant. Everything was safe. Because it didn't mean anything, it had nothing to do with Society. Doreen. A fighter. A commoner. Great almond-shaped eyes, a button nose, well-shaped teeth. A pretty girl. She had her hair cut in a shag. Layered. Most of her other friends did too. She was positively defiant against anything that didn't go her way. Clever, and physically agile, she would compete with the boys. Yelling. Beating up her brother Glen. My parents didn't like her. They told me so. They said she was common. So. I would go to her place. Her parents liked me. Her mother was simple. Stupid. You could say anything to her and she would believe it. Gave Doreen her looks only. Her father was a thin man who chain-smoked and played with his tape-recording equipment all the time. The parents worked in the same factory. Making cardboard boxes. Drove a chipped, pale blue plastic Valiant. The mother would let go of the steering wheel to light a cigarette. The father would smack the kids. Hard. I had never seen a man hit a child on the head. We would get spanked, not hit. I never spoke to him if I could help it. Neither did Doreen.

Their house was strange. It didn't seem real. Tiny. Five rooms only. All plastic. The sofa had a plastic covering. The kitchen chairs, if they weren't ripped, were covered in plastic. The kitchen table was wobbly. With a metal rim. There were always flies on it. And an open jar of French's mustard.

Doreen's bedroom was little. Straight off the livingroom. With little furniture. Pink and white. And a bunk bed. Sometimes when I would stay over her little sister would sleep in her brother's room. He had a single bed. So I guess they slept together.

She and I would often walk down to the school. Public school. Down the Bruce Trail beside the Bartleys'. Below the

escarpment, through the forest, beside the suburban develop-
ments, through the trees, to the school. We'd walk home too.
But it always took longer. Uphill. We'd sing. 'I want to be
screwed by you, and nobody else but you.' Improvised. Elvis
Presley. 'Since you left me baby.' Her father listened to that all
the time. 'You ain't nothin' but a hound dog.' And Doreen
smoked cigarettes. She'd even buy them. Milkshakes and
cigarettes.

Doreen taught me how to steal. No. Not true. I already
knew. She just showed me that you could get away with it.
Publicly. We did it together. The great day. We had gone down
to the Mall. We'd hang out there. Wandering around. She
would smoke. I wouldn't dare. Not in public. Too many spies.
Parental thugs. Reporting Reputation. We had gone into a
clothing department store. Beautiful crushed velvet pants.
Black and very soft. We both wanted a pair. No money. She
said let's steal them. I chose a yellow shirt. She chose a black
one. We went into the change room. With other things. Other
samples. Put them on under our clothes. My gray wool pants
covered them well. Casually going out. Putting the other samples back on the rack. The dumb girls watching. We smiled at
them. Walking casually out. Stopping to look at other items as
we left. A ladies' bra bin. Had a laugh there. Started to giggle.
Running out. But we were safe. Dumb broads. Back to the
house. Glowing. Into her bedroom. Swapping, trying them on
fourteen times. I was frightened to take mine home. So we put
them under Doreen's bed. They'd be safe there. But they
weren't. Doreen's mother found them. A surprise. She never
cleaned the room. But she found them. She burnt them in the
incinerator at the back of the house. She never said a word
about it to me. But she gave Doreen shit. Doreen could handle
it. The Mrs. didn't dare call Mother. Maybe she just didn't
think to. Thank God. We didn't take clothes again.

Doreen and I were friends until she got a boyfriend. Then
she was never home when I called. Or else she was going out. I
resented that. Some friend. Where's the loyalty to me?

Mother had commissioned me to sell lottery tickets for the National Ballet. Forty dollars worth. I gave half of them to Doreen. I sold mine and she sold hers. We did it separately. When I asked her for the money she said she would bring it over to the house later in the evening. She never came. I called her. She said she and her boyfriend had dropped it off by the big pear tree out front. They hadn't wanted to wake the household. I looked. It wasn't there. I called again. She got angry. I called her a liar. She called me a bitch. And I got shit from Mother. I had to pay twenty dollars from my allowance. I never trusted Doreen again. Some friend.

So. I found someone new. I first noticed her in the school cafeteria. I was sitting with Carol. A freckled sandy-coloured plump friend of hers came over. She had beautiful hair. Blonde. Real blonde. We looked right at each other. Immediate. Here was one who understood. She too. We both smiled. I liked too how she dressed. Style. Soft. Cords. Tweeds, wool sweaters, unlike the rest of the crowd. She was from Toronto. That faraway fabled city. Had moved here to Tyandaga. The rich suburb of Burlington. (I always laughed at this idea. The houses were all brand new! Five years at the most. Nouveau riche. Stuffed with tasteful furniture. From Eaton's. Cap T. Tasteful. Just like *House and Garden.* Everything clean and new. Stuffed with perfect little wives and hubbies. With perfect little kidlets. That's how the advertisement looked. Tan-coloured house with chocolate-brown shutters. A light over the garage. Family out front. Husband in blue suit has hand lightly placed on permed woman's shoulder. Her arms crossed over apron with three children in front of her. A family photo. Station wagon parked to one side. Dog pulling on a hose. Click. The Phantom Family.) I became Cindy's friend. And soon found out what goes on behind suburban walls. I spied. Aside from an unnatural paranoia about the intrusion of dirt, the families revolve around the kids and the kids' futures. And then there is the garden. Those little plots were gardened to within an inch of their life. Made into perfect putting greens.

Saturday morning. The men of the house would go out on their power lawnmowers, cut fifteen square feet of lawn and come in exhausted. Dad, on the other hand, would be out all day on the tractor cutting grass. First around the house, then in the fields, then in the orchard. He never complained. He would break only to have a beer. Then we would go do something else. You could tell he had earned his. Really earned it.

There was no sense of independence in these suburban people. They would dress alike. Even in their play clothes. Clean play clothes. That was an odd element. Cindy. She was always clean. Tidy. Ordered in her appearance. Not like Annie, Doreen and I. Her mother would get after her. Her mother would get after me too. Scrub. Scrub. But she was friendly. And she read books. So. We would talk books. She read different books. More philosophy and literature. She was a member of a book club. That was weird. They would have symposiums. Women talking about books. That was different. And she encouraged me to read. I would go there often after school and talk with Cindy's mother. Maybe even while Cindy was out. Learning from her. Drawing on her wisdom. Of books. Spying and stealing. And taking in their suburban difference.

When I turned sixteen I got mother's old Falcon station wagon. The kid van. The Turquoise Turtle. Practising to drive in the fields. In secret. Bumping, dipping. Much more fun than on a real road. Landrover, safari, back country, over the corn fields, back to the artesian well and the sweeping vines. A really great toy. Freedom. Climbing all over it. Inside and out. So easy. Automatic. Not like dad's Benz. Leaping and stopping. With a jolt. Once while in the car Cindy and I got stuck in the mud. Spinning the tires. But no go. Had to go back to the house on foot. David was upstairs. Home from the boarding-school exams. Asking him to take out the tractor to help pull us out. He was furious. He told mother and father. But it didn't stop me. I had a car. No more car links from here to there. No more chauffeurs. No more chains. Cindy and I would skip school and go. Anywhere. Everywhere. Taking backroads just to make sure we didn't get caught. Back to small towns like Milton to buy ice cream. To Hamilton to see a movie. Now that was exciting.

But today everything had changed. Sarah walked up the mud path to the Bartleys' and knew that she wouldn't find Annie. Annie had gone again. To Vancouver. To be with her dying father.

Old Sue was sitting outside at the picnic table with three mongrel dogs panting at her side. People in Millwood called her crazy. Sarah's mother called her crazy. She was a scruffy old woman now who braided her hair in pigtails. She would drive a beat-up jeep and buy her groceries with the antique parrot sitting on the front of her cart. Talking. They would have a conversation. Her children had all left her. Like her husband before them. And she had wandered around the house putting black crepe paper over the ground-floor windows. Eccentric. And lonely. And now poor. Old Sue.

Sarah sat with her at the table. Outside in the warmth of the cold bracing spring sun. With gloves on. Sharing memories. Exchanging moments. After some time she said she had to go.

Sarah slowly walked back to her own parents' house. Over the fields and the fences. There were no horses now. Or cows. But the path was still there. Worn down. She started to run. To canter. To jump. Snort. One of her boots fell off. A laugh. Running several short steps in her lumpy sock and black boot. On the hard cold spring mud.

Annie had tried to kiss her once. They had been playing in the barn. Swinging on the rope. Sarah had fallen into the haystack. Annie caught the rope and swung over her. And had then dropped down beside her. Lying in the hay. Laughing. Annie leaned over. Kissed her. Her fuzzy hair falling on Sarah's face. Sarah jumped up. Frightened. Don't. No one had ever kissed her like that. No one. She told Annie she had to go home. Standing in the hay. Leaving. No words. Hurrying home. To the familiar. Family. But they were good friends. Best friends. So it was soon forgotten. The kiss of friendship. Remembered only now. Annie. Curly. Pudgy toes and paws. Where was she?

When Sarah got home at four she noticed a visitor's car. Her Aunt. Sarah left her boots outside on the step. Leaving the sun to dry the moisture in them. She went inside in her socks. The family was in the livingroom. Her aunt with a sherry. Her mother with a sherry. Her father with a beer. In a stein. They were talking about the morning shoot. 25-25. The aunt's last shoot. She talked of her ailing husband. Her marriageable imminently marketable unmarried daughter. Commanding the room. 'Where have you been?' Fuck you. 'Outside.' Smile. Sarah asked her aunt if they still had the horses. Her cousin had had the privilege. Real horses. They had ridden together as youngsters. At an academy. Taking English riding lessons. Black hard hats with black tapered ribbons. String gloves and jodhpur boots. Round and round a corral. Posting. Cantering. Trot. Walk. And they had started jumping. Sarah had fallen. Smashing into a fence. The instructor had stood laughing. 'That will teach you to keep your arms still.' Sarah had broken a rib. She vowed she would never ride there again. But she still wanted to ride. Like Annie. She told her parents that she wanted a horse, but her parents couldn't see why she would want a horse if she wouldn't take lessons. Her aunt answered, 'Yes, Dierdre will be riding Hunter Class at the Royal this year.' Oh.

Sarah's aunt lived back country. Away from the edge of the escarpment. On a concession. Buried back deep. Their home had once been an Indian trading post. Limestone rocks and Thanksgiving dinners. Fat Puritans raising their mugs over a corn harvest. Stolen from the Indians. Given by the Indians. The Puritans would thank their God while the Indians pondered at the lightning and thunder of the White man's stick. Here, take whatever you want.

They had a buggy. Her aunt. An old carriage for two. One day she had taken her daughter and Sarah into Millwood in the buggy. The pony pulled them back country. Over the railway tracks. Past the ponds. People in Millwood said they were a bit crazy. Old fashioned. But they had had fun. Like the midnight hayrides at Christmas. Pulled by the pony over dirt roads. Throughout the quietly falling snow. Huddled together. Breathing children. And adults with silver whisky flasks. Laughing. Singing carols.

Inside her aunt's house polished Inuit sculptures threw their frozen spears at space during the Sunday teas. Brandy snaps oozed Devon cream. Steamy tea evaporated from painted porcelain tea cups. And a silver Georgian tea service squished a squat mahogany table. Yes. It was all Crown land. Now.

Sarah poured herself a sherry.

She was told that her parents were going out for dinner. It would be only herself and her younger brother and the dogs for dinner. George would be arriving later that afternoon. Sarah nodded.

After her parents had left, and he had arrived, she poured herself another sherry and asked him about school. He was at university now. They were close. Closer than she had been with her older brother. A different closeness though. They didn't play together under the ping-pong table. They didn't play cowboys and indians. They didn't fall down dead in the hall. Or punch each other in the stomach. They smoked and talked instead about the Tubes, Devo, Linda Ronstadt, dope, school, work and relationships.

Her father, as he had left, had asked them both to finish varnishing the rocking chair that was downstairs in the workshop. So after a quick wok-fried dinner they went down.

Switching on the light. Finding a brush. In an orange-juice can. A lot had changed. They talked of their father's cancer. His resistance. His drive. His need to live. The bad family blood. Their father's older brother had screwed him in the family business. And he had gotten all choked up. Had trouble breathing. The doctors had said it was from early years of smoking. But everyone in the family knew. It had been bad business between two brothers. Cancer. The outside world didn't know. But the Family all knew. The older brother had since died of cancer.

That's justice for you.

Now their father was strong. Oddly more vocal. Burping publicly to make himself understood. His new voice. Their mother had trouble adjusting. Straight executive wife to cottager's frau. But she was coping. Had become a born-again watercolourist. Leaving behind her solemn oil portraits. Going to purple rivers, roads and vast yellow fields. But it hadn't been easy. They all knew.

Sarah had been at the hospital with her mother when they had found out the news of her father. The first time they had hugged in years. A mutual grief binding them together. But only for a second. He would not die.

They finished the rocker. Painting under the seat. Running down the curved arms. Jabbing the corners. They knew that their effort would be inspected. Judged. They would get it right. For dad. Smoking cigarettes. Her brother was melancholic. Post-graduation blues. Never would be a football star. Never wanted it. Never be a marathoner. Smoked too much. Never be a pianist. The back room was too cold to practise in. Business school was an alternative, but it wasn't a life. He watched Sarah knowing she had stepped out, stepped beyond some limits. Somehow she was freer. He would always be Stauton. She could become something, someone else. He thought. She watched him. Envying his security, his place, a name. She was never really sure of her place. The house was her mother's. The name was her father's. She knew she could only wander. All over the world. Trying to find home.

They went upstairs and settled into TV. Watching Dallas. JR and the boys. The old gray father damning and praising JR as a father ought to praise a son. Captivating millions as it weaved throughout the American- Canadian- Spanish- Russian dream. Lassoing lonely hearts. JR could be on Yonge

Street, he could be in Paris, he could be in Fiji. Straddling the world. Ride 'em cowboy. Spurs and Cadillacs. Fulfilling a common notion: macho men and bitchy women dominate the world. And only money will ever move 'em. Six gun and sex pots. Ride 'em cowboy, ride 'em.

Sarah and John went their separate ways. To their separate beds. To think. To sleep. To dream.

A muggy clear night. Somewhere south. An island. A seaside mansion. Palms sway languidly on the lawn. The aroma of the tropics musks the air. In the middle. A small fountain splashes aqua-rose light. Water spews forth from a stone boy's proud penis. An animal runs across the lawn. From dusk to dusk. For an instant, aqua-rose. Then gone. Gone.

I am standing on the roof of the house. Near the edge. So that I can see all this. Others are on the roof, but they will not come to the edge to see. They are frightened of falling. So am I. But I can't resist the view.

SUNDAY

She slept through breakfast. And woke with a start intuitively knowing it was late. Sunday. The day of rest. But she had plenty to do. Tony was coming at three.

He arrived in his new car. A silver 1982 BMW. A replacement on his chipped green '68 VW. Blasting into status sphere. The stockmarket had been healthier this year. Bullish. He was pleased to see her. He had brought a bottle of wine for dinner. It was the second time he'd been invited to a dinner with her parents. He felt it was an honour. A sign. Of something. She would never disclose the truth. She had planned it this way. She had wanted a lift back to the city. The GO Train depressed her. All that waiting. Waiting blank faces. She always thought of trains going to Dachau, Auschwitz, Belsen: refugees, persecuted outcasts. Poor people. Abandoned in the open. Going to the din. The furnace. No car. No chauffeur. No. She did not like the GO Train. To go with a friend beside her, chatting and touching. Yes. That was preferable.

He was dressed for The Country. Tweed jacket, wool sweater, loafers, and brown cords. Comfortable. A touch stylish. She had had to wear what she could find around the house. Old jeans and one of her brother's flannel work shirts. She wore perfume to masquerade her lack of foresight to match his costume. Yes. Still attractive. Besides, in his mind it was her place. Her territory. He saw her amongst the antiques, the heritage. She didn't have to work as hard as he did to belong. She slipped on her black rubber boots. Her hand-me-down coon coat. Image intact. Cutting Classic. Babbling about her language class. The party. The walk yesterday. Her parents. Her aunt. He enjoyed listening to her. Her contrived stories and practised movements were the fabric of his idealized perception of her. He attempted to balance with stories of the Big Stock Deal. The car purchase. The reggae show he'd seen the night before. The dope. His Ivy League friends. 'Heh, mia, maka gooda.' I am okay. I am like you. Like me. They bumbled along together. Friendly. Competing. Jesting.

Walking back of the property. Past the pond. The birch trees making the going a bit difficult. Over the caked rows of mud in the farmer's field. Over the fence. Down the hill to the artesian well.

She gave a story. How she and Annie would play back country here. Pulling up pant legs. Splashing in the well. Climbing the trees. Horsing around. All year. Finding new excuses to return to this place. New forts to build. New wars. New escapes. It was close to the Bruce Trail. The blazed walkway that extended from Tobermory all the way to Niagara Falls. Miles of beauty and beasts. But he was a wrong-side-of-the-tracks city boy from Windsor. He didn't know about the Bruce Trail.

They watched a black mare approach them. With a blonde girl bobbing along. Bobbing irregularly. No. It wasn't one girl.

There were two girls. Bareback and barefoot. Riding up towards them. Beautiful twins. Smiling blondeness. Out for a Sunday ride. Sarah had never seen them before. They weren't from these parts. She felt silly in her perfume, twisted hair and fur coat. They didn't seem to mind. They said, 'You two look like you're in the movies.' Tony waved. His tweed jacket arm flying up just in time to reveal a hole at the seam in the armpit. They rode off. Sarah wanted to dump her coat and ask them for a ride. But there was a time and place for everything. Tony was too fixed. Too tame. TV tied. A city boy. He wouldn't. He was allergic to horses. He told her. Made him sneeze.

And she thought of how they looked, those two beautiful blonde twins, riding away through the long grass. Barefoot and bareback. What does that mean: 'You two look like you're in the movies'? Somehow they'd all made it. It was a compliment. Something worth looking at. An advertisement. For the Good Life. Authentic unreality. Those girls hadn't seen the tear under Tony's coat, and Sarah and Tony hadn't heard the argument between the twins as to who would have the privilege of riding in front, as to who would hold the reins, as to who would sit at the back with the other's hair whipping her in the face. You look like you're in the movies. An Image only. Fragment of sight. A frozen moment. Click.

They walked on. Over hill, over dale. Through the woods until they came to the first concession. The dirt road her aunt lived on. They walked over a field that had NO TRESPASSING signs jammed in all over it. She ignored them. She knew where she was going. Back to the lake. The Indian lake. On the crest she stopped and pointed down. 'You can still find arrowheads and work flints around the lake. The Iroquois used to camp here. Centuries ago. Before us. Now it's only part of a country golf club.' They walked down to the lakeshore. Holding hands. He walked over to the water's edge, squatted down and touched the soft mud where the water touched the shore. She watched him. He was a good man. Really. He would be a good father. But she couldn't take his sex. His gentle friendly sex. He could only see her in a limited way. He thought she was kind. A Nice Girl. A lady. She wondered if she should tell him about the child. Quickly considered. No. No point. He would act responsibly. Even if he knew of the other men. That wouldn't be fair. She didn't need comforting. She just wanted to get rid of it. Years of dead semen. A dead child. Entombed in her body.

He picked up a stone. 'What do you think? Vintage arrow-head? Early Canadiana?' He crouched down. Springing up. Flinging it against a bush. 'Got it! Right between the eyes.'

When they arrived back at the house they could smell the woodsmoke. Her mother had already gotten dinner under way. Live-in help was now a thing of the past, but her mother never failed to make it appear as if they still had help. They now ate in the kitchen, but again everything was designed to be enter-taining. Candles were lit. The fire blazed. Placemats were down. The silver was laid out, wine goblets sparkled and the food smell seized them as soon as they entered. The stage was set.

Mother was wearing a one-of-Sarah's-dates-is-coming-to-dinner costume. A long red evening skirt with matching red turtleneck. Crowned with a glass bobble pendant. Behold. I am the Mother Matron. Sitting by the fire, a gin and tonic close at hand. The radio was going. Background music. The musical score. Presto. Enter Father. He hasn't changed from his workclothes but he's cleaner and also has drink in hand. Rye and water. 'How's 'bout a drink Tony?' The men wander off down the hall to the bar. Sarah's mother starts telling her about the luncheon, the tennis, George's departure, her life. Looking knowingly in Tony's direction. 'Is it serious?' she hisses. Wink. Wink. Say no more. Sarah shakes her head and frowns. Why can't she ever leave things alone? She calls to her father. She wants a scotch and water. She goes to the fire to warm her fanny as her grandmother used to do. Getting so warm she can't sit down. Her mother. Hushed. Conspiratorial. 'Have you heard any news from Nicholas?' Sarah looked at her, steady. 'Yes I have, I'm going down next week.'

The dinner progresses. Lavishly served and delicious. Tony rises to the occasion to make a toast. Thanking the cook. Mother sees he's kind. And also too smart to tangle with. Cook my eye. She baits him. 'So tell me, Tony, how did you two meet? At a club? At work? Through friends?' She can guess the answer but she's bored with politesse and wants to drag out the private, the personal, the sacred between them. Everybody can have seconds. Go ahead. Tony explains politely. Aware too that she is testing, is out for blood. Sarah shoves it back at her mother. Hands off. 'More?' Mother's next tactic. The pressure of the stock market, how do you ever cope? Her father sits silently eating. Sarah is never sure if he's conspiring, unaware, or just plain dumb. Tony. 'I scream in my car.' What? 'Yes, I'll be driving on the highway and I'll scream. With my windows shut of course. A blood-curdling scream. For as long as I can, until I feel, well, you know, relaxed.'

The fire barks, shooting a spark clear across the room.

In the car back to Toronto Tony and Sarah smoke half a joint. They pop in a Motown tape. Warming to the day's activities. Yes. It had been fun. 'You were just great. You fit right in. A natural WASP. Handling the family like a real pro.' He was silent. Then. 'That's white of you. Real white.'

He knew she would never let him fit. He would never belong completely. But then. He didn't. He was an Italian from Windsor. Tony Bellito.

They never spent Sunday night together. Not a good way to start the work week. But they kissed good night. Goodbye. She realized that he was getting the idea. Wising up. She knew he wouldn't call for a while. It was better this way.

As she climbed the stairs to her apartment she also realized that she hadn't told her parents about the abortion. It hadn't even crossed her mind to tell them. It would hurt her father terribly. It would blow apart the Good Girl myth, that's for sure. And her mother would want to know all the sordid details so that she could get it right for broadcast. My poor daughter. Oh me, oh my. No. No. No point to tell them. They would never let her forget. Ever.

She could never tell them she had been rather indiscriminately screwing. And that she didn't really know. For sure. The father. What a horror. No. No point. They must never find out. She would look the utter wanton lusting fool. Open. Seeking the hug. The embrace. The thrill of touch. Of belonging with one another. Of being with one another. Man and woman. Woman and man. No. It would be too much for them to handle.

So. Tomorrow. The big day. The hospital.

Sarah fell asleep quickly. She dreamt.

A big old dusty building. People milling about. No furniture. No noise. Half light. She was looking for someone. She couldn't remember who. A crippled midget came up to her. Pulling at her dress. I know where he is. I know. She brushed him aside. And kept searching. Looking. For who? Looking. For someone who was important. Someone she had to find. She went into the hall. Looking in the half light. The midget came to her. I know. I know where he is. She walked past him. And went up the stairs. The broad carpeted staircase. Looking. For. Looking. For. Who. She opened doors. Looking in. No. Not there. She saw people standing together. Silently staring at each other. Looking. No not there. The midget came to her again. Tugging on her skirt. I know. I know. She looked down. Nicholas stood quietly holding her skirt. The fountain flashed aqua-rose.

Sarah turned over.

It was dark. Muddy. Overcast dusk. Half light. A man in a cart. A man with a beard. A wooden cart. With wooden wheels. Going down the dirt road. Slowly. Horse-drawn. Looking back at me. His eyes offering me a lift. Yes. And I was sitting on the wagon. Beside him. That quiet man. He gave me the reins. His thinking eyes were smiling. Soft. I listened to the movement of the wagon. The wheels. The horse. Breathing cold steam.

A fork in the road. Two paths. One path was clear. The other had brambles and thorns growing across it. I pulled up the horse. Drawing in the reins, directing the beast to the clear path. But the horse ignored me. Its head tossed and turned. But its feet plodded on. Straight for the brambles. Straight for the thorns. I was frightened. I looked to the quiet calm man. He smiled. I looked again at the thorns. At him. And I knew that as we approached I was all right. Safe. Protected from those brambles.

The thorns are all around us. But we remain safe.

The Hospital

She arrived at the Toronto General at eleven. In a waiting room.

Christ. I hope there's not much of this. Watching the other blank faces. Young women. Young girls. Tough-looking brats. Foreign women. Some in blue jeans and T-shirts. Fat. Dyed hair. Poor. All sitting in chairs facing one blank wall. The nurse's desk was tucked away at the side. Rise class. Enter great white chief. Doctor. Healer. Murderer. No. Not him. He's too young to be doing this sort of thing. A process of examination. Of elimination. One by one, slipping off into cubicles. Given a number.

Stripped and spread on a squeaky raised plastic bed. A sheet indelicately covering the upper part of the body. Like a corpse. 'Now just relax, we are going to try to get an idea of how old the fetus is.' The militant nurse stands to one side with clipboard holding all vital stats. Grim. No history of high blood pressure. Diabetes. Smoker. No. Sarah stares at the young doctor going in. Cold forceps plowed up. Jesus. Can he smell me? My sex? How many wombs has this kid felt up? How many little children has he mauled and murdered before me? Can she smell me? That pencil-eyebrowed nurse. Like a vet he is. Should I bark for the sake of theatrics, just to confirm the unfit mother jargon? No. No. Serious. This is terribly serious. Maybe I'm in shock. 'Right, that should do it.' A show of teeth.

A smile. They go out of the room. To confab. Serious. Oh so serious.

A black-faced ewe would bleat running along the crusty spring snow, a stillborn lamb dangling from her rear. Blue. Dead. Sarah had gone as a child. Down to the barn to watch. The lambs born. The licking. The cries. The blood. Sometimes her father had to help, pulling, pop. There were many. But only a few ever survived. Sometimes it was too cold. Sometimes the mother lost them. Or abandoned them. Sometimes they just died.

The nurse came in. 'You're lucky, you're not that far on. Get dressed now and make a check-in appointment for Wednesday night. You'll have the D and C on Thursday. You should be out by Thursday night.' Amazing. 'What is a D and C?' 'A scraping.' After she made her appointment she was told to go to the room over there. She went in. A woman stood. Putting out her hand. To shake. 'Hello.' Too kind. The social worker. She had the clipboard in front of her. 'Single?' Sarah nodded. No, twit, I'm polygamous. I marry all men. It said so on the board. Single. 'Well.' Nervous. Why the fuck is she nervous? 'Does your boyfriend know you are having this abortion?' No. 'Do you feel badly – guilty – about telling him?' No. A pause. Silence. 'Is he in the city?' Fuck. No. 'Do you feel this will upset your work schedule? Do you think it would be a problem to get the time?' Pause. 'A magazine. How interesting.' No. No. Not giving a millimetre. As Sarah stepped out she thought she had sure failed that test. D for Deliberate Denial. Shit. Who cares? A young girl in blue jeans was going in. She was smoking. Forbidden. But she had obviously been breaking rules for some time. She could handle it. Some authority should put that social worker out of her misery and give her a paper job.

The first thing Sarah had to do was cancel her English class.

She felt as if she were going on holiday. All the preparations. She was packing bags even.

After work on Wednesday. It took a long time for her to get downtown. Not that she had anything in particular to do. It just heightened the sense of travel. Another land. Out There. Another unfamiliar place. Another unfamiliar bed. Soon to be her own. She wondered if she would know the language. The lingo. Understand the customs. No doubt about it, she was nervous. Or was that excitement? Heading into the white light of no return. She would be altered, changed. Something was ending. Something was over for her.

Discarded but familiar. Known, understood, but now abandoned. Pushed and prodded, pulled forward. The other shoved aside. But really, she thought, it was only the rise and fall. Of wondering virgins.

For so long we know not what we do.

Everything goes in. Our orifices take as much as they can get. Air and food and sex and thought. Sound, sight and smell pamper the consumption. Directing our open holes to the idea of pleasure. Satiation. Our dark tunnels finding traffic. Air. Land. And sea. Taking it all in. Greedy. Swallowing. Pushing it deep. Sucking. To pad our insides. Then closing everything. Shutting the holes. Fastening the hatches. Denying what our eyes still see. What our hands still touch. What our mouths still take. What our bodies still want. While we contemplate and covet. Our treasures. Building inside our models of what's Out There. Making the separate belong. Burping and farting we're so fat and full. Taking a crap. Dropping a load. Spitting. Piss. Busting at the seams. With excess. Until. Finally. Exploding into a trillion and one pieces. Emmanating that fullness. That life force. That brilliant electricity. From our being. Open. Willing. Giving. Free. Children. Wide-eyed and gaping. Only to shut again as we get stuffed. To grow again.

Blinking like a fish gill.

Breathing through scissors.

Dangerously alive.

To have things in our holes. Because we want to take. We want to live. To have. To be. Everything.

Timing is important. Knowing the timing. The cycle. The rhythm. The balance. The thrust. Of giving. The thrust of taking. Completely. A bare smooth bum curves with infinite grace. And melts into another human form. In the half light of dawn. Soft. Giving. Together. Not frenetic zipper sex in a closet or cold stairwell. No. There is the world of difference. She had known it. Tried it. But it is only stolen goods. Greed. How had she ever learned such a thing? How? She had seduced, lusted, used and fucked. She had danced around men. Teasing them with the beat. Waltzing when they jived. Ballet when they boogied. Leaping when they freezed. Second guessing their second guessing. And then scoring too. With that fearful frightful greed. One step. Two step. Three potato four. Left. Right. Left. Right. Giving her body, but not her will. To live fully. Always maintaining the Mind / Body split.

But it was wrong. Terribly wrong. It was sick. Diseased and ugly. It only destroyed, maimed, murdered. Not only outside but inside. So that all that fear, distrust and hatred strangled her. Tying twisted knots in her body. Choking her baby. Her natural beauty. Her flower.

Now it was too late. She would lose something she would never have again. Her first born. But she would live. She would have another chance. To protect the fire. To nurture the flame. She would have to be kinder to herself. Her body. And her mind. Her place in space. There was hope. There had to be. And she had started to listen. Started to learn. Slowly. Carefully.

Why had it taken so long? Why had this happened?

As she entered the hospital she started to cry. Burning tears slipped down her face as she walked down the corridor. Her body glowing with pain for the damage. The irreversible damage of her history. Her female history.

She thought of her mother. She thought of Nick. She thought of the many others. Prisoners of their own skin. Silently crying. Silently dying. To be set free from their frightened loneliness. To hug and play. Only. But locked in. Trapped by the stern voices of others. Taught to believe in others before they could believe in themselves. Never allowed to touch themselves. Never allowed to trust themselves. First. Disciplined soldiers mechanically marching to a demonic drummer. Eyes front. Right. Left. Right. Left. As cripples beg, children cry and lovers wail. Afraid to look, to touch, to step out. To be genuinely and completely solo. Afraid of their singular strength. Their aloneness.

Running to the generals if anyone gets too close. The authorities. The group leaders. The owners. The myth makers. Help me. Help me. They want to touch me. No. No. I can't help myself. I don't know who I am. You know my mind. You have made me what I am. Help me.

A passing nurse asked her if she was all right. 'Yes, yes, I'm fine.' She walked the corridors wiping her face, composing, adjusting.

She was eventually led to a bed in a room that had four. The other women looked at her as she came in. Comrades. Brave women. Once she had settled in they asked her how far along she was. The stories all came up. A young woman. Tough. 'My boyfriend and I are getting married anyway. He wants to. But we can't afford the baby before we marry. But it's okay. I don't mind. I don't want it. Not now.' An older woman. She was to have the saline injection. Frightened. Fat. 'My husband doesn't want another child. We can't afford it.' She squeezed her sheets. She wanted the child. She liked children. She wasn't so lonely. They needed her. She thought. Another young girl. Quiet. Listening. Her mother came in. And gave everyone fruit and chocolate. She told the story. 'It's not fair. She's only a girl. Fifteen. It was her first time.' They all nod. Knowing. Sad. Genuinely sad. Her honest virgin openness. Given, now gone. Sarah disguised her story. Boyfriend. Mistake. Bad timing. More knowing nodding. Not. Any number of warm hard cocks snapping off in my sucking cunt. No. That was a bit much to admit.

Later. Was it dusk or dawn?

The anesthetist. A needle. 'Count down slowly dear from one hundred.' Heavy Scottish accent.

He came to her. Standing naked. Opposite her.

She tried to reach out to him. But her arms were pinned down.

She tried to speak but could not find her voice. So she opened her heart and bled for him.

Flooding. Melting. Flowing. Swirling about him. Slipping under his arms, looping under his feet, blowing through his hair, rushing up his back, embracing the warmth of his body. But he stood still.

Arms fixed. Staring. Only his eyes pleaded.

Love me. Love me. Love me.

And she came to him. Standing naked. Opposite him.

He tried to reach out to her. But his arms were pinned down.

He tried to speak but could not find his voice. Only her eyes pleaded.

Love me. Love me. Love me.

II

Few realize that their life, the very
essence of their character, their
capabilities and their audacities, are
only the expression of their belief in
the safety of their surroundings....
The contact ... with primitive nature
... brings sudden and profound
trouble to the heart.

JOSEPH CONRAD

Listen Nick

It's hazy, but some moments erupt. Remembered incidents. Three years ago in October. At the time I was living with my cousin at Yonge and St. Clair.

A 'circulation manager' for a magazine distribution company. A bullshit job, but it was money in the bank. Good working hours and a company car. Basically acting as a mother to wayward youth. Minors. Who wanted to earn legitimate pocket money. Door-to-door sales. Going from one apartment building to the next, canvassing. From the top down to the bottom. All the way if possible without being thrown out by the landlords. Frank, my boss, told me that I would be a natural for the job. I looked honest. Clean-cut. Straight. All the apartments had kitschy furniture, and usually there were only women at home with young children. The TV always blaring. Something burning on the stove. Curry. Garlic. Pork chops. No presence to these people. You could sell them anything. They were just looking for an excuse to talk to anyone. Smile and the world opened to their pocket books. Learning to be humble. Humility sells big. Gives them a sense of importance, something they'd never had in their entire lives. Once a black guy and I got chatting. He asked me in for drinks. I went. He was good looking, and kind. We sat in the kitchen listening to ska, drinking gin, straight, and I told him about the job. He never made a pass at me. Just wanted to talk, be spoken to. A direct voice. An equal voice, one who listened, one who talked. He didn't buy anything either, but it didn't matter. I told him not to. It was a rip-off no matter how you sliced it. Three years of five magazines for $250. Sign now, pay ten bucks and away you go. But anyway it was a job I found in the paper. I didn't know how else to break into the city without using family connections. I'd been in Toronto at university for four years but I still didn't know anything about getting a job.

Mother had called, so my cousin had said. I returned the call. My parents had been invited to Aunt Jean's son's wedding in Harrisburg, Virginia. Dad was not going to be able to go on account of a medical consultation, would I be able to get a couple of days off? Everything was going to be paid for by my aunt. Sure. I quit the job. We flew down in a plane that was exclusively chartered for Canadians going to the wedding. Michael.

Michael had always been somewhat of a legend. Just that much older that he was beyond knowing. But stories filtered down. A brilliant, precious, precocious guy. Philosophy at Trinity College, PPE at Oxford, a year at the Sorbonne, and an MBA at Harvard. Dad had grunted 'professional student.' Mother had loved it. Her golden godson. Now working in New York for a bank. The source. Marrying a girl he had met here, in Toronto. Janet. An American girl who knew a good thing when she saw it. Clung to him like meringue. Stuck. But she was Cute and Nice and from a Good Family. It all looked perfect. She'd worked hard to nab him. Followed him to New York. So it was really a great occasion.

Mother and daughter left alone at the celebration. No male escorts. Mother and I left to do our thing. Making and breaking it ourselves. Getting jazzed up. Costumed. Dressed for the part. Wealthy relatives. Had to hold up Michael's side of the family. Staying in the old village inn. A turn-of-the-century resting post. For three days the group of us were all taken around and showed the sights: the river, the walks, the hills, the architecture, the history. Meeting the new family. Ivy

League crowd. All American. Backbone material. Espadrilles, topsiders. Mingling with the relatives old and new. The wedding was magnificent. Black-tie affair, some came in white. Afterwards a reception at the art gallery. Looking for action after a couple of drinks. Shaking mother. Going solo. Beautiful women, honest-to-goodness Southern belles. Handsome, courtly gentlemen. Swirl. Most with a certain devil-may-care attitude. But Good Boys. Friends of Michael and Janet's, from Europe, the East Coast, Toronto, New York. A whirl. Late at night. The party moved from the reception at the gallery back to the inn. Aunt Elena's room. As always. The crazed belle of the ball. With a knack for entertaining, and a knack for making all feel larger than life. The party went on. Singing, black ties loosened. Hazy drinking. Corks popping over the swimming pool. Beautiful red dresses. Shoulders bare. Champagne slithering down a bare bosom. Seeing very straight people trying to be crazy. Respectable, responsible people daring. Just a bit risqué. Aren't we having fun? Everyone talking very big. Bigger than big. I too. Yes. I work with a magazine company in Toronto. Smile. Click. Hazy. By the time I got back to the room mother was sound asleep. Tiptoe. Dawn. Changing in the bathroom. Did I vomit? I don't remember.

The next morning mother and I ordered coffee in our room. It all seemed a bit much to dress for that early morning hit. Tumbling out at eleven. Brunch at Charlotte's. Another friend. Pink champagne on the back lawn with scrambled eggs. Jiggling on a joggling board. Everyone turned out from the night before. Looking a bit brittle. Straight, apologetic. Who, me? The last event of the weekend. Okay, okay, the kids are married. Story over. Flight at two. Back to the din. But for a moment. Sunny cool morning. Everyone looking as preppy as hell. Red, yellow, green trousers, horsey-looking broads. Screwdrivers and sunglasses. I sat at a table with a group I didn't know. Getting tanked. I'd been doing a lot of that.

You sat down beside me. I didn't remember seeing you. You seemed a bit out of place. A bit awkward. As if you were somewhere you didn't want to be. Like the wrong seat. Maybe you were hot on a girl who wasn't paying any attention to you. Anyway. We started chatting. Relying on the old lines. How do you know Michael? Janet? You had a distracted air about you. Kept looking off. I liked you. A mad professor look. Old and young in the same breath. Graying hair, slightly longish. Moustache. Friend of Michael's. From New York. Work with a chemical company. Gave me a business card. (Was it strange to be carrying business cards at a wedding?) I charmingly extended an open invitation if ever North. Amazingly loquacious after three days. Opportunism to the hilt. You never know with anyone what will happen. (I didn't have any business cards.) You were the only one wearing dusty top-siders at this cocktail breakfast. Everyone else was wearing polished Bass Weejuns. You knew the hostess well. All friends of Michael's from New York. Wonderful. Mentioned that I hoped to be returning to New York in May with a friend. I failed to mention that the friend was male. But that's another story. You insisted that I call. I said I would. All so amicable. Friendly. Light. Like brother and sister. Hell, we were almost family.

That spring I arrived with Philip. My second visit to New York. The first had been exactly the same time the preceding year. The long May weekend, my last year at college. Also with Philip. He had arrived in an airport limo at my front door. Dressed in a corduroy blazer and ascot. I in total beige. Matching everything. Complimenting each other. Cutting classic. A picture. We were stiff and polite with each other. Public. On our little escapade. Presentable people.

I had arranged in advance to stay with my cousin. Michael. (The only person I knew in New York. Always easier to pull the trump card, the relation, instead of paying for a hotel. Right?) And Michael, when I explained the situation (coming with a man), suggested that perhaps I would prefer the use of his girlfriend's apartment on West 79th and Second Avenue.

Sounded ideal. Philip and I took a cab from La Guardia to the address.

New York. To a girl who's heard of it through TV, mother and the fixed blinders of Hollywood movies. Broadway. Bright lights. Familiar yet unfamiliar names: Greenwich Village, the East Side, Madison Square Garden, Columbia, Soho, Harlem, Carnegie Hall, and of course the Empire State Building from old King Kong movies. The Big Apple. Sin City. Finally arriving. As we drove in I was amazed at how filthy it was. And dark. It seemed to hold nothing of the initial charm of Paris, London or Rome. Only a modern creaky city. Hilly. Coming down Fifth Avenue beside the park. Passing the Pierre. The Plaza. The Carleton. The Algonquin. Gurgling stories from literature confirmed these places. Fitzgerald. Wharton. Kilgallen. Over to Second. Suddenly the streets seemed wider. Cleaner. Driving North. With that striking blue-blazer look. Prosperous. Women dressed in Junior League. A doorman helped us with our bags. Felt like a young lady. Felt a bit decadent. Felt elegant with Philip. Ah, New York.

The apartment was a gem. Lived in. Classic. American antiques with eagles. Accented with Bali prints and paintings. The feel of human worldliness. History. Full of books, albums and a booze tray. Got a feeling for Janet. A loopy note from her given to us by the doorman with the keys. 'Welcome. My place is yours. Call me when you get settled and we'll have drinks.' Philip taking off his jacket. Looking in the fridge. Chablis on ice, a bag of oysters. We were delighted.

The weekend was marvellous. Philip and I were delicate, appreciative, attentive and fascinated by all around us. Walking around the city. Walking until we ached and bitched. Exploring the sights, the sounds, the ambience. Reading the New York Times on Sunday. Spread out in the apartment. Hot coffee and croissants. Philip with his Quebec-Europe influence. I with my English-Europe influence. Being together, listening to Edith Piaf, Cole Porter, and swing jazz. A balanced weekend. With no heavy-duty sex. We weren't lovers. Though we slept in the same bed. Too taken by the experience to want to allow the intrusion of the sexual selves with their demanding expectant here-us politics. No. We were separate but together. We were often mistaken for brother and sister. He was a good boy anyway.

We returned to Toronto. Poorer but happier, richer. Left a decanter for Janet blooming with thanks. We had seen Michael but briefly. He was en route from some conference to another wheeling-dealing venture. We met at the Canadian Embassy. Watching the election returns. What a crowd. Everyone placing everyone else in some year at Harvard, Yale, Princeton. Didn't I see you in '42? On the Cape? At the Game? '47? Baker scholar, who? A lingo I didn't know. A language I didn't understand. But I liked the atmosphere. And I didn't feel out of place, I felt strong with Philip there. He in his silent handsomeness. And his somewhat affected English accent. We wandered. Mingled. Flirted with tortoise-shell types and pearly ladies. Acting the part.

That was our first time down together.

Returning the following year after a lapse in the relationship. We returned almost as a chance to start, renew, something that had been lost somewhere. An innocence? Hard to say. For myself a lot had changed. I had come to know Marcus among others. I saw things differently. Again. A different perspective. I went with Philip to New York to get away from a situation that was oppressive in some ways: its possessiveness, its single-lifedness, the narrow view, the habit. Philip was the reenactment of a romance. Not a passion, but a romance.

This time we weren't going to stay in Janet's place. I didn't even want to suggest it. I preferred to get away from the family tie. I wanted New York alone, with a male escort. Not Marcus. I wanted the elegant, faded grandeur of Philip. I knew we wouldn't spend our time in greasy spoons or hamburger joints talking about money and politics. We would dine well and talk about art and economics. We would putter. Like I used to do when I travelled with my parents as a youngster. I wanted that treat, that lost way of life. Leisure time in New York.

We stayed in a chintzy hotel, the first problem. It was all we could afford. In the East 40s. And we weren't as gentle with each other this time. The quiet caring had been replaced by an opportunism of the moment. We were both working now. Earning money. Our own money. Getting ratty. After two days. Learning late in life that a nickel is only a nickel.

I decided to call you. Arrange a foursome. I called from the hotel lobby. Would you be free for an early dinner? Sixish? We were going to the theatre later. You were charming. Was I with anyone? Yes. Pause. A boy or girl? A male friend. Would it be difficult to get someone? No. Where? The Boxtree? Fine. So simple. I was delighted. Philip was curious. Who is he? A friend of Michael and Janet's. A diversion.

When we arrived at the restaurant I could tell immediately by the hair of the girl sitting at the table that she was your date. Date – you taught me that word. I never dated. Just saw people. Seeing him. Seeing her. Seeing you. Never wanted to recognize the calendar of time. The stops and starts. Just the flow. The come and go. We introduced ourselves to the girl. Jessica. A horsey-looking broad and friendly. The American class beauty. Philadelphia blue. Cheese. Dressed appropriately. But then so were we. Like a parent's cocktail party. On best behaviour. An excuse to dress up. Put on the dog. (What does *that* mean?) Hell, we were almost family. Jessica said you would be a bit late and that we should go ahead and order drinks. Philip was intrigued by this woman who had a Lily Tomlin way of pursing her lips. Twisting her head. Polite, oh so polite. Then you came in. Dishevelled. Springy. But looking good. Comfortable. A day at the office. You Americans didn't get that holiday. We Canadians did. Life is easier when you stick to the Empire, you quipped. Mama's breast, I quipped. Anyway, for the whole dinner, you and I spoke. Philip was quiet, except when Jessica directed conversation his way. You talked about business, your business. I was genuinely interested. A chemical company – 250 employees. You were the president. Dealt with geologists and scientists. Did some nuclear work. Really? Inherited. I could feel Philip tightening up. He always used to say that inheritance made for the poorest of characters. They never have to struggle. Never have to work. But I saw envy in this. Have and have nots. Who has economic control. Power. A closed world. To the uninitiated. The uninvited. The unfamiliar. And Philip was an ex. He had been disposed of before. I found I was attracted. Your eyes, your hair, your family ring. The composite picture appealed to me. (Listen kid, it beats selling magazines door to door.) But what could I do? I was with another man. It really did look as if he was my permanent date. Especially when he pulled out my chair, and rose when I came back from the can. But then so did you. All very courtly.

We were running late. The show. Out on the street, you said you would hail a cab for us. Philip said he would hail the cab. The two of you striding up the street, flailing your arms. Leaving Jessica and I free to talk. Nitter-nitter. I watched you boys play men. Philip was getting pissed off. Jessica said that the two of you were good friends. Nothing more. Leaving the way clear. And Philip? I said the same thing. Knowing the swirl and gossip between good friends. A cab. You said with a smile that if we cared to we could meet later at a punk rock bar. Charming. In our casual classics cutting fashionable. The in crowd. Before I could answer Philip said it didn't seem likely. Oh. You pursued. Mentioned that there was a possibility of coming to Canada in the not-too-distant future. But, of course, you must call. Philip was waiting in the cab.

Then a terrible thing happened. After the show, Philip curt, said let's go back to the hotel. He was paying the cab, who was I to argue? We went to the room. No nightcap? No. Okay. Changing in that puny smelly room that overlooked the garbage. Distant with each other. Crawling into our respective sides of the bed. Then it happened. Philip placed a cold clammy hand on my arm. It moved over to my stomach. I was appalled. What to do? I hadn't the slightest desire to hold him, to do anything with him. The hand moving towards my breast. Oh what to do? He turned, pulling himself up onto me, forcing me, pushing me, spreading me. Thrusting. Entry. Pushing. Panting. I a sack of potatoes. Outraged, bored, disappointed. But polite, oh so polite. He was a good boy. A good boy from Nice Society. Doing this terrible thing. To a Nice Girl. He slid off. His cold clammy hand still on my breast. He hadn't even kissed me. He lay beside me. Breathing, falling asleep. Fucking idiot. The next morning he got up, got dressed, and said he was going down to the cafeteria. Went out slamming the door. I douched, changed, and went downstairs. We had breakfast, not saying a word. We were flying at eleven. We didn't say one word all the way to the airport even while we were packing. Even checking in. Like two strangers. Separate. Singular. Aloof and alone. Sitting in the lobby waiting to board. He spoke. 'Sarah, may I speak with you? Let's walk.' We walked. 'I no longer value you as a friend, and I have no desire to see you at all any longer. Do you have anything you would like to say?' I looked at him. What? He was looking at me. Triumph written all over his face: I've saved my honour, I don't have to run home and tell mommy about this one. Get rid of the broad. I said only, 'I have nothing to say.' Nothing. We boarded the plane. Not a word spoken. I had forgotten my umbrella in the airport lounge. We arrived in Toronto, disembarked, collected our luggage, and walked out like strangers. Philip was continuing on to Ottawa to spend some time with his parents. He swept past me. 'Goodbye,' he said. I barely nodded. Fucking idiot. Friends my ass. The gentleman glamour puffed out. Just another commonplace jerk neurotic about his scoreboard. And mother. I went through the doors, back to Toronto the Good.

The din. The noise was overwhelming.

Late June.

I received a call from you. You were in the city. You suggested we have dinner and perhaps some drinks. A late supper. I was pleased. You'd followed through. A good sign. You asked, where? I scrambled in my mind. Something fashionable. Cool, something that would fit with my conception of a New Yorker. To prove that yes Toronto too is a Big City. I suggested the Blue Angel. Art-deco. Queen Street chic. Moderate prices. I knew dick all about the food but knew too that being good WASPS we'd smother it all in booze anyway.

You came to get me. In a cab. Flying down Avenue Road. Pointing here, pointing there. This is. That is. I have been there. I have been here. Chatting. Friendly. Talking pleasantly about the people we already knew in common. Family. Michael and Janet. Charlotte. Jessica. Philip. You talked about your business. And some of your phantom friends. Steven, John, Adam and Christine. I was dressed, yet again, for one of my parents' cocktail parties. Pearls and all. You were suitably attired. Preppy plus. The way I like my Nice Men.

But I also remember thinking at the table. Okay. I'm bored with this stuff. I'm sick of hearing about your business. I'd like another drink, then some action. You are an Outsider. Ergo safe. I'd lost the Philip escort for Sin City, but I knew that you would be the ideal mate. A native. So I gave you the line. Played it up. Poured it all on. Stuck to the stuff I figured you'd want to hear. Didn't want to shock you with my drug diversions, my late-night ramblings, my sexual escapades. All was painted red, white and blue. All stars. Kin. Of the same blood. Nice people. Giving you the necessary backdrop material. The sales pitch. Displaying my wares. My family, my education, my job. My dedication, etc., etc. You liked what you heard. Especially after I told you I liked perfection. That I liked symmetry, winners, go-getters, success. The top of the pile. Made it sound as if that was where I was heading. And fast. That that was where I obviously belonged. By that time I was working with a nondescript basement-based graphic-arts firm.) You paid the bill. Sold. Wonderful.

Then we started bar hopping. After number four you lurched. My bra strap fell. (Can you believe it, I was wearing a bra. I mean I never wear a bra. Still don't. I was going all out in my conforming to what I thought you were. What you wanted. What you expected.) You kissed me. I thought. Well, well. In public no less.

Within no time you were at my place. Impassioned. It didn't take long to discover what we both liked best.

The next morning you sought me. Sleepy. Heavy. Comfortable. Natural. Bathing, showering in the bathroom after you. Not talking much. We'd done all that the night before. There was no attachment formed. We both knew we could touch. You had a couple of days. And then the weekend. I suggested you move in. You smiled. This was going to be easy. As well as fun. We walked down to Fran's at St. Clair. Holding hands. My suede jacket brushing against you. Not talking much. To my table. My seat. The same one I've used lover after lover. I take the same chair. Get served by the same bespectacled carrot-top crotchety waitress. I get the same order I've gotten for years. You take your seat. It's all new for you. I think of the last one there. I wonder about the one after you. Watching the spectacle. The flow. It's difficult to make small talk with you. I keep asking questions. Not prying, just making conversation. Entertaining you. You have that distracted air about you. Concerned about business I guess. We plan to meet later between five and six. My place.

You with luggage in tow. So. Nicholas Predon enters my life.

I was pleased. Scored. Knew I could hold onto you for a time. If only for your interest in our sex. Knew too that I couldn't keep up the chatter about business indefinitely. It might be tough to keep it entertaining. But I wanted to hold you. Not push. Not pull. Just hold on to you. I wanted New York. A key.

You seemed to be agreeable enough. Never asked me if there was a man before or present. Never asked me anything about my sex life, my private life. Never asked me much when I come to think on it. I volunteered everything. Giving you a performance every time I spoke. Talking about all those safe things. And I showed you Toronto.

That night we went out again. I expectant of preppy plus. You suggested a burger and a beer. Okay, okay. But I felt odd. I was in the wrong costume. Pearls don't suit Burger King. Trapped in an Image. We watched a silent movie. I silent. A bit bored. So where's the action? Bright lights U.S.A.? I kept silent. Figured I would wait my turn. They say patience is a virtue. Okay. I'll wait.

I did handsprings. For a couple of days. Entertaining you. Walking down Yonge Street. Over to the island. A friend of mine lent us her canoe and we weaved in and out of the isles. The water glistening on your arm. The paddles slipping in and out of the cool murky water. Going to a mud landing. Dragging the canoe ashore. Resting in the long grass. In the sun. The birds flocking in the trees. Chirping. Really. Kissing gently. Having lunch. Cheese, bagels and vino.

Taking the ferry back to the mainland. Sailboats taut in the harbour. The lake a golden hue. Bundled at the railing. Not talking much. There seemed no need. There was an acceptance. Both of us willing to bend. To give ourselves. I'll show you what I know and love. I want to share these things with you. Enter my life. Become part of my fabric. I will give these gifts to you. Please. Take.

And then you suggested it. Come down for a weekend. I'll get my secretary to arrange it. I'll pay for the ticket. What? A little weekend romance getting set up here. Wonderful. Allowing me the freedom to see and do what I want during the week and then squeezing you for all you're worth on the weekend. The New York experience. Yes. Thank you. How nice.

Standing on the Scarborough bluffs. Looking along the

146

shoreline. Sitting on a rock. Over the edge. 'Imagine jumping, imagine flying.'

Two. Together. Alone.

Going to the farm for a day. The parents were away. Living together in that big old rambling house. Touching the house in a new way. Seeing the house in a new way. Through your eyes. I could see that you knew these things. You moved comfortably there. No ooh-aah. You did not covet. But then I should have guessed you were just like family.

Eating, sleeping, sitting. In the garden. The white clapboard furniture facing the pond. The willows sweeping the bullrushes. The rabbits on the lawn. Us. Holding. Quiet. Afraid to speak. To break.

Both. Knowing. It would come. But not yet. Not now. For the moment.

We went to the club. To play tennis. To drink lemonade. Neither of us could play that well. But it didn't matter.

Gentle, prodding, poking. Show and tell. How much of the world have you seen? Trying to find boundaries. The limits. I played the piano for you. You played the piano for me. We both played badly. But we played. Together.

The weekend ended. We both had to go back to the din. Our respective noises. There were other demands. Duties. Chores. Families. Responsibilities. Habits. And fixed dreams. There were others intertwined in our history. Others who needed, who wanted. There were other hands to hold. Other people to know. It was inevitable. All things do pass. But you said you would call.

We soon developed a brief urgent telephone manner. Like business. 'Pick up your ticket at the airport. Friday afternoon. American Airlines to La Guardia. I'll meet you at the airport.' Click.

The first weekend.

The Royal York. Airport connection. After getting a time

change in the shift at work. Those boys down there would never understand the life I led or wanted to lead. They are mortgaged to the hilt, with nagging wives and brawling brats. Broken, chipped teeth, overweight and chintzy cotton long-lapelled shirts. No. They would never understand. They thought I was different. Why wasn't I a secretary? Why was I doing that production work with them? A college-educated woman at that. What had she studied? Politics. Well that follows. Politics of what?

I'll give you politics.

A Jamaican boat-nigger with seven kids in seven different ports slips up to Canada to buy a house with a refrigerator and air-conditioning. Easy to immigrate. Marries a white woman with money. Sells his blackness for cash. On the line. Lets her pretend to be Big Mama.

Or. A Brit with an art education in England discovers that the New World blindly believes in the dictums of culture and taste from the Old World. Sells his British supremacy for cash. Of course I understand Canada. I'm its enveloping mother and stern father. Its parent. I'll give you direction. Taste. And make money. Sucking your lack of confidence.

Or. A cowboy who drives a Ford pickup with beer in the back blasts in and out of work from his country home from miles up north. A wife who is into Bible-stumpin' religion and a kid who reads backwards. Making ends meet. A border-liner. A non-conforming conformist. Knows he has to kiss ass. But will kick it the first chance he gets. Likes people. But knows fuck all about them. Stuck in a rut. Knows he'll never get anywhere. Depresses the living delights or is it daylights out of him. Kicks. Gently. This cowboy ain't got no freedom.

Or. Joannie. A generation-gap Japanese. Young and capable, adopting flannel shirts, blue jeans and running shoes. Conforming. Fitting. Her innate Japanese beauty lost between the commercialism and the commercials. Doesn't know the first thing about business, money, power or the Game. To look Japanese, to speak it, to eat it, even in suburbia, but not to know it. Her mother country. Japan. But she is Canadian. Being Canadian. I am Canadian. I speak English. And English is the language of my mother. But she is English.

What a fuck-up.

A free, huge, vacant country with hundreds of thousands of wandering rootless souls. Tied down by memory threads. A, B and C.

I fly south. Los Estados Unidos. The United States of America. A foreign country. A different people. A different language. With indigenous blacks. With Zest, Crest, Tide, Maytag, Ford and Abraham Lincoln. Not Laura Secord, Canadian Cheddar or Louis Riel. An adventure. Forty-five minutes by air. I carry a passport. On the plane beside a blowhard from Michigan. Yak yak yak. Flirt flirt flirt. Dump him. Don't want to make an appearance with him gurgling at my side. Got to look my part. Beauty from the North. The Land of White Quartz. A tundra diamond.

At the airport. La Guardia. I do look my part. People look at me. Good. My Town and Country look. With a leather-crested suitcase. Stamped SES. Monogrammed sweater. SES. My loafers have tassels. Look like someone's wealthy daughter. Gold earrings. (They're actually brass but no one can tell nowadays.) Hair pulled back. Clasp. French. And you're there. A gentle kiss. Hello. You take my bag. Making polite conversation. Not about me. Not asking me anything. I make conversation. How's business? That gets you going. Telling me about the internal problems with one of your scientists. Walking through the doors. You laugh. A tremendous sense of power as the doors swoosh open. Don't you think? You like it. Little Napoleon with collegiate coquette Josephine. Ah New York. Yeah. Sure. Okay. What next? Into the car lot. Well well. Your car. A Porsche. A little red Porsche, top off. Don't want to let on I'm too impressed. Men start to think that's all it takes. No. What next? Into the car. Zipping off through the parking lot. In goes the cassette. The Knack. 'Good girls don't, good girls don't, but I do.' Cracked up. You look at me and smile. Your hand goes into my lap. Squeezing my leg. I lean over and kiss you. You pay the nice faceless man in the booth and we hit the road. You hand me a polka-dotted handkerchief. Do I want to tie my hair back? Casually withdrawn from the glove compartment. I see lady's sunglasses. You don't give me those. I wonder. Trying to read your game plan. What's he want with me? How do I fit into his scheme of things? What side of his personality do I compliment? Not the jealous type, too opportunistic for that. He and I. Both.

Through the city. I play tourist. You play guide. This is. That is. Garbage piled deep, water and garbage smoldering, dogs sniffing. Noisy city in a car. But you turn up the music. Really blaring. At a stoplight. You look and smile. Fiddling with the sound controls, the levels of sound, frequencies. All sorts of gadgets for this one. Fine-tuning Joe Jackson. Yeah. Okay. I like the music. People on the sidewalk look at us. What do they see? An older fellow with a chick. Windblown, healthy looking, music blaring and a Porsche. I'm in with the In Crowd. People's fantasies playing on, tripping over my reality. Cursing, condemning, aspiring, wondering about us. Set apart.

Nick drives fast. And with precision. Knows the car. Handles it as if it were made for him. To the East Side. Upper East. Great. I can handle this treatment. Brownstones. Little brass numbers. Little brass door knockers. Removed from misplaced boat-niggers, lonely cowboys and Canadian Japs. Looks decent and clean, somehow familiar. Inviting. Permanent. Paid for. Moneyed.

In the East 90s. Stopping in front of an old house. Rented to a group of young professional people by a dotty old broad from Vermont. Inside the triple-latched locked front door stands a floor-length Victorian gold-framed mirror. We enter. Click. You point across the street. A diplomat's home. Greek. Great parties. Crashing them in black tie and sneakers. Smile. Up the stairs, past the livingroom. A guy reading *The Wall Street Journal*. Open-neck oxford-cloth shirt. No socks. Hellos exchanged. Easy. No problem with having a woman in the house. I'm designed not to shock. Looking presentable. One of them. Up more stairs into Nick's room. Opposite a library. Closing the door. Asks me if I'd like a beer. Hmm. Real college type. Not even sherry. Or wine. For the ladies. No thanks. Looking around. Getting the picture. A masculine room. Brandy and cigars on the mantelpiece. Tidy. Cleaned up. Nothing personal. Nothing exposed. No private parts. Wondering how he'd changed things for me. Setting the stage. Removed things. The last girl. Nothing to indicate another. A poster on the wall. Framed. The Predon collection of Japanese prints at the Chicago Art Gallery. Hmm. His heritage leaps forward with a roar. A four-poster Early American oak bed. Covered with a navy-blue down. Deep blue curtains over deep-set windows. A good place for a read. Quiet. Removed. An antique phone cradled on the bedside table. Hoping it doesn't ring. I don't want any distractions. No Others. Asking me. God, what a fright. Asking me if I want to wash up. Yes. He points to an open door. Walking through to the bathroom. Through the clothes cupboard. Clothes neatly arranged. Private school training. Boarding school would be my bet. Or maybe there's a maid. Maybe. All kinds of attire. Tux, tweeds, flannels, jeans, leather jacket, suits, running shoes, gold-clasp Guccis and cowboy boots. Hmm. I thought of mother's cupboards. Her endless wardrobe. Her costumes. My costumes. My costume. Hmm.

Spying. The bathroom. Splendid. Black, smoky tile, gold mirrors. And a deep sunken bath. Archaic fixtures, but all pleasing. Accented with ruby red towels. Smelled soapy, after-shavey. A wooden toilet seat. And eucalyptus fronds. Yes. I do.

Sitting on the toilet, congratulating myself. On this prize. All for a lay. I mean I could hardly call him a friend of mine. So. Great. What next?

The problem with getting what I want is that I get bored. I want more. Natural, no? Or I want to be left alone to enjoy what I have. To be me. Just me. I hoped Nick would decide we needed something. Wine, oysters, champagne or contraceptives. Something to make him disappear, to leave me alone. So I could spread out on the bed, kick off my shoes and luxuriate. Have a bath. Put on the stereo. And, assuming he'd disappear for good, enjoy. Plan my entertainment. The idea of being alone in New York with a Porsche at my disposal plus a place to stay suited me no end. I wanted to play it out. Go to the best restaurants. Go to the worst restaurants. Go Broadway. Go off-off Broadway. I wanted to wander the streets in jeans. Slither underground. Buy groceries. In a Porsche. Yeah. Look. See. Romance, sex. One plus two plus three plus more. Artists, businessmen, old and new. Deviance. Yeah, why not? And class. All the good society shit too. Clubs, luncheons, yachts, families. Jewels and joys. I wanted New York. But how? Flushing the toilet. I had no dough. It was only by virtue of my open thighs that I was here. Could I figure this one? Nick. For a summer? With him madly in love with me. Keys to his heart, car and apartment. Wondering if it could be managed. Would have to check him out. Find the spot. The tender spot. Snow him. Yes, darling, this much. I do. Submissive coo-coo. He must trust me. Too late for this year, this summer, but for next year, next summer. In the interim I would have to work on it. He must confide in me. Be vulnerable. While I entertain, amuse and tickle him. Sell myself. Not giving up too much. Holding back the sacred. But that would be tough. Because he was close to the family. Of the same blood. There was always the risk of. Exposure.

I emerged from the bathroom. He had changed, more relaxed. Slugging beer. Small talk, me being polite and preppy. Abruptly he stood up, pushing me down on the bed. Hurried. Lifting my tweed skirt. Pushing. Deep.

We slept half-clothed for some time. I nestled in his arm. Confident of the seductive powers of my thighs. My ability. My learned experience. Whoring. Loving it. Waking. Again. No words. o touch me.

A strange one. Seems tight. Closed. No small talk. Snuggled, I asked how many women he had known. A leading question. But it was asked matter-of-factly, not acquisitively. He looked at me. Looking off. Shrugged. I wonder. Ten? No, more. Twenty? He didn't know. He got up from the bed. Went to the cupboard, pulling out a pair of black velvet pants. And said, 'A girl from Washington who was in love with me made these.' Okay, okay. He went into the bathroom.

I laughed. God. Making pants for a man. Ridiculous. Never. Velvet. More ridiculous. He holding them like a fucking trophy. Maybe that was his game. A list. Like mine. An international hit list. The Who's Who of the bedroom circuit. A connoisseur of naked natives. No. He couldn't be like that. Not this beer-slugging preppy. No. He was not enough of a loner. He did not have to keep off that roar, that separateness, the Mind / Body split. With the touch of clinging sex. No. Not him.

You emerged. Suggested dinner at your parents' house. Wonderful. That should be entertaining. Families always are. Seeing the flow. The idea and the realities. Making it with the 'rents. Convince them, and then you're in. Where? In the city? No. Up the Hudson. In the country.

Dusk falling over the city. Buildings agleam. A slowness in the air. The Grand Exodus. People walking North. With food parcels. Hurrying home. On roller skates. In sneakers. Skate boards. The core dying. Ebb and flow.

We took the bridge over to New Jersey. Headed north along the Hudson. Looking back at the city. What a prize. Glowing golden in the sunset. Roof off. Music blaring. Fast. Hand on my leg. I placed my hand on your leg. You placed my hand on your balls. You smiled. Unzipping your pants. Cradling your strength. I liked the openness. There was no sense of boundary. Touch me now. No, don't touch. One hand on the wheel, one hand in my lap, searching. Upward. Warm and wet. Hard. Jesus.

You pulled over into a roadside stopover. Other cars parked

there. Their noses pointing down the Hudson towards the city. I was appalled. (Visions of high school, groping, lunging, all bubbling in my head. No. Not here. No. No. No.) You stopped the car. I had pulled away. Quiet. Didn't stop you. 'Come on, don't tease me.'

'I hate necking in parking lots,' I said. 'Hate it.' Frozen. Turned off. Disgusted. This I would not do. Not in my game plan. Ever. One time that I will not compromise. Firm.

Getting out of the car. Walking. Looking back at New York. You came up beside me. Putting your hand on my hipbone. Pulling me to you. 'Sorry Nick. Making it in a car is just not my style.' Kissing me. Pulling for an embrace. Jesus. Doesn't he ever let up? 'Let's go to your house. Away from here.' We get into the car. Lunging at me again. 'NO.' I push. Not here, you thick-headed jerk. You pulled back. Changed the tape. Turned on the music. Talking Heads. You looked in the mirror. Pushing your fingers through your hair. Didn't look at me. A nonentity. Pissed off that I wouldn't give. Fuck. I was worried. I still had the weekend. And I wanted a lot from this dude. What to do? Pulling out of the lot. Fast. Rolling down the window. Moving fast. Didn't offer me his bandana this time. Didn't acknowledge me. No forgiveness. Fuck. I am dealing with an arrogant preppy. Another Joe. Who just wants the lay his way. Okay. I hear you. Loud and clear. We drove into the parkland. A beautiful drive. Soured. Passing cars. Music. Blaring. Popped out cassette. Popping in Berlioz. Adjusting frequency. The waves. Eight speakers. Crashing. No words. Lost in the swirl. Separate souls floating.

Driving off the highway into a little town. Cornwall. One question. Like a punch. 'Do you want to eat in or out?' Looking at him. Trying to read the signals. Figured he would be placated with his familiar surroundings. Family. 'In.' I put my hand on his leg. Again. Smiling. My best. Giving. He looked in the mirror, out his side mirror, sighed and continued on. I withdrew my hand. Jesus.

Up a country lane. Up the hills. Like driving the Grande

Corniche in the south of France. Sweeping impressive views of the Hudson. North and south. Pink sky. Breathtaking. I wished I was driving. Alone. I wished I was popping the tape. Wanted the Stones. He moved on to Wagner. Driving fast up the roads. Could feel his anger still. His disappointment at not getting what he wanted. A live wire. The car screeching. Tearing the dusty roads. I holding on to my seat. Frightened. Imagined flying off the cliff. Tumbling car. Headlines. 'Unidentified Canadian Girl with Clean Underwear Found Dead.' Should I talk? No. Impossible. The music was too loud. The Walküre.

Up a dip. Around a corner. Past a clapboard house. Dogs barking. Flashing grass and spinning wild lilies. Through gates. Old stoneposts. Years ago. A lost century of grandeur. A limp chain hanging to one side. Crumbling at one corner. Gravel. Huge beautiful trees. Hanging, looming, over the road. Dusk. Sun almost set. Wagner. A house rose up. A big house. A monstrous home. Three silver Honda Accords were parked in the circle at the front. Glistening. You drove past them. Down the hill. And stopped. Beside an ivy-shrouded door that looked as if it led into the cellar. Turning off the car. Wagner trumpeted our arrival.

Taking my bag out of the car. You marched through the doors. I turned off the music. You yelled. 'Bring the tape.' Ja wahl Herr Capitan. I note. This is only for the weekend. A dutch door with a cast-iron latch. The top half swung into a livingroom. I peered in. Entered. I loved it. First sight. Dark panelled walls. Crinkled red-leather cushions lining the window boxes. Animal trophies hung on the wall. Tusks. Deer. Spears. Tribal masks. Oil paintings. Landscape. A bear rug. Ratty, but a bear rug. A huge brick fireplace faced a beige sofa and two old Spanish leather chairs. A man's room. Conquistador. Conquerer. Big game. A desk at the back. A sand shark's skeletal beak on display. Beside a monogrammed ink well. Books. Tucked away below. Architecture principally. English philosophy. Eighteenth century. Art books. Well, well. What

have we here? A culture hound. Tidy, musty, lived-in space.
Where are the parents? You took the tape and popped it into
another munching sound system. Blasting through the room.
Terrific. Terrifying. Power. You walked through a door at the
back of the room. With my suitcase. Ergo. The bedroom. I followed. Entering a diningroom. A long wood table. Iron candelabra. Benches on either side. A portrait of a woman. Tall,
elegant, blue. With her hand on a Great Dane. The dog. Posed.
Fitting one full wall. A delicate Japanese print on the facing
wall. A tranquil boating scene. Damp smelling. Old. Familiar.
Down a hallway. Into a bedroom. Symmetrical. Ordered. Two
single beds. What? Bookshelves. Heavy academic worn leather
sitting chairs. Three windows opening out. god. the view. I
hadn't realized we were up so high. A bird's eye view of the
valley. For miles. Up and down the hills. Caressing with my
eye. Magnificent. Sunset. You turned. Pushing me. What?
Down on the bed. Pushing me. Disrobing me. Frenzy. Frantic.
Pushing. I could smell your skin. Your hair. On my bosom.
Your hair falling down over me. Pushing. Confused. I off guard.
Taken before I could recover. From the sunset. Remask. Pushing. o nick.

Clinging.

You lay on me. Quiet. No words. In me. Soft. Sweating.

I kiss you. You turn away. Withdraw. Slowly. Then you
push yourself off the bed and stand up. You look at me. Then
away. Outside. Twilight sky. The wind only. And Wagner. I
lay before you. In my nakedness. I smile. You look away. And
you leave the room. I lay quiet, wondering. A different man. A
difficult man. But I liked it. Liked what I saw. Felt. Be careful
Sarah, you're supposed to be doing the seducing baby.
Remember that.

I rose. Changed into a cotton skirt and different loafers. Still
prepping it. Keeping the image constant. Don't want to shock
you. You are giving a good show. Don't want to startle you.
Make you insecure. Conscious of an Other. So. Into the
kitchen.

Your favourite meal. Spaghetti. Pesto. Your parents? 'Upstairs.' I looked at him. What? Parents tucked away in a closet? Chained to their beds? Invalids? I wonder. Brothers or sisters? 'Sister. She's crazy. Older than I. Thirty-six. Has an imaginary pet beaver. She lives with her fruity husband in town.' Bravo. A mad relative. Dickens comes to life. Better than a ghost. A real spectacle. Good stories. I stir the spaghetti. You put one hand on my breast. Swoop around and place the other on my crotch. Jesus. Horny little bastard. Felt a bit like an object. A bit stiff. You pulled away. I stirred madly. Setting the table. Silver. Candles. Wine. From the cellar. Like Pineridge. Familiar. French stick. Sitting opposite each other. On the benches. You say, 'Entertain me.' I look at you. What? That's my line. An open look. Too open. You look away. I look down. You then tell a story of a friend of yours who got laid on a diningroom table. You thought it was funny. Exotic. Okay. Tit for tit. I tell you a story of a friend of mine who got laid in a sail locker. You smile. 'Tell me more.' Jesus. What have I got here? No small talk. I can't resort to the usual bullshit stories. Just couldn't break into the pretty tales somehow. The polite stories. Felt I was dealing with a swaggering pirate. I, a captive maiden. The wench. Good, good. Wagner boomed in the background. I reached. I did not want to be trite. Stupid. Female. Goo-goo. I wanted to be recognized by this fellow. Seen. Familiar. Equal. But there was no opening. No invitation. You changed the tape. I washed the dishes.

Some things never change.

You on the sofa. Falling asleep with your feet in my lap. A heel nudged into my crotch. We're watching the late-night movie. *The King and I.* Sleepy. You caress my breast. Pull me to you. Beside you. We lay on the sofa. Squished together. You put my hand on your crotch. No shyness here. So. Unzipping your pants. But you say not here. In the bedroom. Sleepy, we stand up and go to the room. Sleepy gentle sex. It's late. I'm sore. Tired. But still. Jesus. We don't talk. As we glide. Not even goodnight. The wind outside. You rise and open another window. You come to bed, kiss me, and then go to the other bed.

And fall asleep.

I feel abandoned.

Used.

Sure a single bed is a tight fit but shit, just the warmth. You breathe heavily on the other side of the room. Asleep. Over there.

I can't and don't approach you. A sternness about you. An inaccessibility. So I lie in this foreign bed alone.

A wind lullaby blowing through the room. Open billowing curtains. Papers flutter. An owl somewhere. You breathing. I wide awake.

Wondering. Feeling the night. Being. Alone.

Well. At least there were no toothpaste formalities. And I think of the men I have fucked. Who I have turned away from. Not trusting. Not caring. About those male objects.

In the morning. I slip into your bed. 'Good morning.' You smile. Feeling my body. Touching.

You say, 'We'll breakfast with my parents.' We shower. Clean up. Get presentable. The layered sweater look. Lipstick. Feeling sore between my legs. Yellow and blue bath towels. Like mine. Identical.

It's still early. About 8:30.

We go outside. Gravel, grass, swinging trees. Full-bodied air. Early-morning crisp sun. Air. Silent. Quiet. Peaceful. A beautiful dawn.

Melancholy slaps me. No. No.

This is not for you. A slap. No.

Leave me. This is a flash of time. Nothing more. Nothing less. Nothing permanent. That was lost long ago. There is nothing here of yours. Nothing. Stop Sarah.

Into the house through a big screen front door. In the hallway a grand piano. You tell me that your mother hides the silver there. You sit and play a sloppy Chopin. Intermittent thuds. A man comes out of another room. A study. A big man.

Graying with spectacles. He is dressed oddly. Suspenders and moccasins. A Mexican shirt. No greeting to me. He addresses Nick. 'Good morning Nicholas.' Deep baritone. Nick speaks. 'Father, a Canadian cousin of Michael and Janet's. Sarah Elizabeth Stauton.' I hear choral music from somewhere. It seems appropriate. We exchange nods. He speaks. 'Nicholas, your mother wants to speak with you. She is in her room.' Nick disappears. The big man looks at me. Okay. Dialogue. Handsprings kiddo. Make it with the old boy. Smile. 'A beautiful house.' Sweeping gaze. Appreciative. Acknowledging the treasures. Fine, oh so fine. And all yours. Very nice.

He looked at me. I was startled it was so direct. Not a father's gaze.

'Yes. We had to take off the top floor because of the heating bills. But not a bad place. Can you cook?'

Curious this.

'Yes, after a fashion.'

'Well. Cook Nicholas and I some breakfast. This way.'

Fuck you buddy. But I was in no position to argue. Guest and all.

Dug into the fridge.

He asks, 'Can you make shrimp armaud?'

Shit. This was pressure. I knew I should have read that last issue of *Gourmet*.

'I make a mean Spanish omelette.'

'Sounds good. With creamed corned beef?'

'What's that?' Sweating. God, these bloody foreigners.

'I'll prepare that.' God, these bloody tourists.

Little mice in the kitchen. I dutifully aware of my place. Wondering about the pots and pans. A propane stove. Spices. Old gadgets like Pineridge. I would have settled for toast and coffee. But when in Rome....

He asked, 'How did you sleep?'

Flooded by images of dancing girls. The green pepper sizzling. Brunettes, blondes, redheads, yellow, fair, black-skinned beauties. How many girls get asked that question by the old

159

man? He aware of his son copulating below him. His son scores. Another one bites the dust.

'Well. Thank you.' I respond as if he'd asked me if I like roses.

Nicholas enters. Springy. After the mother ritual. And this guy's thirty-two? Opens the fridge, pulls out the mustard. The milk. Proceeds to make himself a sandwich. I explain that I'm making an omelette.

'That's nice. I'm having a sandwich.'

You mean I have to eat the damn thing. Not the bacon and eggs crowd.

Nicholas and his father jockey for position in the kitchen. Bouncing into each other. Awkward. Tension there. His father doesn't flirt with me. He is too occupied block-checking his son and carrying on his eating ritual. Nicholas curtly suggests we go out to the stone verandah.

Through a dusty sitting room and wow: that breathtaking view across the valley. A glass-top table. I see myself sitting. Toast and coffee, a paper. A book. Looking. But not yet. Not now. With them. I'm trapped in courtesy. A beautiful sunny day. No wind now. Crisp morning. Nicholas returns to the kitchen to get more mustard. I stand staring, soaring. Alone. Sucking in the beauty.

Nicholas calls me. 'Sarah, come inside. Mother wants to meet you.'

Finally. The moment that every woman waits for. The Other woman. Mother. The only other contender for the prize. Man. The blood-bonded woman. Son from her loins. From her sweat, pain and sex. I expected something.

A graying little woman with haughty green eyes emerged. Moving slowly. Aged. In blue pants, slippers and a soft silk blouse. Bronzed, weathered. Extending her arthritic hand. 'Gut morning.' Syrupy German accent. I didn't like her. And she didn't like me. But I had to pay my dues. Gay, polite. She asked, hands clasped, 'Have you had breakfast?' Whining. 'Nicholas is such a terrible host. And also a terrible cook. He eats so badly. There is nothing his poor mother can do.' I swear she is going to pat him on the head. Nicholas glowing. A Mother's Word. This was going to be tougher than I thought. She knew a lot about me. 'Down for the weekend from Toronto, aren't you? On business?' Bitch. Smile. Nod. 'Nicholas has so many girls calling him, it's hard to keep them all straight.' Still smiling.

Who is this broad? Why is she trying to shake me? Sure a protective, possessive mother. But there is tact baby. Maybe she just doesn't know about that. No. She is clever. She knows exactly what she is doing. Nicholas glowing. She asked me if I could cook. Why? Do you need kitchen help? Dying to say it. Or just a little hand servant? Beck and call. My spine erect. Stiff. Claws pop out. Ready. A mother all right. Like Mother. False powermonger. I wouldn't take her bullshit. Wanted to leave. Get some balance. A walk. The contact-lens excuse. No. No. Nothing serious, just have to rinse my eye. Wash out the dirt. (Get it?) Out the screen door. Well. I sure blew that one. Didn't make the great impression. Back to the Retreat. Downstairs. Angry. Restless. Wanted to get something. Do something. Anything. Frustrated energy. Wanted action. Physical.

Nicholas arrived. No. God. No touch.

He wasn't interested anyway. Maybe he had been put off. Watching his mother and I. How many others? Sons love it. Crossed swords. The potential battle over him. For blood. He asked me if I wanted to go for a bike ride. I wince. Bicycles? No – a motorbike. Sure. Now that's more like it.

Gave me a helmet. Shoei. The best money can buy. This guy knows. Outside. The morning crispness warming up. Moist. 'You'll need more protection.' He gives me his leather jacket. We go into the adjoining garage that topples down the side of the hill. A little white MG buried under cardboard boxes. An old car. His. From his student days. Oh really. And a BMW 750 motorbike. Dragging the beast out. Straddling it. I behind him. The big boy's toy. Told me of motorbiking in Europe when he was sixteen. Whoosh. With another guy. Whoosh. I remember my motorbiking. But I don't tell him. My male history.

A bike always feels good. A warm rumbling horse. The sense of power. Speed, strength. Slowly down the driveway. The gravel can be dangerous. Hold on. Popping the clutch. Holy Jesus. Screaming up the country road. Dipping, ducking, swerving, bouncing, floating. I holding on for dear life. Sliding into him. Compact. Sliding away. Pulling on his stomach. Our helmets occasionally click. Tilting, left then right. The road rushing by. Wild grass. Wild lilies. Streams. Embankments. The speed. Down a road then quickly off onto a dirt path, into a forest. Bumping. Under a foot bridge. Up a hill. Holding on. Beside a lake, slowing. Stopping. I don't want to let go. Ever. Enjoying it. The rush. Yes, the thrill. Clinging. He takes off his gloves. His helmet. I finally release and get off.

Asking me, as we walk up the dirt path, what I like in the way of romance. Oh shit. Do I answer this honestly or give the pat reply? Hell. What difference? They come and they go. I say I hate repetition. Convention. Hate the candlelight serenade. I like living with someone for limited periods of time. The intimacy of being. Together. We walk. Up and up. Puffing. He ahead of me. Putting in a good stride. Okay. Mount Olympus with Hercules leading the way. I ask him. How do you like romance? He says honest. Yeah sure. Ask a stupid question.

The wild park around us. Flora and fauna. I wish I knew more names for these things growing here. I wish I could see more. But it is difficult to see when you can't identify distinction. The trees. The types of grass. The flowers. The wildlife. The birds. How to live in the woods. How to survive. Euell Gibbons. And his merry band of men. I would like to try that one day. Why not? Walden not? Puffing ever upward. Saving our strength. Not talking. Breathing. My prep image getting dishevelled. He too. Mud on sneakers. Hair loose. Stray. Shaking up. Getting smelly.

Onto another path. Where are we going I ask. 'Up.' Ask another stupid question. Up. A narrow squeeze through a rock. Then the open. The top. I stop. Stop puffing. Looking. For miles. Storm King Mountain. We sit on the rock. I am happy. Very. But suspicious too. Just another broad, show her the sights. Nicholas tells me he wants to be a conservationist. I look again. Out. Beyond. This beauty is worth saving. I understand. Forest below and beyond. Gray roofs occasionally emerge. The Hudson languidly caresses the toes of the mountains. All under the Sky. Stupid romanticism. Sentimentality. But I can't help myself. I am overcome by the sheer beauty. Thank you.

He kisses me. Presses me.

Please. A moment's peace. No. Not yet.

He is good. Stops.

Asks me if I would like to smoke a joint. I look at him.

More potential than I thought.

Or have I just been missing something. No. I am too good at this game. But. He is good too.

He pulls out two well-rolled numbers. A box of wooden matches. Lighting up. Inhaling. Looking away down the valley. Toking. Back and forth. Back and forth. Inhaling. Breathing. Drawing in. Sucking it up. All of it. The landscape. The sun. Him. Yes. I am ready. Now.

He leans against me. We look Out There together. I stroke his hair. That speckled mane. Graying. Long earlobes. He quiet. Looking. I touch his face. Caressing. Looking at him. But I don't dare say it.

Gives it all away. Never. Ever tell them that they've done it right. Become insufferable afterwards. Expect you to fall backwards when they show you a picture postcard of a sunset. No. Never say it. Never make it easy. Keep up the mystery. The unobtainable. The inaccessible. The Female Mystery.

I detest doing it. But no. Even when tempted. There is nothing left if you give it away. If you say yes uncategorically. Nothing. It is really too much for someone to bear. Yes, I give myself to you. No. Never say it. It is so much more than just spreading.

We sat for some time. I noticed that you were not wearing a watch either. Not talking much. I briefly wondered if you wanted me to talk. To perform. But I kept looking. Looking and forgetting to talk. Holding you. Quiet.

Your stomach grumbled.

You moved. Lunch time. 'Let's go.'

These moments come and these moments go.

Not saying much. Standing. One last look. Never want to forget. Working on an epiphany. Thank you.

You start down. Standing for a moment alone. Looking. Out. Away. Breathing in.

Then moving too. Back to the house. First stopping in the little village for an ice-cream cone. While sitting on the curb. You asked what other dope I had done. I say, 'Coke, hash, mushrooms.' You ask me if I have done chemicals. No. Don't like the idea. Poppers? No. Looking off. You looking off. And you? Yeah, I've tried them. A real biker. Leather jacket. Sitting on the curb. Us. Hanging out. Me. Talking dope with a long hair. Licking ice cream. Close to high-school days. The hockey-game crowd. Southern Comfort and dopeheads. The cool guys and gals. Here today. Gone tomorrow. Up in a puff of smoke.

To the house. Avanti. Slinging over a leg. A biker's chick. Yeah. But. Not like Paris. Not like Cozumel. Not like Rome. This is all American.

Bumping up the driveway. The cars were all gone except for the Porsche. Opening the screen door. A silver dish on the side table. A note. European script. 'Pool.'

Brevity seems to be the mark of this family.

Leaving the bike. Changing from our biker outfits, back into the clean cut look. Not talking much. Just doing. Walking down to the pool. Along a path. I make polite conversation again. About biking. How many years have you had a bike? Stupid questions. Hating it. But figured he'd not like the silence. Dutifully answered. Not asking anything in return.

Through the stone gate. Onto another foot path. Could hear the pool. Kids. Splashing. Yelling. Through the trees.

Decked out under an umbrella. Heaps of food on a white tablecloth. As we approached other people around the pool stopped swimming. Staring. Okay. On show. Strolling the Sarah stroll. Gets them every time. Yup. It's working. A young man. A young family man comes over. 'Hi Nicholas.' Staring straight at me. The baton race. Passed on and on. The Big Stick's gettin' around. No. That's his line. Charming, politesse. Smiling, we drift towards the parents. Got the feeling that Nicholas is reputed for arriving always with girl in tow. Resented that role. The chick. No. I'm not with him. Nor his family. I'm on my own. Separate. Always. Look at me as me sweetheart. That's all there is. Well. Sure. Like everyone else I drag along sticks and stones of clattering fossils.

His mother. 'You're late Nicholas.' The father to me. 'Do you like Serrano ham? Gazpacho? Help yourself. There's also some steak tartar.' He gave me some wine. Pouilly-Fuissé. I raise my glass. 'Santé.' Switzerland finally pays off. The father raises his glass and gives me five salutations in five different languages. See, I'm international. Na-na-na-nee-na-na.

All interrupted by a car screaming up the dirt path. Past the change house. Nicholas looks at me. 'My sister.' Screeching to a halt. Out emerged a hefty woman. Black hair kinked out. Her bust spilling out of her sloppy T-shirt. She opened the back door. 'Come on.' Nothing happened. She slammed the door. I was curious. An abrupt greeting exchanged between family members. Teresa introduced herself to me. 'So, you're Nicholas' new date?' I liked her. She introduced me to her pet beaver, Oscar. The imaginary one. Nicholas had told me not to humour her about it. Ignore it. The family watching. Teresa watching. I looked to where she was pointing. I looked to her. Smiled. A genuine one. I liked her. Almost a wink. She smelled. But I liked that too. And bad breath. A person. A real person. Her brother teased. 'Teresa, you must forget about

your car-racing days. You're a married woman.' She exploded.
'To a miserable wimp. And I haven't seen him for days anyway. I don't want to see him. He went to his aunt's last week
and didn't even take me. Why? Because he's frightened. She
despises me. Always has. From the moment I told her that I
would suck her nephew away from her.' Nicholas' mother.
Cool. 'That's enough, Teresa.' The crowd at the pool. Quiet.
All aware of this performance. I liked it. Full marks. She
abruptly turned towards me. 'Do you like champagne?' I nodded. 'What kind?' She asks. How the fuck should I know.
Scrambling in my brain for something reasonably witty
without goofing. Am I supposed to know labels, years, grapes,
houses; how much do they know? To say Dom Perignon
seemed far too easy. I smiled. 'Canada Dry.' All in a split
second. Yes. It was all right. They laugh. I passed. For a while
anyway. Shot my chances at being a sophisticate. Thank God.
Canada squeaky clean. Wholesome. Not Paris left bank. Bag-
dad or Madrid. Hating this process. The labelling. But so it
goes. Seeing me in one way. Judging. A necessary evil. Otherwise all hell breaks loose. I see them too in fixed parameters. It
all makes it so much easier to use each other. No?

Conversation started percolating around the pool. A group.
Talking about political education. I zeroing in. Nicholas zeroing out to the two lithesome creatures draped beside the pool.
'The trouble with the private-school system today is the
liberal-minded teachers. They don't know a damn thing about
the necessity of ownership. They do everything in their power
to dislodge a child from his heritage, past and present. They
are filled with cockamamy rubbish. Political and economic
realities ought to be drummed into these kids. Not romantic
idealism. They should have cadets like we used to do. Com-
pulsory. Get rid of their soft ideas. They are the next
generation's leaders whether they want to be or not.' I said,
'What's wrong with the idealism of Saint-Exupéry?' The man
looked at me. A woman. Ignored me. 'We have to go back to
the basics. My kids are having trouble reading. They read by

word structure for Christ's sake. Word structure! What the hell's that? What happened to the alphabet?' I said, 'Maybe it's got something to do with television. You know, Sesame Street.' Wondering too if he'd allow anybody else a chance to pick it up. Nope. He looked at me. A woman. Ignored me. I realized I was dealing with a type. MCP. Male Conservation Police. Spread 'em and bed 'em. Barefoot, pregnant. Controlling my outrage. Frustration. Imagine what kind of father he would be. To his boys. To his girls. Apartheid. The kind of person I could kill. With his pounding perpetration of Right. Encouraging centuries of distrust and hate. Breeding half people, mental midgets. With long tails. I look at Nicholas. What does he think about all this? He is talking to one of the girls. Bikini boobs. Another day, another lay. Everyone placidly sitting listening to this old fart. Looking around. Teresa. A cigarette in a cigarette holder. Looked preposterous in relation to her size. Buxom. Heaving. Arched neck. Eyes piercing. I liked it. Style. 'Henry,' she said calmly, firmly, 'you don't know the first thing about it.' I almost clapped. With glee. He rolled his eyes and reached for his drink. 'Oh Teresa.' Her mother interrupted. 'Teresa for God's sake do something with that T-shirt, you look god awful. You don't.... ' Etc. Etc. So. The Mother. Another she-devil. Slowly getting the picture. Respect one's elders piled on in another form. Don't do this. Don't do that. It doesn't matter what they say, or do. By virtue of their age they think they are entitled to special treatment. Bullshit. I'd had enough. Turned off.

Went to the pool and dived in. Something about water. Swimming underneath. Playing dolphin, water-babe, obliterating, washing. Clean. Cool water melting around my body heat. My hair swaying like a weed under the water. A skin voyage to the other side of the pool. Bubbles up. Bursting out. Nick patted me on the head and walked away. 'Come on, let's go.'

Walking through the woods again, another path, under a rose trellis. Onto a tennis court. Four players bouncing about.

They stop their game. Hail Nicholas. Shake hands. A divine Omar Shariff type hops the net. I melt. 'Hi Nick. Not here for a game are you?' Nick polite. Checking out the women. I checking out the men. Wondering about this new man's casual confidence. His stance. His Lacoste arrogance. My motor revving. Later baby, later. One of the women players approaches and places her hand on his shoulder. Mine. Okay. Okay. An attractive, healthy, moneyed blonde. A handsome couple. They stood before us. Aware suddenly that Nick looks goofy. Flabby, buck teeth, flat feet. Wanting to be disassociated again. Look see. I'm on my own. I'm okay. One of you Beautiful People. Nick puts his arm around me. There we stand. The Couples. Yeech. Standing still. Polluted air. But got through it all, bid adieu, and then we walked on.

Flowing in and out. To and fro. Ebb and flow. Aware that now I wanted solitude. A chance to play the piano in the hall perhaps. To tinker. Not impress, express, impose or challenge any longer. Nick hugs me and suggests a siesta. You mean sex, I thought. Oh God. I couldn't. I shrugged. 'I don't sleep in the afternoon.' Not looking at him. Closed.

Back to the house. The Retreat. Downstairs. Walking through the livingroom and out the other side into a small garden. Overlooking the cliff. And the valley. Wild orange irises in profusion everywhere. Get him to talk about the garden. Away from those lustful thoughts. It worked. Nick rambled on about planting, cutting, trimming, moving trees. Like dad. I sat on the wood picnic table. The sun blazing. Warm. We lay down on the table. Side by each. Belly up. He falls asleep immediately. God, how does he do that? Age? Clear conscience? Worn out? How? And he hadn't even tried anything!

Wakened from our peaceful snooze by his mother calling from the window upstairs. 'Nick, Nicholas.' Henreee. He trotting to his mother. I stayed put. Luxuriating. He returns. His mother wants him to pick up some groceries in the village. Do I want to go? No. 'Okay, I'll be back in a moment.'

I steal peace. Eyes closed. The wind. The trees. Birds. Bliss.

Lovely. All mine. Slowly rising. Looking up. Then. Going inside. Taking a shower.

I hear the car. I emerge from the shower. Wrapped in swaddling clothes. A brilliant yellow towel. Nicholas arrives with fresh strawberries. Taking a strawberry from him. Aware of the picture. Wet, bronzed, sun-streaked beauty with gold mesh chain stands barefoot. Dripping. Moisture dripples down my nose. Onto green topped strawberry. Head tilts. Nibbled. Plucked. Sucked. Emerging from the Primal Bath. The first moment. Water. Woman. Warmth. Won't you?

You pop a tape. Rodrigo. *Fantasia para un Gentilhombre.* Swelling. Standing. Looking at me. I look at you. We stare at each other. Then you turn and leave the room. Poof.

So. Nick's father's birthday. Sixty-five. A party of friends. A square dance. Followed by dinner at the Predons'. Nick reappears with a long red-checkered skirt over his arm. Here. His mother's. Too large to fit her. I change. Perfect fit. Hair draped back. White moccasin slippers. A loose silk blouse. Nick waiting in the livingroom. I emerge again. Turn. You stand up. Pleased with the end effect. A suspicious thought flickers in my mind. Is it me or me in your mother's skirt? Can't dwell on this. He gives me a woman's navy-blue cashmere sweater. Another suspicious thought. Oh rusty cynic. Shut up. You expect more? He hands me his leather jacket and a helmet.

Outside. Straddling. Hitching up the skirt to my thighs. Tucked in. Tucked under. Isadora style. Off.

Bumping down the driveway. Dusk again. Down the hills, looking at the view. North. Soaring. Hugging. Through another gate. Many cars. An open garage. To see. A fiddler. Caller. Record blaring. Country western. Bobbing heads, children, elders, squatters, and a peach punch bowl.

Nick's father. Standing. Great White Chief. Arms crossed with little beady-eyed squaw standing beside him. Guatemalan garments. The clan pay tribute. Nick and I go to dance. Square dancing. Losing each other. Familiar faces from the pool. Swirl. Hop. The Toad Hall Association. A private, communal pool. A tax write-off. For many. One of the family friends is a lawyer. Fixed it. A member. Whirling dervishes. Blonde children. Protected, sheltered, groomed, chained to believe without question. In their families' Rightness. Position. Happy hopping. Pigtails and cowboy party hats. Bliss. For a while anyway. Until they pick up the reins. The purse strings. And learn too to become cheap millionaires. Ride 'em cowboy. Protecting, sheltering, grooming. The Rightness. With limousines. Private school. Months on the Cape. Siempre. Centuries. Happy hopping.

Talking to the parents. Who are you anyway? Getting the stories, the myths first hand. He, the chief, is retired from the family business. Formerly an anthropologist. Worked with Mead in New Guinea. Sleeping on leather hides. Squatting on bamboo tripods. Has published. I nod. Wondering about the dough. The business. His father? A great man. Great. A connoisseur of Oriental art. Particularly Japanese silkscreen. In his day. Priceless collection. Sounds to me like a robber baron, sir. Someone had to rip off someone somewhere, Mr. Gentleman Sir. And the broad? The squaw with you? Met on Broadway. Yes, that fits. Backstage romance à la Hollywood. Gene Kelly and Ginger Rogers. She. He says. A great European actress. Austrian. Vienna. With a promising career studying under a Great European Director. She gave it up. For me. He asks. Do you know? He names a name. This Great European Director? No, sweetheart. Before my time.

That generation always expects you to know everything they know. Their heart-throbs at twenty-two. Like me asking a child what do you mean you've never heard of Mick Jagger? Twirling fact with fiction. Toe touching the water. The Who's Who of My History. Before my time sweetheart. Like Churchill. His books line the library. Rumour has it he saved the world from German imperialism. He's long dead and buried by the time I get to him. Sure, written history and photos and recorded radio broadcasts to prove. The Glory. The Great that was. But it's like Napoleon, Caesar, Alexander, Jesus or Zeus.

Lost in the dead calm. The muck of time. Circumstance and consequence. Muddy murky myths.

Is Life, the immediacy of our lives, so very different from then? What freedoms? Is there a New Humanity? Is there no tyranny? Is there freedom? Sure, electricity and mirrors have changed some things. Well, haven't they?

What do I care if I am English or German or Russian? If I am I am. Someone's opinion doesn't change that. I was born and live in a WASP Canadian tradition. So? Born somewhere, moulded like clay to become someone's idea of somebody else's idea of security. Rightness. Stamped with a name. First and last. Sarah Elizabeth Stauton. But what does it amount to? You die anyway. Singular. Alone. I could be Jewish, Chinese, Mau Mau, Greek or Newfie. In a sense I am. But to look for notoriety because of it. No. In this life. It's no big deal. Ethnicity. Fossils. Look at the cycle. Created for someone else's idea of Family. Created in someone else's Image. To be them. Midgets with big tails. Long tails. I, another shadow of Stauton. You, another shadow of whoever. Love? Who are you kidding. It's very tricky business. The rich and powerful are desperate to keep it that way. They'll do everything to keep it that way. You can't trust a damn soul. Your own blood is some security. But. Don't bank on it. Children can make mistakes. Believing that they are separate. Solo identities. Doing it alone. Solo. Stamped as Fools by Elders. Disinherited. Banished. From having Things.

I think of Nick in the family business. He once told me that he had always wanted to be an architect. In this life he'll never be an architect. I ache for his stumped self. The sacred bashed in. Never given a choice. Never allowed to like himself. As he is. Overruled. Stoked with fear. Fear of losing what he has materially known. Promised more Things. Governing his life. Pumped and propped by like-minded types. Terrified. Where is that strength that allows him to say no? Never allowed to like himself. His own ideas, his own fantasies, his own dreams. Drummed. Keep your fantasies as fantasies kid. Dreaming is not reality. Another form of apartheid. Keep it all separate. Sure, be yourself. But only under my wand. The Mind / Body split. At all costs smash wholeness.

And the mother? An actress really? You bet. She and Mother skipping towards the bright lights like Shirley Temple. The dusk of an era today. They may have wanted to be Here and Now. But somewhere along the line they confused it with others' recognition and acknowledgement. Looking for themselves Out There. Bright lights and promises blurring their perception. Someone else deciding who they would be. Believing that they were Above and Beyond the Call of Duty. That's for sure. Breaking in. Using everything they've got. Cunning, beauty, thighs. Bigger than big. Better than best. Top of the pile. Selling themselves. Their souls. Promote the wrong rights. Say, do anything, to win, to get it. To be seen. As part of Society. The grand applause. You've done it kid. You've done it. You belong. You've entered the slave trade. Then. Told that they're alive. Believing that there is here. Tomorrow is today. Sweet Jesus.

I will never grow up. Growing up means working the way others want you to work. Being what others want you to be. Servitude. Female bondage. Human bondage. No. I am a conniving innocent. I will always play. And do my own thing. Imagine someone sitting on you all the time. Nagging, scolding, complaining, correcting, bitching. Not if I can bloody well help it. Never allowed to believe in yourself. Never allowed to speak. No dialogue. Commands only. 'Look at me, I'm a perfect person, you little worm.' Squish. Imitate me, mimic me, but know that you'll never be as great as I am. Pathetic. Absurd. Running scared. Hiding behind titles. These public people. Sold out years ago. To the God of Images. Rules, regulations, customs, conventions. Keeping things separate, hidden. Fences. They forget how to speak with meaning, and forget, no, refuse to listen to meaning. Here doesn't exist. They are not now. At this moment. It's only baked yesterdays and half-cooked tomorrows. Listen to this man. This great white chief identify himself. Only time past. He is not here. Here. This gray man.

Something like that.

I tell a joke, twist my third-generation pinky ring and get dragged back to the dance. Nick's mother scolds above the din. 'My son, and you don't know the Viennese Waltz?' Strauss slipped in for the elders. Rickety heart conditions. These adults. Jesus.

Nicholas doesn't have a clue about dancing. His sense of rhythm lost. Not really listening. Trying so hard to listen in another way. I don't know what the hell he hears. But he moves spastically. As though there were no music at all. Maybe he hears his mother. Feels her. Try waltzing with that. I am the ball in a rugger match. Twisted, bounced, tugged, turned, ducked and dodged. The punch too having an effect.

Given the hi sign. Returning back up to the house. The Predon house. Through a screen door. The crowd from the pool, plus several other beady-eye types. A small Joycean character and I start, god knows why, talking about Dante's rings of hell. I said nine. He said seven. As soon as I said it I stumbled. Caught myself. Playing bigger than big. Guessing. Flinging bull. Head down, horns up. Torro. Brute to brute. No Sarah, not this way.

In the hall. A makeshift table. Coolers full of ice and green bottles. Twelve crates. Champagne. Everyone given a blank card. Labels have been peeled off. Guess the best. Grade 'em. Spittoons placed about. But, let's face it, who was going to take this seriously?

A buffet spread. Piled higher and deeper. Salmon, salads, eggplant, devilled eggs, pâté, turkey, ham, aspic, potatoes. The silver, the bone china. A presentation. Nicely done. Full marks. A pat on the head. Head of the class. The proper names begging to be announced. Hi, I'm a Caesar salad raped from the pages of Julia Child's 1964 Annual. Hi, I'm one of millions of Louis XIV forks molded in a twentieth-century industrial furnace to be pretty and seemingly traditional. Hi, I'm a dead

173

turkey slaughtered in New England for your great birthday feast. Yes. Everything has origins.

Nick is instructed by his mother to sit with the treasurer of the company. Protect the Family Business. And his wife. Make them feel at home. Part of the Family. I tag along. She's a hysterical broad. No personal dignity. Dying for the pat. Mad about the Predons. Talks about when she was young. Star-struck. Going to acting school. But never as good as the missus here. As for him, he'd given up. Talking about his sons, his daughters, stuffing his face. What schools they had gone to. What colleges. What profession. Talking at me as if I were a dumb daughter. Back to the polite stuff. I was getting pretty bored. Hungry. Not for food. Looked around for the MCP. Or Teresa.

A contemporary of Nick's, Jake, whirls about collecting the slips of paper. Pops a bottle. And the winner is.... Nick interrupts the wife's reminiscing and offers me ice cream. Yes. He sneaks off. The cad. Exit stage left. I nod. Nodding. Fifteen minutes later he returns, I am still nodding. Mrs. Predon notices his absence, his gesture to me. Comments, 'Nick, offer Mrs. Treasurer some ice cream.' 'Oh no, dear, I couldn't. My figure.' Listen baby, you lost it years ago. I was dying to get away. Jake pipes up. 'How 'bout a swim for the younger generation?' I could have kissed him. A quick clear-up. Distributing the colourful liqueurs and bottles. Jake, Nick, Teresa and myself. A passing thought. Where is Teresa's husband? Nick doesn't know. Doesn't care. Hmm. Incest is best. No?

Jake, Nick and I walk over. Saunter. Stumble over to the pool. Teresa takes the car. A glorious night. No house lights, only stars, warm air. My little paw engulfed in Nick's hand. Tight. Jake and I discover a mutual experience. The Outward Bound School. Wilderness training on Hurricane Island in Maine. A survival course designed to teach you of your limits, if you dare admit you have any. A physical and mental endurance test. How far can you go? Boys from Chaud and St. Paul's selected to build the outpost. Jake had been one of them. Nick tells me that his kooky sister has written several survival handbooks. She carries a fishing line, a pocket knife, matches and a half litre of fresh water everywhere she goes. Survival kit. Great. I squeeze his hand.

At the pool. Jake suggests we go skinny. Yes. Teresa drives up. Screeching to a stop. Slamming two car doors. Leaving her car lights on. Sending a fuzzy glow of half-light over the pool. She comes out of the car brandishing an emergency flare. Icy blue flame. A bursting firecracker. Jake off the diving board. Holding the torch. Screaming 'Geronimo.' Nick quips. He never got over his Nam period. I quip, you mean his Numb period. Jake's body silhouetted by the blue flame. Madness as we all jump in. Divine. The flare still burning. Under the water. A champagne bottle appears. Presto. Popped in the pool. We pass the bottle. Shaking it up. Fizzing. Frothing. Bubbling. Laughing. Water and champagne. Nick kisses me. A kiss of champagne. Of water. Squeezed between our lips. Yes. I like your style.

Sitting in the lawn chairs. Naked. The car light settling like a frost on us. Hash. Toking. More champagne. Nick squeezing my leg. I am getting blasted. The three of them paly. Belonging together as family, friends. Glowing. My mind starts floating. Looking at the stars. They tell stories. Poolside stories. Jokes. The night around us. I am high. Very.

Sitting on the lawn chair. Feel it coming on. The Me. The Being. The Fullness. I say to Nick that I'm going for a walk. Standing. Moving. Away. Towards the night. Away from the light. The cool grass beckons. I want to roll in it. But not yet. Not now. Get away, away from the eyes, the judging. Not self-conscious, I am Other-conscious. I want the Self. I want the Conscious. Wandering. Naked. Into the woods. Through the grass. The cool envelops. To a clearing. Standing. Naked. The stars. Aching now. With the Fullness. Tickling me. The moment is here all around me. I am alive. Living. Breathing. Being. Without beginning, without end. I am Everything. Free. Full. I open my arms. Wide. Turning. Up to the Sky.

A voice. A quiet voice. A gentle voice.

My name.

Sarah.

Focusing. Where?

On a shape. A presence.

Nick.

He approaches me. Slowly. Moving. Growing bigger. I see me in him. Him in me. Oh no. Please. No. I mustn't. I stand. Staring. No. No. No.

A sadness swelling up. He is dressed. Sarah. Closer. Opposite me. Leaning. Stop. He kisses me. Enters my aching. Stop. No. You mustn't. Again, kissing me, Nick. Please. Nick stop. I can't. You mustn't. Touch. Stop. Respect this. Moment. Respect. It is great. Greater than me. Or you. Again, kissing a gentle kiss. Battling the intrusion. STOP. Is this what you want? Is this your price? Stop. Your prize. Stop. No. I have never. Never. I can't ever. I must never. Give that. Much. Never. Ever.

He speaks. 'I've been calling you for half an hour. They are waiting.' No. Nick. No. He speaks. 'Wait here, I will get your clothes.' Gone.

I stand. Arms at my side. Quiet. Trembling.

When Nick returned I was sitting on the grass. Staring through the trees to the house lights far below. I dressed quietly. And we walked back towards the house. Through the trees. I carried my shoes. Feeling the earth turning, moving under my feet. Quiet.

The party was still going on. Nick walked up to the front door. I wouldn't. Feigned toilet. Pee-pee. Slipping down into the Retreat. The dark room flooded by the starlight. A quiet place. I wandered. Still very drunk, stoned, high. The thrill of that moment, or was it moments, lingering with me. The record player light was on. L.E.D. I turned the volume and switched over to the tape deck. Looking through the window-box collection of tapes. Blues, Broadway, Classic, Ethnic, Folk,

Female, Funk, Jazz, Gamelan, Gongs, Kinky, Organ, Swing, Reggae, Rock and Roll. Zithers and oddballs. I was impressed. I chose Keith Jarrett, Lausanne Concert, Side 3. Dangerous music. Piano. Free-form jazz. But I was alone. Going into the kitchen as the music started. The fridge light illuminating my dirty hands. Grass stains and dirt. Taking a beer. Thank god for preppies. Back into the livingroom.

There was a candle burning on the table in front of the fireplace. Nick sitting in its gentle light. I shut him out. No. No entry. Leave me alone. I heard voices. Jake and Teresa muttering outside. Approaching. No. No entry. They came in. Looking at me, still speaking. I looked out the window. Away from the gathered assembly. Feigning stoneness. Listening to the music. Pushing them away. Looking outside. Listening very hard. Very hard. To the music. Catching it. Swaying. Moving. Starting to move. Looking outside. The music in me. Each note. Each silence. Caressing my mind. Tickling. Leaving language behind. Again. Moving away. Dancing. Lifting my arms and dancing. Swirling to the movement. The current of sound. The winds of music. Melting. Dancing with the stars and Sky. I turned to them. The people. They were watching me. I closed my eyes. You are such prisoners. Listen. Listen to this. Gift. I danced at them. For them. With them. With my heart. Know this. Opening my eyes. Dancing. Before their seated staring bodies.

But. The sadness was coming. Swelling. No. Do not do this. Not with them. They hurt too much.

They do not understand.

I am unable to give. Anymore. I mustn't. I battled with it. The music pushing me. No. The rhythm. The wind. No. No. A war. A tempest. A fury. I swirling, swinging, losing control. Yes. Losing control. Use that. Nausea. Come. Claim me. I ran from the room to the kitchen. Vomiting, retching, good. Nick's hand on my back. Yes. It's all right. I am hidden again. It's all right. I must lie down.

Into the bedroom. God, my head is really whirling now.

Feeling as if I would fall. Nick pulling me. No. I must lie down. Yes. Lie down. But stand up. I am standing up. Helping me. Thank god for alcohol. Finding the bed. The nausea again. No. I've been sick. I'm all right. Leave me alone. Now. I am not frightened.

I lay on the bed. Nick lay beside me. Cramped. I hogging the space. Sensing the betrayal already. Aware. They will have a story now. 'Nicholas' Canadian girlfriend got stoned and started dancing like a maniac. Can't hold her liquor. Vomiting. You should have seen....'

Who really gives a shit?

I awoke alone.

The morning. Sunday. Too young for a hangover, but not for monge-mouth. My clothes wrinkled. My paws filthy. I went for a shower. Washing off that residue. That nighttime madness. Scrubbing my arms. White. Clean. Scrubbing my crotch. Soaping. Bending. Stretching. My feet. Stealing shampoo.

Stepping out of the shower. Looking in the mirror. Staring.

I look okay. I'll survive.

And I am hungry.

Barefoot in the kitchen. Wrapped in a towel. Making tea. Toast. Found some honey. It's early. I'm sore. Stiff. The sun not full yet.

Going outside into the garden. Sitting on the table. Sipping tea. Looking at the view. Blanking. I don't want to think. Anything.

I think when I'm at home. Toronto. When the mundaneness and monotony almost kill me. There I like to sit with memories and moments. Like a brandy snifter. Savouring. Saving the thinking for later. On my turf. Now. Just squeezing this early-morning moment. As I have done so often before. It's special here. It's good. I must suck it all in. Before I leave. Before things change. Again.

Into the house. Slipping into the bedroom. Nick asleep on

the single bed. Naked under the sheet. Mouth open. I look at him maternally. Seeing a little boy growing into this big man with moustache and flat feet. Did he wear corrective shoes too? I wonder how many nights he's slept here. What number of buddies and broads has he had here? His bookshelf sags under the science fiction, adventure stories, horror stories, *National Geographics*. A little boy's room. He sweats slightly when he sleeps.

Each one is so different. No two mythologies or bodies are identical. I'm impressed with this one. So far. We're keeping up to each other. Displaying our selective memories. Dangling. Bait. I wonder how I'm doing on his scoreboard. How was my performance last night? Well. He got a real glimpse. Our similarity is stealing my edge. I go over to the bed.

He'll want his morning's morning that's for sure. That's why I'm here. I want to touch this sleeping man. With his slowly heaving chest. Nick. Touch me.

After his mustard sandwich he suggests we pack up. 'We're going to Steven's. A friend's place. For a sail, dinner and a swim.' Sounds good.

Off in the Porsche. Not saying anything to the parents. Isn't that rude?

Off we go. Nick tells me he hates his father. A pat idea pops up. Isn't that Oedipal? Someone else's thought stealing over me. The obvious answer. The reason. I don't get into it. He does not offer any further explanation.

Back down the Corniche, south. Over towards Long Island. More beautiful scenery. Catching myself. Come on kiddo. A stranger in a strange place. That's all. The novelty always wears off. Second or third time around. Then you always see the dirt. The highway blasting past.

The moment I've been waiting for. Nick offers me the wheel. I handle it well. Nonchalant. Like I've done it all my life. Sports cars. Fast lane. Cruising. I change the tape. Rolling Stones. Picking up speed. Nick tucks down for a snooze. Strange. He not saying anything about last night. And neither do I. Mum's the word. Is this some form of consideration? Or does he just not delight in regurgitating memories? In either case I appreciate it. I had nothing to say. Maybe that's why he didn't ask. Knowing this. Sensitivity or indifference? The former is a rare breed, I'll put it down to the latter.

Speeding. A black Firebird draws up. Beside me. Wanna drag sweetheart. Okay buddy. We tear along. Weaving the other obstacles. The other cars. Yeah.

Nick wakes up. Watching me. The boys in the other car. Riding the fantasy. Rich chick running the gun. Laying it on. Smoking. And then, Smokey. Under the fucking bridge. I didn't see him. My inexperience. Cherry-top. Pulled over. The other cars slip away. The Firebird flies past. The boys smiling. I quickly resume the preppy look. 'Miss, the speed limit is fifty, not ninety-two. Let's see your licence.' I don't even have it with me. The officer talks to Nick. Nick gives him his and does a delicate snow job. Trying to get out of the fine. I meditate on the problems I seem to have with cars. Always getting caught. By the Law. Smashing up a dune buggy in the Bahamas. Speeding tickets in Uncle Derek's Caddie. Ripping a door off the Benz. Blowouts in France. And breakups in Switzerland. I can't seem to help myself. I like power. Force. Movement. Agility. Used like a rodeo horse. Ducking, swerving, speeding. Ride 'em cowboy. Maybe it has something to do with my political voice. Listen, my car, or whoever's car I'm driving, is a symbol of my citizenship. My place. Zoom. Through the automatons. Zoom. The lifeless careful drivers. Zoom. Helter Skelter. Zoom. Speed. Zoom. Life. Zoom. Spurs and Cadillacs. Zoom.

Nick drives the rest of the way to Long Island.

Long winding drives, old trees, homesteads. Reeking of Old World. Old Money. Old Family. Props and Property.

Pulling up to the Rices'. Walking in the back door. No one was home. Nick helps himself to a beer in the fridge. Met my surprise with 'I'm like a son.' Wandering around the house.

Taking our bags upstairs. To the guest bedroom. He puts his bag in Steven's room. Winking. We hear a car come up.

Meeting Steven in the front hall. Straight as they come. Crewcut square guy. Totally enamoured with the Predon myth. Steven was cute. Seemed gentler than what I had been meeting so far this weekend. Gracious. Charming to me. The tourist. With small talk. To the guest. We're all polite to each other. Even Nick.

Out to the back garden. Stretching down to the Bay. Paradise. An immense lawn. Landscaped for the view from the house. A dog, a Lab, came running up to us. Friendly. Like at Pineridge. Careful Sarah, careful. Down to the dock. 'A Canadian dinghy but still a good sail,' says Steve. I listen to the patronizing patriot. With gilded humour. Nick says he's going up to the house to get some more beer. I ask him to grab my sweater. He smiles. 'Sure, just call me your beast of burden.' Steven taking it all in. Watching. I smile again. Christ, give me a break you guys, I just want to sail.

Off in the Tristar. Out across the Bay, past the yacht club, past the heritage, the human, going for the Open. The Sound. Rough. The Ocean. Exhilarating. I was pleased. Steve letting me tiller. Arching. Reaching. Ploughing. Flying. Riding the waves. Getting soaked. Steve telling me stories of the area. The Roosevelts, the Vanderbilts, the Moneybelts. Entertaining. Me, the voyeur voyageur. Nick takes the bow. Nose forward. For hours. Thus.

Finally. Back to the house to change for dinner. The parents and the sister greeting us as we come in soaking. Mr. Rice is charming. Gracious. The wife, younger, prettier. The sister preppy. Not as possessed as the Predons. More willing to genuinely give. Shooed upstairs to change, invited down again for drinks before dinner. I take a hot shower. Standing in the bathroom. Drying my hair. Nick enters. Smiling. Closing the door. Is this wise? He grabs me. Nick, please. Turning me. Kissing me. Pushing me up to the Laura Ashley wallpaper.

Tasting my wetness. Nick. He touches me. Nick. Shit. But then what do I care, this is why I'm here. Letting go. Giving up. Giving. Taking. Down. On the bath rug. He licking my breasts. Pushing into me. o nicholas.

Pulling away. His hand sliding up my leg. 'That reminds me. I came for my razor.' He digs around in his toilet kit. Pulling out a jar. 'Want a snort?' Poppers. Sure. Why not? Embracing, touching. A Quick Blast.

Once dressed and downstairs. Sitting in the livingroom being civil. I have tremendous difficulty focusing. Aware only of Nick's sex in me. Of the blast from the drug. In me. Around me. You horny bastard. Wondering if these nice people could tell. That well-dressed woman. That courtly gentleman. That intelligent sister. We talked of Japan, industry, oil painting. Entertaining each other. Polite. Politesse. Politics.

Later, after dinner. And the parents have gone to bed. Steven asks if we'd like to swim. I'm waterlogged. But Nick says sure. Steven gets some pink bath towels and gives them to us. 'Have a good time.' Odd. How many times has he done that before? Giving strangers the run of his place. Or is it just Nicholas and his dates? There's no time to think. We go down to the pool. The lights are off. Surrounded by an apple orchard, hidden from the house. Nick goes over and stands on the diving board. I stand at the shallow end. We drop our clothes. Naked in the moonlight. Staring at each other's nakedness. Aching for each other over the stretch of the pool. 'After you,' he says. 'After you,' I reply. We meet half way. Embracing. Kissing. Swimming. On top of each other. Below each other. Like dolphins. Sliding into each other. Brushing liquid skin. Enjoying ourselves. Playing.

Noiselessly rising from the water. Draped in towels. I tousle his hair dry. He tousles my hair dry. All of it. Rubbing me. Smiling. 'Come on.'

Tiptoeing to the bedroom at the end of the hall. The guest room. Closing the door on the Rices.

Nick woke early. Slipping out quietly to the other bedroom.

For appearances only. I loved it. Good boy plays bad. Wenching. Like me. Good girl plays bad. Whoring. And such Nice People too. Playboy, Playgirl. Having such a fucking good time.

Breakfast. With the old boy. Donning the Stauton look. The wife appears in a dressing gown. Apologizes for not dressing for breakfast. Proper. Civilized. A bit of smudged eye makeup under her left eye. Aha. Orange juice and coffee. Bacon and eggs. Told I was welcome anytime. Grin. Grin.

Nick driving me to the airport. At a stoplight. Beside a Stingray. 'Watch.' Popping the clutch. The two cars whizzing down an early dawn intersection, through a yellow light, around a bend, through a green light. Nose to nose. Nick looks at me. Smiling. Then. Zoom. We're away. Waving to the tiny fading car.

At the airport. I say. Thanks for the weekend. Sure. He smiles, kisses me gently, briefly. I step out and grab my case. Turning. Away. So.

Back to the din.

Our telephone conversations were brief. Efficient. Like business. Click.

I tried not to tell anyone. I wanted you all to myself. My sexy secret. Private and sacred. It worked for a year. But word got out that I was going to New York regularly. Mother began her sleuthing. She knew I wouldn't tell her much so she dug into her bag of friends to see what she could find.

'Michael's mother has said that Michael's wife told her that that man Nicholas Predon, you know, the one we met in Virginia, is quite keen about you.'

'Did you know he was a Baron?'

'I understand he is from an old New York family.'

'Runs a chemical company doesn't he? He must be quite rich.'

'He'd be a good catch. A 32-year-old bachelor. And he did seem charming.'

Shut up. Shut up. SHUT UP.

Mauling you with her ideas. Mauling me with her plans. Making us both objects of matrimony. Sterile man and wife. Miniature statues stuck into a million-dollar wedding cake. Staring. Frozen. Her hand on your mother's hand holding that knife poised for the waiting photographers. Leering. Just like the front cover. Of *Time-Life.*

And when I saw you I started seeing two separate people. The public myth Predon began to dominate the private Nicholas. I hated being your publicity mate. Seen as The Couple. The Match. I hated the spying gossips. I just wanted to sleep with you. But it was difficult. Because I too wanted to be your mate. I wanted to be a couple. The match. I wanted to believe in you. But I didn't know if it was their idea or my idea. Or your idea. Juggling minds and bodies. I don't know. But I do know believing in someone is first cousin to needing someone, demanding from someone. I only wanted to hold you. I didn't want to need you. Both of us hating the nagging expectations. The snares. The fixed orders. The Rules. The more time we spent together the more we exerted our volatile individual selves. After all. We did live in separate countries, separate cities, with separate lives, from separate mythologies. And yet. Whenever you would turn away from me to go, my shadow would cling to your shadow. Wait. Wait. Don't go. I don't want others. I want only you.

We had nearly two years together.

On a first-name basis.

But then the families got into the act. Seeping in the side.

Tugging. Rooting for Sarah Elizabeth Stauton and Nicholas Pierre Predon. Pulling us into the public arena.

I had company holidays. Two weeks. Can you manage some time? You were bogged down with a lawsuit. And you were moving into another apartment in the village. But yes. Some time. Come to New York. I came. You bitched about work. Your father. I unkindly reminded you I was on holidays. You complained about the moving. This was precious time.

Valuable time. No din here. No din. Please. You couldn't stop. Smothered by the problems. Overwhelming you. Consuming you. I had no place. So. I left. Went to the Bahamas and stayed with an old male friend. Tanning, reading, enjoying my limited freedom from the yolk. You called me. 'I'm going to Mexico on business. Will you fly over and join me? I can send you a ticket.' I hesitated. No din. Please. Mexico on business. I would have to play a role. A part. A pattern. 'Listen,' you said, 'call me back tomorrow and let me know.' Hung up. My Bahamian friend took me out to dinner, kissed me, told me he loved me, would marry me. I always enjoyed him. I decided to stay in the Bahamas for my holidays. I called the next day. To the country house. Your mother answered. You were out. I was told to call back later. I had five hours to reconsider. I did. I changed my mind. I was supposed to be your date. All the family knew. Besides if you'd be fool enough to tempt me with plane fare to Mexico, of course, I'd take it. On top of which it must be important to you. It would be my second trip to Mexico. This time I would be going first class instead of student class. That would be novel. I called back and accepted.

You told me later that you had been aware that I would at first say no. You had deliberately not been there when I had called. You also knew that with time I would succumb. You could buy me. And I had bought it.

We made love in the five-star hotel of Mexico City to the accompaniment of honking cars and a muffled marimba band. Touching my tan. Trailing your fingers along my swimsuit mark. And then we dressed and went for a business dinner with another American business family. I played. I dressed up. Nick's Date. His healthy wealthy Canadian sex kitten. Vavoom. A long evening dress with gold trim. Bronzed, beautiful. Hand lingering on your arm. Your trophy. They were boring people. And they bought it all. I did my bit. They were nice and polite. Charming in fact. But that wasn't surprising. After all. Nick was their boss.

We went to Acapulco for a week. It was horrible. You were

so caught up in the business. Of carrying on the myth. Nicholas Predon and Company. Getting a tan to show the boys back home. See-vacation. See-business. At the Top. Suck ces. And I was caught up with the contrasting ways of using Mexico. As Outsiders. We stayed in a luxurious English-speaking condominium complex. Free. Courtesy of your American counterparts. Courtesy of your employees. Not in the centre of town as I had done before in my student days. We ate at five-star restaurants, Americanized, not like the local fish pocket bars I had known before. We spoke English everywhere we went, not struggling to understand as I had done before. No. Not buenos dias todos. But 'Good Morning, Señora, Señor'. You were concerned about your stomach getting upset. Tourista. Montezuma's Revenge. I wanted tacos, empañadas and tequila. We were bored with each other. The set-up was too easy. Too conventional. There was no thrill. No challenge. Nothing new. Surrounded by the All-American standard in the midst of muddy Mexico.

We sat on the verandah at dusk. Like honeymooners. Except that we buried ourselves behind books and papers. A blazing spectacular sunset. And a blaring radio with American music. Reading science fiction and Voltaire. Well. Here we are.

It all fits now. We are public lovers. Everyone knows we're here. We've made it. Acapulco.

I told you you would make a terrible father. You told me I was fat. And we lost touch with each other. Completely.

Walking back to the condominium after a burger dinner. You walked fast. I walked slow. You kept going. Moving away from me. I maintained my pace. By the time I got back you were in bed. Asleep. Lights out. So. I slept in the other room.

I woke early. Going out on the verandah. Looking down at the pool. A poor Spanish-Indian family were chipping away at the cement walkway. Making a design. Several tattered children smashed chisels into the etched-out pattern. Heads bent. Working hard. All day long they would chip. Occasionally stopping for a Coke. Or a Macburger. Chipping. Rhythmic.

Peasants. For peanuts. Completely unaware of our bored civilized North American romance.

I went down to the ocean. Lying out in the cool sand. In the
heat. The sun. Alone. I jumped. Startled. A boy. A dirty toothless grinning Mexican boy had placed his hand on my crotch.
'Wanna fuck missus?'

They are completely aware of our bored civilized gringo sex.

You came down much later. Placing a towel down beside
me. I cool. Eyes closed. You apologised. For last night. I said,
through closed eyes, it didn't matter. Cool. You went down to
the ocean for a swim. I sat up and watched you. Diving into the
waves. You turned. You waved. I waved back. Watching. I
loved you so very much and I didn't have the slightest idea
how to say it. How to show it. How to tell you. How to reach
you. So that you would know. Absolutely. Completely. I
didn't know. How.

Standing on the steps waiting for the cab that would take
me to the airport. You were to fly back a few days later. After
more business. Holding hands. Quiet. Both of us so proud. So
hidden. So singular. Denying any connection. Denying belonging to anything. Denying trust. Holding hands. Quiet. Hesitantly I speak. 'I always feel I've got something terribly important to tell you just before I leave you. I know it's urgent. But I
can never remember.' I look away. You look away. Holding
hands. A weak smile met by a weak smile. Goodbye. Nick.
Sarah.

The magic moments faded as we became more public. I
invited you to come to the family Christmas dinner. And stay
for the weekend. Black tie at the club. December 20th. Friday.
The whole gang. All forty-three of 'em. Come as my date. Yes.
You would come. Predon and Company in tails. Tra-la.

Arrangements were made. You would come at four on Friday. Rent a car, change at my place, in Toronto, and we'd go
out there together. One of your minions called. You would be
late. Seven-thirty. The message was to meet you at the airport.
I took the airport bus from the Royal York in my black evening

dress and pearls. My fur coat snug around me. Fuming. We would miss the dinner. That was obvious. They were Family. They were all dying like flies. It's not every day now that we get together. My corporate corporeal blood Family. I want to be there. How rude of you.

There was no explanation. A sheepish grin. You changed into your tux while I drove. Your red underwear shooting up into the light of the highway as you changed your trousers. You thought that funny. Fun. I was fuming. I decided to take a short cut. To save time. Ironically I got lost. By the time we reached the club, some of the Elders had left. Others were lingering about the fire sipping nightcaps and coffee. I could have cried. My Family. My Life. My memory. My broken compass.

Sarah arrives with her glamorous boyfriend from New York. And we were so shamefully, disrespectfully late. You started passing out your business cards and talked of U.S. bank rates. I mingled with the gracious Grand Dames and the aging wry Gents. Familiar faces peering. Everyone finally meeting the man they'd heard so much about from Mother. Predon and Company in tails. Tra-la.

I started drinking.

We left and went to another Christmas party. A young people's party. We were the only couple in black tie, but it didn't matter. More familiar faces. Cocktales. You were my date. Showing you off. Look see. Paired off. With me. Public mate. Number 1. Everyone saw. Everyone ogled. Everyone would now ask in whispers. 'Predon who?' Waiting. Holding their breath. Is this serious? Holding their breath. Wanting to be the first to announce. The news.

Shut up. Shut up. SHUT UP.

I don't want to be a prisoner, a wife, a good girl. Nice.

Nick told a story to one of the family friends. How he'd skillfully managed to sidestep a shotgun wedding in Belize some years ago.

I kept drinking.

Dancing to the Rolling Stones. 'Never be your beast of burden.' It was late.

We were staying at Pineridge for the weekend with my parents. So. The pressure to be on good behaviour. But by the time we got back to the house I was drunk.

After I had vomited in the downstairs bathroom we stood in the hall under the Dutch star hall light and kissed goodnight. I teased you. With a full vomit-tasting kiss. Slinking away. Temptress ducks out. But you held me. Wanted me. I pushed you away gently. Confident of my control. My Rightness. This is my parents' house. I can't fuck you here. It is not Proper. I turned and swayed away. Going upstairs. Satisfied. Ready for bed. Ready to tuck in. My parents' bedroom door was closed. The floor squeaking as I slipped down the hall to my room. Stripping, tossing the evening dress on the chair. Crawling into bed. Snuggling. Surrounded by the warmth of the pillows and the blankets. Ready for sleep. Turning my head. The dogs' chains jingling. Bouncing up the stairs. Groaning as one lay down in the hall. Weary old pup. The other coming down the hall toward the room. I knew why. This dog liked comfort. Came to sleep on the warm wool rug. Stealthfully jingling into the room, finding her spot and settling down. Quiet.

Sarah heard him. In the hall downstairs. Walking slowly by the drink tray. The floorboards squeaking. He paused at the bottom of the stairs. And then he slowly came up. Heavy steps. An owner's foot. She was entranced. Tense. Listening. How brave of him. Bold. In Father's house. In Mother's house. To come to me. To take me. What if they should hear him? What would it make me look like? He arrived at her doorway. And came in. To her bed. Standing there. She whispered angrily. 'What are you doing here?' She realized that her control in the downstairs hallway had meant nothing. He had disobeyed her. Violated the House Rules. He wasn't even challenging her, he was telling her. His presence. He put his hand out to her in the darkness. Touching the bedspread. Seeking her. 'Nick, get out!' she hissed. 'Get out!'

The dog hiccuped at the end of the bed. Sarah instantly sensed trouble. The hiccup meant more. The dog was epileptic. Hiccups came before the seizure. The noisy, violent, messy seizure. She jumped up. She struggled, pushing him away. 'Get out you ass, the dog's going to have a fit.' He didn't want to understand. 'Sarah, don't tease.' She could feel it working in him. Was this a ploy? She was desperate. The dog had stood up. Hiccuping. Jesus. The noise. The parents. Finally caught. Red-handed. Guilty. Whore. Labelled. Cheap. Common. A slut. 'Please Nick. Nick. Get out. Please!! I'll be down in a moment. Please.' He left. The dog hiccuped.

The dog arched its back. Sarah went to the cupboard and took out her dressing gown. Doing it up, she coaxed the dog to the top of the stairs. That's all she needed. To be caught naked in her room with Nick. Sitting bolt upright while the dog writhes and yelps in pain. On the white wool rug. Lights on. Blinking. Exposed. Must get the dog outside. She stroked the animal and murmured, 'Ssh, it's all right, ssh, ssh.' The dog seemed to be settling down. She managed to get it downstairs. The hiccups weren't so rapid, or so convulsive. She led the dog into the livingroom. Nick was sitting in the chair. The lamp was on beside him. She crouched down, stroking the animal. Talking to it. She glanced at Nick. Coping with the situation. He was watching her. 'You look so beautiful.' Pause. 'I like your dressing gown.' She frowned. Looking down. Stroking. Thinking of the gown. Yes, it was exquisite. Japanese embroidered gold. Raw silk. She liked it too. But damn him. Where was his shame? His sense of decency? The dog settled down. Quiet. She stood. Looking at Nick. Erect. Beautiful. Proud. 'The dog should be all right now.' She felt strong. Right. He had no business in her room. Not tonight. 'Goodnight Nick.'

In bed. She lay there. Alive. Awake. He had come to her room. In this sacred house. Breaking all Rules. To take her. To have her. He had wanted her. Or. Was he just resisting being dismissed? Cast off. Told to go to his room. How proud he is.

How he fights. She lay in bed. Drawn to him through his denial of her. Of his Rebellion. Yes. She wanted him. He was worthy. He reached beyond. He said no to the boundaries. No to the rules of formality. No to her upbringing. No to the laid-on Niceness. It was entirely possible that he was using her. Abusing her. Yes. He was bad. Unimpressed and disrespectful of Family. Stealing as much as he could get. Spying on her life. A playboy. How thrilling of him. How brave. Taking on a good girl whore of his own.

He was equal. No stronger. Greater. More daring. Than she.

Later. Dusk. The stone house was silent. Still. Her parents were out. They were alone. Sarah led him up the stairs to her room. To her bed. She climbed onto her throne. And drew him into her cave. Opening her arms to him. Completely. Giving and taking with his every breath. Breathing. In and out. Melting. Flowing. Giving up. Yes. I breathe your air. And yes. The magic words. Never before spoken. Yes. Never before uttered. From the depths of my sacred centre. Yes. I do. Love you. Nicholas. I do. Give. My love. To you. I you. Nick my love.

And he did not speak.

They went walking back country in the snow with some family friends. He took her and threw her down. Laughing. Falling upon her. She squirmed under their eyes, under his weight. He had done it for the others. See, look, we're in love. Romantic Kittens Romping in the Snow. See how happy we are. What a Lovely Couple we make. She snapped at him, 'Get off.'

Later they all went out for dinner with family and friends to a chalet. They were standing at a salad bar. He placed his hand on her waist. Moving his hand down her rump. Slipping his finger along the ridge of her skirt. His hand going inside. Touching the lip of her underwear. She pulled away. No. Curt. 'Nick,' she whispered, 'these people are Family.' He looked at her and said she was a bore.

They were talking at the table. Dinner conversation. She was arguing about Poland. He put his hand on her neck. Play-

ing with her pearls. Teasing. Playfully tugging at her earnest-
ness. Damn. 'Can't you see I'm busy?' Please. I live here.
Amongst them. I know their cunning. They will destroy
everything that is good about us. Everything. Know that.

The Family were sitting in the livingroom. Her mother was
talking about France. Did he know? Her aunt was talking
about England. Did he know? Her uncle was talking about
wine. Did he know? Her cousin was talking about business.
Did he know? Sarah's father was silent. Nick machine-
gunned them, with his stories of Gstaad, his aristocracy, his
connections, his business, his private cellar. And then he
stood up. And excused himself. He had to pack to go back to
New York.

When he had left the room. All family eyes were on her. Yes.
Chase him. He fits. He has breeding. One of us. Of the same
stock. Blood. Kin. Use your thighs. Sell your soul. Get him.
Own him.

For the Family.

At that very instant Sarah knew she had lost him. Because
he too had seen. He too had known. Now. Every gesture she
made, every nod of her head, every ounce of flesh would be
seen as a snare. A trap. A confidence trick. Love me – I am of
good stock – marry me. Buy me. Own me. And let me own
you. He would never believe her. How could he? She had seen
it before in others. And now he would see it in her.

He did not call at Christmas. And all the Family asked.

He did not write any letters. And all the Family asked.

He did nothing. While all the Family asked.

The noise thundered.

Sarah wrote. Trying with her voice to break, to reach him.
He did not answer. She went twice in the spring to see him.
She paid her own fare. The first weekend he had surrounded
her with his family and friends. Their contact was cold. Lifeless. Brief. He was closed. When she had put on Roberta Flack
he had replaced it with the Rocky Horror Picture Show. She
had to hold her own ground. Forced to be Stauton. On Show.

He put her there. Stauton-on-Show. And he had left her there. Getting another drink. Disappearing. He did not want her now.

She went a second weekend. Paying her own fare. Some mutual friends had invited her to come to a harp concert in Nick's apartment. He said she could not stay with him. He would be too busy. Preparing, entertaining. So she arranged to stay with an old male lover. She took him as an escort to the party. Elegant. Chic. On show. She chatted, she cocktailed, she whirled, she watched. Nick came to her. Cool. Public. A quick kiss. On the cheek. 'Hi Sarah. Pretty scarf.' Moving on. Swirling with other guests. Another woman put her hand on his shoulder. Sarah choked on her drink. Her date came to her. There were only two men at the party wearing wool tweed jackets. Her escort and Nick.

She had another moment with him. Standing together in the midst of the hum of people. Tinkle, tinkle. He asked if she'd liked what he'd done to the apartment, rearranging, remodelling, altering. Yes. She did. Her date came over. She introduced them. But when she looked at Nicholas she was unable to remember his name. He stuck out his hand. 'Nicholas. Nicholas Predon.' The two shook hands. Pause. Sarah chatted nonsensically. Filling the void. Nick excused himself. 'Help yourself to the bar, nice to see you both.'

Sarah was sweating. Heaving inside. She went home and fucked her date. Marcus. The Hemingway figure. He. Going for the Big Time in New York. And he held her. Cupping his hands under her chin. Looking into her eyes. He exploded into her, she exploded into him. Then. Quiet. Staring. Solemn. He ran his finger along her nose. They were quiet. She kissed his finger. 'You know, it doesn't really matter what or who you are, Marcus. I'll always have a tender spot for you. Always.' He kissed her. Gently. 'Sarah, you are such a prisoner.' She touched his moist lip. 'So, my dear, are you.'

One Friday after work she impulsively hopped a bus to New York City. She arrived at 2:45 a.m. in the Port Authority and took a cab straight to Nick's apartment. Climbing the stairs. She banged on the door. He had been asleep. She pushed past him and went into the livingroom. Looking for the trophy. The gift she had given him many moons before. A small purple clay heart with red ribbon. Given between lovers. It was in a silver urn on the window sill. Another fucking trophy. No. NO. She took it into the kitchen and with a broad stainless steel butcher knife smashed it. Pieces flying all over the place. She dropped the knife. Clattering into the sink. He was sitting in the livingroom. Silent. She wanted so much to kiss him. To hold him. To touch. But no. This was business. Real business. I am not one of those. I am not to be included on your hit list. I am not on your hit list of lust. He did nothing. She slammed the door.

She went down again for a third weekend. Under the pretence of business. She invited him to lunch at the Tavern of the Green. In Central Park. They were polite. Talking about their families, the economic situation in Iran. They did not talk about the clay heart. Or their hearts. And Nick casually invited her to be his date at the Vienna Spring Ball. She accepted, casually.

Sarah awoke. A white coat. 'You just rest now, you'll be out in no time at all.'

Hot burning tears blurred her eyes. And blood oozed from her open empty hole.

The nurse told her she had a visitor. Impossible. Who? No one knew. Howith came in. He was carrying a huge yellow torch of forsythia. He came over to the bed, kissed her. Smiling.

She took his hand. 'Howith, you must never tell. Ever. Never.'

He looked at her. Bewildered. His eyes slowly clearing. 'Listen Sarah, I thought it was your back acting up. I called you at work. I called you at your apartment. Finally I figured you'd be here.' Fuck. Always. Always. Leaping before looking.

Always. He was quiet. 'Who is it?' She answered, 'You don't know him.' He looked at her. Grateful. He was clean. Uninvolved. Bastard. His hand going over her face. He placed his big hand along her cheek. Bending forward and kissing her eyes. Her nose. Her mouth. He got up. Pulling the white screens around the bed. Private. Jesus. What the fuck is he doing? He placed the forsythia on a chair. Took off his shoes. She started speaking. He shshed her. He got on the bed beside her. Placing his arms around her shoulders. Holding her. His weight beside her.

He then told her of a dream he had had about her. He had been at a funeral. A pallbearer. Other young men were helping him carry the coffin. Sarah's mother came up to the coffin crying. She started beating the men. Shouting, 'Let go. Let go. You men. You horrible men. Stealing my poor baby's light.' Sarah had committed suicide. The other pallbearers had been other lovers.

Sarah looked at him. 'Well. That's quite a story.' He looked at her. 'Yes. It is. Sarah. Listen. I don't want to hurt you.' Sarah knew this line. She knew too she should dive for cover.

He spoke. We met at a party. A couple of drinks. He had taken her up north. To the family cottage. First kissing under a full moon, did she remember? They had come back to her apartment. The love nest. At first they had been slow. Sharing. Giving. But as time had worn on. They found each other's limitations. Their prejudices. Their blind biases. Sarah knew she would never take him home. He'd never cut it. And he had discovered that she couldn't adjust to his athletic jockdom. The more she evaded the issue of taking him home to meet Family the more he sought it. Knowing full well that he was being denied something, some part of her. He was greedy. Likewise the more she had indicated that she wouldn't mind sailing or playing squash at his clubs, the more he resisted taking her. She was greedy. Too. Let me see. They had started fighting, arguing over petty things. Each looking for the final word, the final say, the final decision. Struggling for control.

She would use music to shut him up. He would use sex to shut her up. Moving in. His big hands on her. Sssh. They competed. Each wishing to win. Not to be the one hurt. Not to be the one left behind, forgotten, dismissed, used. Their early affection had turned into a flippant cruelty. Performers. They had wanted applause. Total acceptance through deception. They had both been clever. Because neither was vulnerable. Neither really cared.

At first he had been generous. Given her presents, to win her over. And she too had been generous, giving her body. Then he had started saying he couldn't pay for dinner, shows, drinks, drives anymore. She wouldn't pay. After all, she was giving herself. So the only thing they had left was sex. That, they both understood.

'We're a total failure as a couple,' he said. 'A disaster. Our inability to be open and giving with each other has stopped any true generosity or caring.' She had once pulled his hair. He had once tweaked her breast. Neither willing to let the other be. Wanting both to leave their mark somehow. Some memory. Some scar. Defined. Fixing the other in time and space. An object to be moved and used at will. With no concern. 'We have never been a couple, Sarah. We have just used each other.'

Well. This is really something, Sarah thought. What next? 'Sarah, I think we should stop seeing each other altogether. I don't like being cruel. I am not a cruel person. And I find I am cruel with you.'

So. 'That's the nicest kiss-off I've ever heard.' By this time the hole had stopped bleeding and Sarah marvelled that she had been alive long enough to get socked in the mouth. 'Fine, yes, Howith, fine. Yes, yes. Whatever you want. Yes.' Slam. Shut. You've been a True Gentleman. Not a gentle man. That has nothing to do with it. You have only gentle man pretensions.

After he had left she lay in the bed remembering. Playing ping-pong at his house. She had beaten him. He called her a bitch. With a laugh. He had kissed her. And then gone upstairs and phoned his mother.

One of the other girls in the ward asked her if he nod-nod was her boyfriend. What did it matter? 'Yes.' 'He's good looking.' 'Yes,' she answered, 'he knows it.' He had once asked her if she was aware of how difficult it was to be so handsome. He had been serious. Who does he think he's kidding? He uses every inch of it. Aware of his performance all the time. He had also said that if he hadn't been an architect he'd have been an actor. Yes. That just about said it all. He'd fit right in with the others. He'd play the games. Padding the walls of his experiences with others' blood in order to become an interesting person. A handsome hero. An enigma. A ladies' man. And she hadn't just got sacked. She had got dumped. Another one bites the dust. Filed neatly away.

It was like eating an egg. You have to eat to live. So you eat life. Coons eat eggs. Foxes eat eggs. Fish eat eggs. Tearing off life and eating it. Even vegetables. Corn, lettuce, eggplant, tomatoes. Killing beef, lambs, pigs. Given and taken. A slug of fire. Ripped off and raped. Stuffed in. To live.

The only thing that made any real difference to survival was caring. It changed everything. Real caring. Real caring meant something. It respected life. In whatever form. A living creature. But where today? Where? A good, honest man or woman with virtue? A plain man or woman without decoration? Who is self-educated? Self-governed? Self-controlled? Who loved. With faith, trust and caring. Who didn't watch TV. Who believed in the sacredness of Life. Where? Who? The only man she could think of was her father. Well. That figures. She nodded acknowledgement to Freud and the boys. The only woman was Alicia. Dear, sweet Alicia.

She entered her apartment. Shaking her head. It's all such a poetic paradox.

She went into the shower. Dropping her clothes. Turning on the water. The heat. Fogging the mirror. The windows. A waterfall. Washing her clean. Hidden in the mountain of apartment buildings. Hidden in a forest of faceless people. Like a little animal. Washing. Paws. Clean. No soap. Just water. Rain falling over her body. She put the plug into the bottom of the tub. Slowly filling with the cool water. Rain water in a pond. She sat down leaving the shower running. Squatting in the rain. Falling on her. Coming down on her. On her lips. Her eyes. Down her neck. Alone. Quiet. Thinking.

Air. Non-air. Splashing on her face. Turning her head. Warm rain. She turned away from the spray. Letting the rivulets run down her back. Over her closed eyes. Curling up. Sitting down. Sitting in the pond. In the water. Breathing easy. Comfortable. Warm. A tiny fetus in the world womb.

Sometimes it comes like an explosion. It's all I can do to contain it. Bubbling. Then pow. I'm there. Me. Full. Without beginning or end. A bouncing brain and a booming heart. And I am content. Happy.

Like sitting. Drawing. Thinking. Striving with a problem.

But then someone walks in on you. Caught you. Red-handed. Being yourself. The subsequent flush, the embarrassment. You haven't had time to cover yourself properly with a mask. With the expected. Scrambling with words. With motion. Facial distortion squishing into a smile. Covering. Hiding the immensity of your being. You can be so vulnerable then. As you scramble under. Looking for shelter. For cover. Hiding Life.

Fear pushes that mask right up front. As you tuck under. You are not self-conscious. You are Other conscious. The eyes of another person watching you, catching you, be private. A spy. Seeing all reactions: the body bobs, the hand-head movement, the smile. The clothes. The sex. Instantly chained, judged, analyzed, challenged, coveted. Yes. It is a question of intimacy. Of involvement. Of trust. Between two.

It is so important to overcome the cringe. That fear. That denial. Accepting the thousand and one ways of being together. By selecting parameters one dies. Losing curiosity, losing strength, losing life. Fixed borders indicate finality. To seeing. Walls, fences, masks. All codes to qualify. Judge. They stand as obstacles. Between the seeing and the seen.

Knowing that people are immense helps. It's like listening to music. Music allows the involvement. You can be yourself listening to music. Pushing yourself to all kinds of crazy limits. What is it about rhythm, song, melody? A good sax can drive you crazy. Screaming out an ecstasy. Becoming so public. Like holding light. It's such a gift. Such an accomplishment. Of giving. To have that which is so private and dear become so public. So freely given. Clean. From one human to another. With no strings.

Looking again. Beyond the blinders of our own experience. Attempting to break the patterns. That visible history. Our own qualifying codes, our conscious codes of who we think we are. Going beyond our composite historical selves. Moving beyond that into the quiet zone of humanity. Where lovemaking typifies the open merge. The blending. Moving into the primal, the mythic relationship, the melting moment. Where origin is all. And every movement is new. Limitless. Giving and sharing intimacy. Gestures moving the mind and the body. To touch. It is the closest articulation of giving we can ever know. Of this I am sure.

Nick.

Would he be able to recognize me here? A naked child sitting in the rain? Soft, vulnerable, wide-eyed, wondering? Could he genuinely smile with me and just let me be? Could he be kind? Or would he try to take what I have created? What I am? Sarah touched herself. She was sore. Empty. Of all that rotten dead semen. And she was pure again. She was a virgin. Free. Clean.

And she would be seeing him in a day. Nicholas. Would he be kind? Could he be kind? Could she?

There is a world of difference between saying 'I am' and 'you are' – and 'I will be with you.' It is always such a personal wrestling match with time and space.

The Final Meeting

They were to meet in Boston.

She had arranged with some married friends from Europe, Lawrence and Renana, that they stay with them. On Beacon Hill. Nick had said that he would be late. After midnight. She went out on the town with her friends. Dining at the Union Oyster House. Larry was an American businessman she had met in Paris some years ago. He had married an attractive German woman, Renana, who worked for Lufthansa Airlines. They were a Couple. Well matched. They leaned into each other often. Soft. And they talked about making money. Making it. Together. Success. They had original Lautrec lithographs hanging on the walls to prove it. Success. Egads. Sarah was eager for Nick to come. But by two she guessed he wouldn't be in till the morning. He was driving up from New York. So. She went to bed. At four the doorbell rang. She jumped. Running to the door, not wishing to wake the others. Opening the door. He stood with his initialized suitcase. Button-down shirt and loafers. He stepped in and kissed her. He had been drinking. She responded, but pulled away. She put her finger to her lips and led him down the hall to the guest room. She opened a cupboard and pulled out some blankets. 'There's a bathroom around the corner.' She started to leave. He looked at her. 'You mean I have to sleep alone?' She smiled.

'Yes.' She knew he wouldn't like that. But that was tough. She had a lot of explaining to do. A lot of talking to do. Some how.

She woke early. She could hear Larry getting ready to leave. He was flying to Dallas for business. She rose quickly. Poking her head out. Thanking him for letting her and Nick crash there. 'No problem,' he whispered as he slipped out the door. Renana was making coffee in the kitchen. She and Sarah had a light breakfast. Nick eventually emerging. Doesn't want breakfast. Only a mustard sandwich. Renana attempts to be polite. Nick somewhat reticent. Wanted to get going. Away from Hospitality. Renana trying to entertain them both. Gosh. She's really trying. Sarah reciprocates. Telling stories. Internally and externally torn by a monopoly of memories. Aware of Nick. Aware of Renana. Aware of herself. All that detail is so important. All of it has a message. All of it telling her something she doesn't know. Even the givens. Like electricity. Or gravity. Jeeze. How does one explain that water is wet or that air is there? These ideas are mind boggling. Where to begin? And yet. They sat. The three of them. Separate souls believing that within their historically manufactured, fabricated spheres they were secure and safe. Entertaining each other with buzz words. Renana asks if Sarah would like more coffee. Sarah glances at Nick. No. Thanks. We should probably get going. Sarah wants to be alone with him. Nick.

In the car. Heading off. On the highway. The sun shining. The roof down. Music blaring. The Beach Boys. The All-American pastime. Cruising. I ask him if he's feeling the gas pinch. He looks at me. No. I wonder if he's ever read Schumacher's *Small Is Beautiful*. No. He reads science fiction. The last great American frontier. Conquerors of Space. They've already conquered Time.

He showed me more sights. The Cape. His adolescent playground. Wandering around Chatham. Pointing out the exclusive clothing stores. Marks, Fore and Spike. The Sail

Loft. Prep Plus. Do I want to buy anything? I buy a pink button-down shirt like his.

He suggests we stop in on the parents of some friends of his. The Hanlins. We're invited in for a beer by a calm gentleman. Of the Roosevelt era. The second wife wasn't so keen to see us. The cat slipped out the door. We running to retrieve it. And all the while I wanted to be alone with him.

We continued our drive. Maintaining some distance. I frightened to touch. To be too affectionate. Sexual. He removed. Quiet. Driving. I watched his hands on the wheel and remembered them on me. Sometimes rough, sometimes not. Concerned with their own pleasure. And giving pleasure. Wanting them on me. I thought of Nick, I thought of Howith, I thought of Tony: I became absorbed by the flow of emotion for them all. Each so gifted, each has so much. Really. But I recognized it also as a unique moment. My thoughts and feelings for them all fluctuate and I know I only feel for them when I give myself up. How to reach. How to do it with meaning. How to create genuine loving trust. That does not sacrifice oneself. It is not a given. That I know.

We stopped for lunch. A beer joint. Over our hamburgers we talked about business, family, friends. You were excited about the party. You were an original sponsor. You had done a lot of planning. You asked me what I was going to wear. I described the outfit. Knowing you wanted to get the Image right. The costume. Cutting classic. Would I be glamorous enough to wow your friends? Yes. But I said I didn't have any jewellery. No diamond tiara or emerald clusters. You smiled. Said. Wait here. Came back with a box. Oh shit. Jewellery. I opened it. Yes. A gold necklace with gold beads. Christ. I guess it was the idea. I stood and kissed you. Thanked you. You smiled. Sipping your beer. I was suspicious. Saw it all as another fucking trophy. I on display. Back to basics. I went into the bathroom to try it on. I mean. That's the idea. How it looks. I need a mirror to see how it looks. The Image. It looked great. Isn't that what one's supposed to do when you get jewellery? Of course. I came back. On display. Like at Birks. You were pleased. I wanted to say. It's the nicest collar I've ever had. But I knew too you'd say you ungrateful bitch and ask for it back. But no. Now I had a trophy. A necklace. Look at my loot.

I tried to be light. You don't like the heavies. You get annoyed, removed, when I make it obvious that I am thinking.

'Relationships are like Broadway.'

'How do you mean?' Sipping beer.

I laugh. 'Let me entertain you. I'll give you an audition. And you'll give me a break. Give me a pat on the back, give me a part to play and then I'm trapped. Cause I got to keep performing or else I lose the leading-lady status. Frankly, Nicholas, I don't need that kind of pressure.'

He looked at me. Eyebrows up. Told me to relax. He asked me if I wanted another beer.

Yes. I laughed. I drank. Slowly. Thinking how.

On the road again. To Wood's Hole. Changing in the car. Warmer clothes. Taking the ferry over to Martha's Vineyard. Vineyard Haven with a six pack. Deciding to walk to Edgartown in the fading daylight. A rising full moon to our left. A setting sun to our right.

I really don't *want* you, Nick. But I do want what you've got. The lifestyle. The ease. The security. The money. The freedom to choose. The freedom to be. I'm so fucking tired of having to perform every time I turn around. To bob, bounce and smile. To please, placate and plead. I don't want to be anything other than what I am. I don't want to deny. I don't want to pretend. Anymore. I don't want to be right or wrong. I don't want to have meaning. Or goals. I don't want a direction. I don't want decisions. I just want to be. It is enough for me. All that other stuff is just padding. Like the clothes you wear. I don't want to be *anything*. Any thing. It is a false state to want to belong to anything. Can't you see that? To a definition. To a group. To a custom. A fabricated world. A business. A movement. A family. Another person. We are all separate. We are all alone, independent of each other. Naked solitary animals. Our trust and distrust, our sharing and our greed are directly proportional to our understanding of this primary state. It's what we think we are that governs what we want. Hey darlin' can you hear me?

Do you like yourself? Do you hear yourself? Can you amuse yourself? Can you be your own audience? Can you entertain yourself? Or. Do you need to suck. Before you'll have form? Identity? Do you need to suck people? On television, on radio, in media, in advertising, in life? Do you need that audience out there before you'll perform? Do you need them believing in you before you'll have that power to believe in yourself?

A lot of people say yes. You need the others. To know you are alive. To complete you. To compliment you. To ward off singularity. But that's bullshit. You don't *need* anyone. Think about it. You are complete. You are a full human being. Sure you have natural parameters. Skin. Skin holds you together and apart from others. But remember. *Your* brain sits in *your* body. Bubbling with blood, electricity, and life. When you respect that, you don't *need* anyone else. What can you want from them? What can you need from anybody? You are complete. You are human. You are the one who is breathing. Feeling. Knowing. Ah, I hear you say. The problem. You can only ever have half of the total human experience. You are only of one sex. Your body form is one sex. That form tells you are either male or female. But listen to me, that's all it tells you. The rest is outside information about what to *do* with it. Layers and layers and layers of perceptions are dumped on you. You are told to believe this. Act this way. Be feminine. Masculine. Seductive. Macho. We are all employees of the sex perception business. T.V.V.D. But I'm telling you. Revolt. Make it your business. Take over. It is your body. And your mind. It is your body. Understand it. Listen to it. Know it. Touch it. Be kind to it. Listen. It's the only one you've got. It is life. Love it. There is no Mind / Body split.

Meanwhile Nick is walking forty feet in front of me. I haven't opened my mouth yet. Why? What am I afraid of?

Well. I'm afraid of my performance. My inability to express properly. To reach. I'm afraid he'll look and say – you nutter. You crazy hedonistic broad. And he'll ask me don't I need him? Aren't you afraid your audience will walk out of the show and leave you on stage ranting and raving alone? And I would say. But look. We are alone. Forty feet worth. Over the earth. The sun and moon between us. And I would say. Do I need you? No. Yes. I don't need you. I have no need of you. But I like you. I like how you respond to the universe. I like how you occupy space. I like how you think. I would like to touch you. I would like you to touch me. I would like to have children with you. Yes. Create life. But I don't want to have to impress you. I don't want to have to win you over. And I don't want to take anything from you. I want only that we be friends. Sharing time together. Lifetime companions. No more fucking around.

He is still forty feet ahead of me and I am muttering to his back.

You stop and sit down. I walk up, pick a single flourishing sea beach pod and give it to you. 'You know, you can eat these.' It is the nicest gift I've ever given anyone. 'It's filthy,' you say, and throw it on the ground.

And I don't know where to begin. Standing on the edge of the galaxy, teetering on a pinhead of light.

You proceed to tell me of a Greek friend of yours who owns an island in Greece somewhere. Okay. Okay. You then tell me about friends of yours who are getting married. Tying the knots.

I sigh. I suggest we keep walking. It's getting to the quasi-dark point. The twilight zone. We decide to hitch the remainder of the way to Edgartown. A van. Two guys, a girl and a dog with a red bandana. Soft, friendly people. They drop us right at the door of the Colonial Inn after giving us a few tokes on a passing joint. We get the room under the widow watch. With a view second to none over the harbour. The bed was beside the window. The window was open.

You, unlike our last New York encounter, are warm. Er. Warmer. Hugging me. Good god. Joy. I hug back. Holding. The quiet cling. We kiss, and decide on supper. After dinner we walk through the darkened, cool streets of Edgartown. Affectionate with each other. Warm. Natural. Giving. Not demanding. Calm. Oh Nicholas. I do so love you.

Upstairs. I drop the bombshell of the D and C. You don't even know what it is. So. I am more explicit. I can't have sex for six weeks. I have had an abortion. It doesn't bother you. You don't even ask if you are the father. You say that you knew a girl from Oregon who had one. I am suspicious. But you hug and hold me. Not in a pitying, patronizing way. Just for the warmth. The tenderness. o nick. I melt. Wanting so much to give you pleasure. So much.

We slept well. Holding each other. Lying in the morning sun. Awake. Quiet. The early morning breeze coming in off the sea. Touching gently. Quiet.

But we had history before us. And behind us. And our families all around us.

And the big night. Ahead. The Vienna Spring Ball. A public rant and rave event. In sin city. Manhattan.

Driving in. Working on our face burns. Wanting to be part of the beautiful people scene. In the apartment. I hang out the dress and know I need some sleep before the party. Nick goes to his club to shower and shave. But he doesn't leave before giving me a token farewell peck. A tiny thoughtful gesture. I notice the kindness.

The evening began with a dinner party at a restaurant. Right. On Show. Nick's Date. La Canadienne. Va-voom. As the evening progressed we moved further and further apart. He surrounded by his licking friends. I alone. Some token conversations. Some token flirts. But one thing was certain. This was his show. I started getting into a guy who wrote for *The Wall Street Journal*. A Harvard glad grad. Bespectacled. Kind. He taken by the Beauty of the North.

At the Hotel Pierre. The Grand Ballroom. Pastoral wall murals, brass candelabras, and a sixteen-piece orchestra. The costumes were fabulous. The ladies in pastel. The gents in white. Thank goodness I didn't know anyone. Made the whole thing so much more enjoyable. Didn't have to go through the routine – Oh Jennifer, where did you find that.... I was left to fend for myself. Alone. Felt suddenly like Ian at the Gatsby party. So. This was what it felt like to be an outsider. As Philip would have it. Uninitiated. Like Marcus. An outlaw. I was damned if I would sit like an obedient wallflower. No. So. On the prowl. Hustle. Swirling. Chatting. Chewing. Chasing. Who can I leave an imprint on? Who will see me? I dance madly. I see Nick disappear with a woman. He reappears and asks if I would like to take a stroll outside. Yes sirreee, hop to it date. Adjusts himself as we go down in the elevator. Walking on Fifth Avenue beside Central Park. In white tie and evening dress. So. This is it. Glam New York.

Nick sees a group of tough boys coming. Suggests we go back. Upstairs again. Just before entering the ballroom. He lets go of my arm. We appear singularly, walk in separately. He off again. I go to the bar. The bartender doesn't know me. I have to tell him the drink. Scotch and lime cordial, no ice.

The party finished. The Vienna Spring Ball in New York. Wow. Whoopee. Twirl.

After the floor closed, Nick hustled together a group to go to a dance club. We go. And dance. Loud, gyrating, beautiful plastic people. Sticking their pelvises up each other's nose. Nick passing out poppers. Everyone getting blasted. You think it's easy being so beautiful? So wonderful? Forget it. Blow your brains out first and then it's not so bad. I lost him again. But fuck. I'll dance anyway. A strange man joined me. I didn't care. My wonderful satin dress started falling apart at the seams. I didn't care. Just wanted to dance. To forget. To dance. The only cause of pain lies outside us. Ergo. I will turn off the outside.

o nicholas, know that I am not so strong.

We take a cab home at four. Not talking. Spaced. Flying through the evening in our heads. Upstairs. Up the long winding grotty staircase. He running up. I coming slowly. Heavy.

He dropped the keys on the desk. Started pulling off his tie. Loosening his starched vest. He stripped and entered the bathroom brushing his teeth. I watched. This naked, singular animal throwing back his head and gargling. Is that the primal savage roar? He crawled into bed and asked if I was going to join him. I stood in all my frail finery and said with true sincerity, 'Nicholas, I feel like a virgin coming to you.' He threw back his head and laughed. I went into the bathroom. I changed. Putting a towel around me. Profoundly aware of my nakedness. My pubic hair. My breasts. My vulnerable, soft, female form. My open innocence. My fragile, tender love. I went out into the bedroom. The lights were out. I slipped into bed quietly. He pulled off the towel and pulled me to him. Brutal. Running his hands over me. No. Nick. No. Please. Not like this. Please. He panting. Like a dog. Humping. Cold. Mechanical sex. I a sack of potatoes. When it was over I got out of bed and went over to the window. Looking out over the bright lights of New York City. Sin City. His sex running out of me down my leg. From the bed he snored.

This is so fucking useless. It's even beyond crying over. Useless.

We are no further. We have not moved at all. There is no respect. None.

No caring. No anything. He is incapable of understanding.

Listen Sarah, you're getting fucked. And that's all there is to it.

So. Back to the din. Toronto the Good.

To say no to anyone who asked. No. We are through.

I call him in a drunken stupor. 'I want to live with you.'

Dead silence.

Aha! A clue. You mean you're not going to fall backwards over the idea.

You finally respond. You reject me. 'I think you love me. Listen Sarah, I don't love you. I was initially attracted to you, but I am no longer. Just let the whole thing go.' Click.

Bang. What to do? How to react? Refuse to let go. He really does want me. I can offer him so much. So many things he doesn't have and doesn't know. I'm not just another body. Another mind.

Bang. Listen kid. He doesn't need you. At all. Get wise. You don't fit. You aren't necessary.

But what about a playmate, what about a friend, what about his sacred voice, his quiet spot, what about our history, what about us?

Baby, he doesn't care. Dig that.

But I care. I don't want to be just another open hole for some hard jerking cock. I am not separate from him. I do think of us. I want to share. To care. He can't get what I have to offer just anywhere.

Baby listen. He's got money, tradition and power. As long as he's got that he'll have more people around him than the press. He won't even hear you. He can buy love. Both nice ladies and wicked women. He can buy experience. He can buy virgins. He can buy trust. He bought you. Remember that.

Oh Nick.

What about the fire? What about the children? What about Life? What about Love?

Listen. Are you ready for this? Are you ready?

It's only economic sex.

That's it.

I plopped down in the chair. Sure. We are all naked, singular, pleasure-seeking animals who want only to roam and fuck. We just learn how to get what we want. Stock up. Eat the meat and throw away the bone. Sure. I get it.

I will never make such a silly mistake again. Believing. Caring. Sharing. You only get hurt if you trust. Maimed, mangled. Falling head first onto concrete. Smashed. Cracked, broken. No. Never again. Never vulnerable again. Never.

So.

Goodbye cruel world.

On the other hand. I am too much of a suck to take my own life. really. Besides, think of all I've got to live for. Rent, phone bills, hydro, car payments, dental and medical expenses, groceries, three meals a day, a boring meaningless job, mindless nothing men, and a tyrannical family. Now that's one hell of a lot to give up.

Besides, I may get a better more meaningful job tomorrow. And I may even get more money. If I marry rich. Which well enable me to buy more security. Like my own business, life insurance, stocks, bonds, options, a mortgage, a vacation, some freedom, and maybe by the time I'm forty I can have a two week break from my C.A. hubbie to go to Maine Chance for a facelift.

Friends and lovers? Salt and pepper. On the steak of life.

Who'd want to give up a feast like that?

It doesn't matter that the cow is emaciated and lives off chemical grass, that salt is bad for your heart, that pepper makes you sneeze.

You've been given a feast. So gobble it all up. And flush it down with piss, semen or champagne. It all goes to the sewer anyway, kid.

Sarah went to a bar, ordered a drink and met Jerry.

Do you want to fuck?

And she dreamt.

Of a room. No windows. Two doors at either end. Six chairs. Three facing three. Three women on one side. They are all dressed identically. White faces covered with gooey makeup. Masks. I am sitting on the middle chair facing the other three.

The door opens.

Your father, Nick, comes shuffling in, closing the door behind him.

The other door opens.

My mother comes twirling in, closing the door behind her.

They face each other.

The three girls stand and stiffly bow.

I stay in my chair. Cross my legs. Relax. And light a cigarette.

Your father and my mother embrace. With passion.

The other three women are standing. Straight as pins.

I am watching the closed door.

I am wearing a turquoise evening dress. It fits like a glove. My hair is loose. Falling gently about my neck and shoulders. It shimmers. I am tanned, bronzed by the sun. I inhale. The smoke curls languidly out. Sliding upwards.

You enter.

My mother and your father are still embracing. You stop at the doorway and watch everything. You see the three women. Who are now staring at you. You see me. I am looking at the other door.

You come over to me, pull my head back and kiss me gently on the mouth. Your father and my mother stop embracing. They stand beside each other. Watching you. Your father asks you where your mother is. You tell him it's a secret and you can't tell. My mother laughs. I inhale on the cigarette. The smoke curls out. Upward.

You go over to the girls. Take one to a chair. She is pleased to have been chosen by you. You both sit. You whisper to her. The secret. She whispers back. With a giggle. The other two rush over. The four of you whisper. Madly together, at the same time. Cackling.

My mother and your father embrace once more. Your father is frenching with my mother. I am watching the other door. Waiting. But I see everything. One girl has her hand on your shoulder. One girl has a hand on your knee. The last one is whispering to you.

I sit quietly. Inhaling, exhaling. The dress moving slowly with every breath. The hair shifting slightly. Watching the door. Waiting.

Your mother enters. You rise. She walks straight over to me. And slaps me on the face. Hard.

The other three women applaud. You embrace your mother. You have your hands on her ass. Squeezing her, pulling her up to you. Kissing her. Frenching.

The three women come over to me. I am sitting quietly. One pulls at my dress. She tears it off me. Ripping it. Another rubs black coal dust in my hair and tangles it. The last takes my cigarette and stubs it out on my knee. I sit quietly.

You and your father have stopped kissing the women and are watching.

Your father comes over to me. Mother tries to hold him. She appeals to your mother. Who shrugs her shoulders. Mother is holding your father. He takes her arms and throws her down. Crumbled. Whimpering.

Your father comes over. He slips off his suspenders. He unzips his pants. He kneels in front of my casually crossed legs. The three girls are watching. He puts his big hands on my knees and with a jerk pulls them apart. I am quiet. Watching.

You step forward and say no. Your mother is holding you. Sshh.

The three women are running their hands down my body. Palms open. Over my shoulders. Down my neck. Across my breasts. Around my thighs. He is kneeling between my spread legs. He bends over and kisses me. On the inside of my thigh. His big nose moves towards my hip. He licks my belly button.

My mother, your mother and the three girls are holding you. You are standing, watching your father. Staring at me.

I shut my eyes.

Your father licks along the top of my hair. His hand touches me. Gently. Touching my moistness. My lips. My fertile wetness. He puts his fingers in me. Gently. Feeling me. Playing. Prying.

I slowly start to move. Rocking gently. Loving the maleness. The touch.

I open my eyes. You are staring at me. There are tears in your eyes. The women are holding your erect penis.

Your father thrusts into me. He uses the back of the chair to pull into me. Tight. Hard. Pushing in. Going deep.

My head falls back. I close my eyes. I feel your tears running through me.

He is a big man. Your father. A big man.

Your mother lets go of you, she comes to me and puts her fingers around my neck. She tightens her grip. Your father is thrusting. And I sit quietly. My eyes closed.

I hear you.

And your tears run through me.

Crystal rapids tumble thousands and thousands of metres. Through me.

Crashing, leaping, sweeping, thunderous clear water pounding through me.

And I open my eyes and I am wide awake. Jerry is rubbing my neck. He tells me I have been saying your name.

But I never said your name. I never said your name in the dream, I never said anything to you. Nicholas. Nothing. Not a damn thing. Nick. Not one word. Ever. I don't know how. Nick.

III

The fire sparked in the whites of their
eyes, gleamed on patches of white
skin seen through the torn shirts ...
A high, clear flame, an immense and
lonely flame ascended from the ocean,
and from its summit the black smoke
poured continuously at the Sky.

JOSEPH CONRAD

In the Beginning Before Noise

Sarah was promoted at her job. No longer one of the assistants. She became managing editor. She moved to a new apartment. She took a vacation. She kept her nose clean. No more sniffing curiosity. She joined the Tory-Liberal-NDP party. Nothing there for anyone to disapprove of. To gossip about. To judge. Sarah Elizabeth Stauton in the public arena. Respectful. Responsible. Thank you. Yes. Thank you. I belong to you.

She had public dates. Other poisonalities. She was wined, dined and shown the sights. By handsome, respectful kiss-ass men.

Six months.

A year.

Other men hovered. Knocking. Waiting at her door. With the pitch.

Gimme shelter. From the storm.

Two years.

And she did not let them in.

She wrote to him periodically. Just a hello note. He never answered. Except today. A postcard. From Chile. Written in caps.

DEAR SARAH. CHILE IS A WONDERFUL COUNTRY. THE PEOPLE ARE WELL OFF. GOOD COOKING. THE LANDSCAPE IS BEAUTIFUL. I HAVEN'T BEEN TO THE SOUTH WHERE THIS CARD IS FROM, BUT I

SPENT SUNDAY DRIVING FROM VISTA DEL MAR IN THE CENTER
ALONG THE COAST TO PORTILLO. FLOWERS AND VINEYARDS. CIR-
CUSES. PEOPLE ON BICYCLE TOURS. HOPE ALL'S WELL. NICHOLAS.

Numb. She thought of his sacred spot. The spot she had once
known. The spot she had loved. Did love. She read the card
again. Shaking her head. He is so frightened. So buried. Smothered. o nick.

She went to her study. Thinking. She looked at the debris.
Maybe I should phone. No. He needs me. He doesn't need you.
He only wants to fuck you endlessly with no emotion. With
no giving. Look at the postcard. Well. At least he wrote it.
Listen Sarah. Aren't you tired of crumbs? She smiled to her-
self. Beggars can't be choosers. We're all starving.

She sat down at her desk. Thinking.

Finally she picked up her pen. And slowly wrote

Disciplining Gods

As far as I can tell. That's the problem.

From birth to death we are harnessed.

Draped in lies and fear. Scolded and slapped. We are taught
self-loathing. Yes. We are. And then. We are bridled. By con-
cepts of success. Fame. Fortune. Acceptance. From Out There.
By Family, first. Then School, and Church. Then Work. Then
Politics. And Nations.

But.

It is only an umbilical tug of war. Between have and have
nots.

The taut rope is Greed. For Treasures. For Things. For Information. For Knowledge. For Wisdom. *For power over more
than one mind.*

From day one we are taught how to be. From Out There. We
are taught when to speak. When to eat. When to pee. And we

are taught to want. To need. We are taught to want more than we need. We are even taught to want more than we want, so that Greed itself becomes a Need.

Once our greed is properly nurtured we are then taught not to want. We are taught to wait. For someone to give. Have to have nots.

This is called kindness, love, charity, and learning. From have to have nots.

It is the justification for Established Society. For Family. For Power.

For Control.

'Yes, we will look after the children. But they must do as we say. They must obey. Above all, they must not step out of line and stop needing us. They must remain subservient dependents.'

After we are taught about how awful we are, we are taught to be good. Obedient. And we are rewarded. With things.

We are taught to give ourselves. Our brains. Our bodies. To them. We are taught to be slaves. Puppet performers. Taught to kiss ass to get. To fill our greedy need. Learning to lie, cheat and steal. To fill our greedy need. And we are taught to believe in Greed. As Truth. A Fact. A Right. A Human Condition. A given.

The haves equate 'getting ahead' (stocking up) with 'good.' They equate 'progress' (power) with 'better.' All these terms are infused with an understanding of control. And the ultimate – judgement. From the top. Giving rewards. And punishment. Both monetary and social. Recognition. To those who have risen from have nots to haves. Slapped on the back. Arrived. Limelight. The Bright Lights. One of the Stars. Success. And now too one of Power. And Control. One of the big boys. And girls. Eager to perpetrate. To maintain. Forever. The same. Power. The same. Greed. For Control. Having Power over more than one mind. Disciplining Gods. Yes. It is so.

The haves nurture greed in the have nots. Owners perform tricks. They entertain us with media. They nurture our greed.

They feed us with Images. Of how to be. Out There. They make us look for ourselves Out There.

And they tell you that growing big like a hero, like them, is what it's all about. A Hero in Society. In a made-to-measure million-dollar suit. And then they say. Work hard to be like me kid. To be Rich and Powerful.

Work hard.

And then one day you'll be like me. And you'll know.

Rich Powerful People own and have things.

Rich Powerful People own and have plenty.

Rich Powerful People own and have the world.

Rich Powerful People own and have humanity.

Rich Powerful People own and have Life.

That seems to be quite a haul just to figure out you have life.

We have to go back to basics. To the very beginning.

We have to understand who to trust. Who to believe in. And why.

We have to choose between Life and Death.

People or Things.

Civilization or Annihilation.

Yes. We have to make these decisions.

It is time.

We have to overcome our inherited fears. We have to overcome our self-hatred. We must learn to trust and more, respect, our own individual questioning thinking minds buzzing away inside of our bubbling bodies, giving us warm intelligent life. We are Here, not Out There. We have Life. Here. We breathe. Air. At this moment. Together. All of us. And yes. We think, feel, love, touch, explore, learn and know all alone. We are Alone. Together. Always. There is no reason to be frightened of this. At all. It is our singular beauty.

You have to trust yourself first. You have to believe your own eyes. Your own ears. Your own voice. And close off that outside hype noise. Blow a Tell-a-Vision fuse. Listen to your own mind and body. Flow. Don't worry. You will be safe. Protected by the demons and beauties of your own imagination. Your own vision. Don't resist. Flow. To your humanity. Respect your human life. Let them speak. It is your body. Let your body speak. Listen to it. The more you listen the more you'll hear. The more you see the more you'll know. The more you touch the more you'll feel. There is no Mind / Body split. Exploring is the first form of your own power. Personal Power. Your curiosity to know, to understand, is a gift. It is you. It lets you be any form. It loves to be known. It is the secret and joy of life. Not only reaching out but pushing out. Breathing out. Air. Fire. And Life.

Believe me, it feels great to roar. Really.

Listen, I know we must give up this destructive, unnecessary, all-consuming Greed. We must reject this inheritance.

We do not need it. We do not want it. It will destroy us.

Sarah put down her pen. Then slowly she turned.
I too put down my pen.
And slowly turn to look at you.
Eye to Eye. Within the Sky.

I believe we have greater deeds to do. You and I. As givers and takers of life.

Editor for the Press: Homer
Typeset in Trump and printed in Canada

For a list of other books
write for our catalogue or
call us at (416) 979-2217

THE COACH HOUSE PRESS
401 (rear) Huron Street
Toronto, Canada M5S 2G5